WHAT PR

'CARL! GET INTO cover!' Nayl was yelling.

Thonius slid out the vial of adhesive and wiped the drooling nozzle down the side of the grenade ball.

He leapt out of cover into the face of the dreadnought and lobbed the grenade. It hit the front casing, and adhered there, stuck fast. Mathuin threw himself out of cover and tackled Thonius, bringing him down behind a pillar.

The grenade exploded.

'You see?' said Thonius. 'You see how *thinking* works?'

But the dreadnought wasn't finished. The blast had split its belly plates, but it was still moving, still striding, still firing.

Thonius shrugged. 'Okay… we're dead.' – *from* **Thorn Wishes Talon** *by Dan Abnett*

G'HAIT'S MIND REELED, lost in a web of confusion. He was certain that he was missing something, some piece of this puzzle; but all his focus was bent upon anger at the Cardinal's betrayal, blinding him. The need to understand – itself a product of his unique and freakish biology – was crushed; buried beneath a landslide of rage.

And then Arkannis winked at him.

And the world went mad. – *from* **Elucidium** *by Simon Spurrier*

IN THE NIGHTMARE world of the 41st millennium, humanity is locked in a desperate struggle for survival against a relentless tide of aliens. Read tales of heroism and valour in this action-packed selection of savage science fiction stories ripped from the pages of *Inferno!* magazine – plus two brand new tales!

More Warhammer 40,000 from the Black Library

• WARHAMMER 40,000 SHORT STORIES •

STATUS: DEADZONE
eds. Marc Gascoigne & Andy Jones

DARK IMPERIUM
eds. Marc Gascoigne & Andy Jones

DEATHWING
eds. Neil Jones & David Pringle

WORDS OF BLOOD
eds. Marc Gascoigne & Christian Dunn

CRUCIBLE OF WAR
eds. Marc Gascoigne & Christian Dunn

• GAUNT'S GHOSTS by Dan Abnett •

The Founding
FIRST & ONLY
GHOSTMAKER
NECROPOLIS

The Saint
HONOUR GUARD
THE GUNS OF TANITH
STRAIGHT SILVER
SABBAT MARTYR

• SPACE WOLF by William King •

SPACE WOLF
RAGNAR'S CLAW
GREY HUNTER
WOLFBLADE

WARHAMMER 40,000 STORIES

WHAT PRICE VICTORY

Edited by
Marc Gascoigne
& Christian Dunn

A BLACK LIBRARY PUBLICATION

First published in Great Britain in 2004 by
BL Publishing,
Games Workshop Ltd.,
Willow Road, Nottingham,
NG7 2WS, UK.

10 9 8 7 6 5 4 3 2 1

Cover illustration by Scott Johnson.

A CIP record for this book is available from the British Library.

ISBN 1 84416 077 7

Distributed in the US by Simon & Schuster
1230 Avenue of the Americas, New York, NY 10020, US.

Printed and bound in Great Britain by
Cox & Wyman Ltd, Reading, Berkshire, UK.

See the Black Library on the Internet at
www.blacklibrary.com

Find out more about Games Workshop
and the world of Warhammer 40,000 at
www.games-workshop.com

IT IS THE 41st millennium. For more than a hundred
centuries the Emperor has sat immobile on the Golden
Throne of Earth. He is the master of mankind by the
will of the gods, and master of a million worlds by the
might of his inexhaustible armies. He is a rotting carcass
writhing invisibly with power from the Dark Age of
Technology. He is the Carrion Lord of the Imperium for
whom a thousand souls are sacrificed every day, so that
he may never truly die.

YET EVEN IN his deathless state, the Emperor continues
his eternal vigilance. Mighty battlefleets cross the dae-
mon-infested miasma of the warp, the only route between
distant stars, their way lit by the Astronomican, the psychic manifestation of the Emperor's will. Vast armies give
battle in his name on uncounted worlds. Greatest amongst
his soldiers are the Adeptus Astartes, the Space Marines,
bio-engineered super-warriors. Their comrades in arms are
legion: the Imperial Guard and countless planetary defence
forces, the ever-vigilant Inquisition and the tech-priests
of the Adeptus Mechanicus to name only a few. But for
all their multitudes, they are barely enough to hold off
the ever-present threat from aliens, heretics, mutants –
and worse.

TO BE A man in such times is to be one amongst untold
billions. It is to live in the cruellest and most bloody
regime imaginable. These are the tales of those times.
Forget the power of technology and science, for so much
has been forgotten, never to be re-learned. Forget the
promise of progress and understanding, for in the grim
dark future there is only war. There is no peace amongst
the stars, only an eternity of carnage and slaughter, and
the laughter of thirsting gods.

CONTENTS

THORN WISHES TALON

Dan Abnett

THE PAST NEVER *lets us go. It is persistent and unalterable.*

The future, however, is aloof, a stranger. It stands with its back to us, mute and private, refusing to communicate what it knows or what it sees.

Except to some. On Nova Durma, deep in the leech-infested forests of the Eastern Telgs, there is a particular grotto into which the light of the rising daystar falls once every thirty-eight days. There, by means of some secret ministry and ritual craft that I have no ready wish to understand, the blistered seers of the Divine Fratery coax the reluctant future around until they can see its face in their silver mirrors, and hear its hushed, unwilling voice.

It is my fervent hope that what it has to say to them is a lie.

THAT NIGHT, THE waste-world called Malintei had six visitors. They left their transport, dark and hook-winged, on a marshy flood plain, slightly bowed over to starboard where the landing claws had sunk into the ooze. They proceeded west, on foot.

A storm was coming, and it was not entirely natural. They walked through streamers of white fog, crossing outcrops of green quartz, lakes of moss and dank watercourses choked with florid lichens. The sky shone like filthy, tinted glass. In the distance, a pustular range of hills began to vanish in the rain-blur of the encroaching elements. Lightning flashed, like sparks off flint, or remote laser fire.

They had been on the surface for an hour, and had just sighted the tower, when the first attempt was made to kill them.

There was a rattle, almost indistinguishable from the doom-roll of the approaching thunder, and bullets whipped up spray from the mud at the feet of the tallest visitor.

His name was Harlon Nayl. His tall, broad physique was wrapped in a black-mesh bodyglove. His head was shaved apart from a simple goatee. He raised the heavy Hecuter pistol he had been carrying in his right fist, and made a return of fire into the gathering dark.

In answer, several more unseen hostiles opened up. The visitors scattered for cover.

'Were you expecting this?' Nayl asked as he crouched behind a quartz boulder and snapped shots off over it.

+I didn't know what to expect.+

The answer came telepathically from Nayl's master, and seemed far from reassuring.

'How many?' Nayl called out.

Twenty metres away from him, another big man called Zeph Mathuin shouted back from cover. 'Six!' echoed his estimation. Mathuin was as imposing as Nayl, but his skin was dark, the colour of varnished hardwood. His black hair was plaited into strands and beaded. Both men had been bounty hunters in their time. Neither followed that profession any longer.

'Make it seven,' contradicted Kara Swole as she wriggled up beside Nayl, keeping her head low. She was a short, compact woman with cropped red hair. Her voluptuous figure was currently concealed beneath a long black leather duster with a fringe of larisel fur around the neck.

'Seven?' queried Nayl, as whining hard-round smacked into the far side of the rock.

'Six!' Mathuin called again.

Kara Swole had been a dancer-acrobat before she'd joined the band, and ordinarily she would defer to the combat experience of the two ex-hunters. But she had an ear for these things. 'Listen!' she said. 'Three autorifles,' she identified, counting off on her fingers. 'Two lasguns, a pistol, and that...' she drew Nayl's attention to a distinctive *plunk! plunk!* 'That's a stubber.'

Nayl nodded and smiled.

'Six!' Mathuin insisted.

+Kara is correct. There are seven. Now can we deal with them, please?+

Their master's mind-voice seemed unusually terse and impatient. Not a good sign. One of several not good signs that had already distinguished this night.

The two other members of the team sheltered against a gravel shelf some distance to Nayl's left. Their names were Patience Kys and Carl Thonius. A slight, fussy, well-bred young man, Thonius held the rank of interrogator and was technically the master's second-in-command. He had drawn a compact pistol from inside his beautifully tailored coat, but was too busy complaining about the weather, the mud, and the prospect of death by gunshot wounds to use it.

Patience Kys suggested he might like to shut up. She was a slender, pale woman, dressed in high leather boots of black leather, a bell skirt of grey silk and an embroidered black leather shirt. Her hair was pinned up in a chignon with silver pins.

She scanned the view ahead, and located one of the hostiles firing from the cover of some quartz rocks.

'Ready?' she yelled over at Nayl.

'Pop 'em up!' he replied.

Kys was telekinetic. She focused her trained mind and exerted a little pressure. The quartz rocks scattered apart across the slime, revealing a rather surprised man holding an autorifle.

His surprise lasted about two seconds until a single shot from Nayl hit him in the brow and tumbled him leadenly onto his back.

With a spiteful grin, Kys reached out again and dragged another of the hostiles out into the open with her mind. The man yelled aloud, scared and uncomprehending. His heels churned in the ooze and he flailed his arms, fighting the invisible force that yanked him by the scruff of the neck.

There was a blurt of noise like an industrial hammer-drill, and the man ceased to be, shredded into pieces by heavy fire.

Mathuin had shot him. His left hand was a burnished-chrome augmetic, and he had locked it into the governing socket of the lethal rotator cannon that he was wearing strapped around his torso. The multi-barrels whirred and cycled, venting vapour.

The firing ceased.

+They have fled for now. They will return, I have no doubt.+

The master of the team moved up amongst them. To the uninformed, Inquisitor Gideon Ravenor appeared to be a machine rather than a man. He was a box, a smoothly angled wedge of armoured metal with a glossy, polished finish from which even the approaching lightning seemed unwilling to reflect. This was his force chair, his life-support system, totally enclosed and self-sufficient. The chair's anti-gravity disks spun hypnotically as he advanced.

Inside that enclosing chair, one of the Imperium's most brilliant inquisitors – and most articulate theorists – lay trapped forever. Years before, at the start of a glittering career in the service of the ordos, Gideon Ravenor had been struck down during a heretical attack, his fair and strong body burned and fused away into a miserable residue of useless flesh. Only his mind had survived

But such a mind! Sharp, incisive, poetic, just... and powerful too. Kys had not met a psi-capable being remotely strong enough to master Gideon Ravenor.

They were sworn to him, the five of them. Nayl, Thonius, Kara, Mathuin and Kys. Sworn and true. They would follow him to the ends of the known stars, if needs be.

Even when he chose not to tell them where they were going.

THE DIVINE FRATERY *practises a barbaric initiation process of voluntary blinding. Sight, as one might expect, is considered their fundamental skill, but not sight as we might understand it. Novices sacrifice one of their eyes as proof of their intent, and have that missing eye replaced by a simple augmetic to maintain everyday function. The one remaining organic eye is then trained and developed, using ritual, alchemic and sorcerous processes.*

An initiated member of the Fratery may therefore be identified by his single augmetic eye, and by the patch of purple velvet that covers his remaining real eye at all times except for circumstances of cult ceremony. A novitiate, self-blinded in one socket, must work to fashion his own silver mirror before he is allowed his augmetic, or indeed any medical or sterilising treatment. He must cut and hammer his dish of silver, and then work it with abrasive wadding until it is a perfect reflector to a finesse of .0088 optical purity. Many die of septicemia or other wound-related infection before they accomplish this. Others, surviving the initial infections, spend many months or even years finishing the task. Thus, members of the cult may additionally be identified by blistering of the skin, tissue abnormalities and even significant necrotising scarring incurred during the long months of silver-working.

It is also my experience that few Fratery members have codable or matchable fingerprints. Years of scrupulous endeavour with abrasive wadding wear away hands as well as silver.

OVERHEAD, THE SKY flashed and vibrated. Kara could hear the thunder now, and felt the drizzle in the wind. Fog-vapour smirched out the distance.

With the toe of her boot, she gingerly rolled over the body of the man Nayl had shot. He was dressed in cheap,

worn foul-weather clothes made of woven plastek fibre
and leather. He had one augmetic eye, crude and badly-
sutured into the socket, and a velvet patch over the other.

'Anyone we know?' asked Nayl, coming up behind her.

Unlike the others, Nayl and Kara had not been
recruited for ordo service by Ravenor himself. They had
originally owed loyalty to Ravenor's mentor, Inquisitor
Gregor Eisenhorn. Somewhere along the line, a decade or
more past, they had· become Ravenor's. Kara often
thought of Eisenhorn. Stern, fierce, so much harder to
bear than Ravenor, Eisenhorn had still been a good man
to follow. And she owed him. But for Gregor Eisenhorn,
she would still be a dancer-acrobat in the circuses of
Bonaventure.

She often wondered what had become of her former
master. She'd last seen him back in '87, during the mission
to 5213X. He'd been a wreck of a man by then, supported
only by his burning will and fundamental augmetics.
Some had said he'd crossed a line and become a radical.
Kara didn't believe that. Eisenhorn had always been so…
hard-line. She thought of him fondly, as she did the others
from that time. Alizabeth Bequin, God-Emperor rest her,
dear Aemos, Medea Betancore and Fischig.

They had known some times together. Great times, bad
times. But this was her place now.

'Face doesn't ring any bells,' she said. She reached down
and lifted the eye patch, just out of curiosity. A real eye,
wide and glazed, lay beneath.

'What the hell is that about?' Nayl wondered.

Kara reached up and sleeked the short, red strands of
her rain-wet hair back across her head. She looked across
at Mathuin and Thonius beside the other body. Thonius
was, as ever, elegantly dressed, and as he crouched in the
mud, he fussed about his shoes.

Thonius would Ravenor's pupil, which supposed that
one day Thonius was to be promoted to full inquisitor.
Ravenor had been Eisenhorn's interrogator. Kara wondered sometimes if Carl had anything like the same stuff.

'If you'd left him a little more intact, we might have made a more decent examination,' Thonius complained.

'This is a rotator cannon,' Mathuin said bluntly. 'It doesn't do intact.'

Thonius prodded the grisly remains with a stick. 'Well, I think we've got an augmetic eye here too. And what's either an eyepatch or a very unsatisfactory posing thong.'

Thonius's caustic wit usually drew smiles from the band, but not this night. No one was in the mood for laughs. Ravenor, generally so forthcoming with his team, had told them virtually nothing about the reasons for coming to Malinter. As far as anyone knew, he'd simply diverted them to this remote waste-world after receiving some private communiqué.

Most alarmingly of all, he'd chosen to join them on the surface. Ravenor usually ran his team telepathically from a distance via the wraithbone markers they all wore. He only came along in person when the stakes were high.

+Let's move on.+ Ravenor said.

THE GROTTO IN *the Eastern Telgs is deep in the smoking darkness of the forests. The glades are silent except for insect chitter, and wreathed with vapour and steam. There are biting centipedes everywhere, some as long as a man's finger, others as long as a man's leg. The air stinks of mildew.*

Once every thirty-eight days, the rising star comes up at such an angle it forces its pale and famished light in through a natural hole in the rock face outside the grotto. The beams streak in down an eighty degree angle to the azimuth and strike the still freshwater of the pool in the grotto's base, lighting the milky water like a flame behind muslin.

The Fratery cowers around the pool – after days of ritual starvation and self-flagellation – and attempts to interrupt the falling beams with their silver mirrors. At such times, I have observed, they remove the purple velvet patches from their real eyes and place them over their augmetics.

*Their flashing mirrors reflect many colours of light. Having
ingested lho seeds and other natural hallucinogenics, they glare
into their mirrors, and begin to gabble incoherently.*

*Voxographic units, run on battery leads, are set around the
grotto to record their ramblings. As the light fades again, the
masters of the Fratery play back the voxcorders, and tease out
the future truths – or lies – that they have been told.*

THE TOWER, AS they approached it, was far larger than they
had first imagined. The main structure, splintered and
ruined, rose a full half kilometre into the dark, bruised
sky, like an accusing finger. At the base, like the bole of an
ancient tree, it thickened out and spread into great piers
and buttresses that anchored it into the headland. Crumbling stone bridge-spans linked the rocky shelf to the
nearest piers.

There was no way of defining its origin or age, nor the
hands – human or otherwise – that had constructed it.
Even its purpose was in doubt. According to the scans, it
was the only artificial structure on Malinter. Older star
maps referred to it simply by means of a symbol that
indicated *ruin (antique/xenos)*.

As they picked their way through ancient screes of rubble and broken masonry towards the nearest span, the
rain began to lash down, pattering on the mud and driving off the raised stonework. The rising wind began to
shiver the glossy black ivy and climbing vines clinging in
thick mats to the lower walls.

'This message. It told you to come here?' Nayl asked.

+What message?+

Nayl frowned and looked at the floating chair. 'The
message you got.'

+I never said anything about a message.+

'Oh, come on! Fair play!' Nayl growled. 'Why won't
you tell us what we're getting into here?'

+Harlon.+ Ravenor's voice sliced into Nayl's mind and
he winced slightly. Ravenor's telepathy was sometimes
painfully sharp when he was troubled or preoccupied.

Nayl realised that Ravenor's thought-voice was directed at him alone, a private word the others couldn't hear.

+Trust me, old friend. I dare tell you nothing until I'm sure of what we're dealing with. If it turns out to be a trick, you could be biased by misinformation.+

'I'm no amateur,' Nayl countered. The others looked at him, hearing only his side of the conversation.

+I know, but you're a loyal man. Loyalty sometimes blinds us. Trust me on this.+

'What in the name of the Golden Throne was that?' Thonius said abruptly. They'd all heard it. Ravenor and Kys had felt it.

High in the ruined summit of the tower, something had screamed. Loud, hideous, inhuman, drawn out. More screams, from other non-human voices, answered it. Each resounded both acoustically and psychically. The air temperature dropped sharply. Sheens of ice crackled into view, caking the upper sweep of the walls.

They moved on a few metres. The keening wails grew louder, whooping and circling within the high walls, as if screaming avian things were flying around inside. As lightning accompanies thunder, so each scream was accompanied by a sympathetic flash of light. The psychic shrieks seemed to draw the storm down, until a halo of flashing, jagged light coruscated in the sky above the tower. Corposant danced along the walls like white, fluo-rescent balls.

Kys, her psi-sensitive mind feeling it worse than the rest, paused to wipe fresh blood off her lip with the back of her gwel-skin glove. Her nose was bleeding.

As she did so, the hostiles began trying to kill them again.

THE DIVINE FRATERY, *may the ordos condemn their sick souls, seek to chart out the future. All possible futures, in fact. With their mirrors and their abominably practiced eyes, they iden-tify events to come, and take special interest in those events that are ill-favoured. Disasters, plagues, invasions, collapses of governments, heresies, famines, defeats in battle. Doom, in any guise.*

The masters of the Fratery then disseminate the details of their oracles to the lower orders of their cult. By my estimation, the Fratery numbers several thousand, many of them apparently upstanding Imperial citizens, spread through hundreds of worlds in the subsectors Antimar, Helican, Angelus and Ophidian. Once a 'prospect' as they call them has been identified, certain portions of the 'cult membership' are charged with doing everything they can to ensure that it comes to pass, preferably in the worst and most damaging way possible. If a plague is foreseen, then cult members will deliberately break quarantine orders to ensure that the outbreak spreads. If the prospect is a famine, they will plant incendiary bombs or biotoxins in the Munitorum grain stores of the threatened world. A heretic emerges? They will protect him and publish his foul lies abroad. An invasion approaches? They are the fifth column who will destroy the defenders from within.

They seek doom. They seek to undermine the fabric of our Imperium, the culture of man, and cause it to founder and fall. They seek galactic apocalypse, an age of darkness and fire, wherein their unholy masters, the Ruinous Powers, can rise up and take governance of all.

Five times now I have thwarted their efforts. They hate me, and wish me dead. Now I seek to derail their efforts a sixth time, here, tonight, on Malinter. I have journeyed far out of my way, pursued by their murder-bands, to carry a warning.

For I have seen their latest prospect with my own eyes. And it is a terrible thing.

LASER FIRE SCORCHED across the mossy span of the bridge arch, sizzling in the rain. Some of it came from the ruin ahead, some from the crags behind them. Stonework shattered and split. Las-bolts and hard-rounds snapped and stung away from the age-polished cobbles.

'Go!' yelled Nayl, turning back towards the crags and firing his weapon in a two-handed brace. At his side, Kara Swole kicked her assault weapon into life. It bucked like a living thing, spitting spent casings out in a sideways flurry.

They backed across the bridge as the others ran ahead. Mathuin and Kys led the way, into the gunfire coming out of the dim archways and terraces ahead. Mathuin's rotator cannon squealed, and flames danced around the spinning barrels. Stone debris and shorn ivy fluttered off the wounded walls. Kys saw a man, almost severed at the waist, drop from an archway into the lightless gulf below the bridge.

Ravenor and Thonius came up behind them. Thonius was still gazing up at the screamlight tearing and dancing around the tower top overhead. He had one hand raised, as if to protect his face from the bullets and laser fire whipping around him.

+Concentrate!+

'Yes, yes… of course…' Thonius replied.

Mathuin ran under the first arch into the gloom of the tower chambers. His augmetic eyes, little coals of red hard-light, gleaming inside his lids, immediately adjusted to the light conditions and revealed to him the things hidden in the shadows. He pivoted left and mowed down four hostiles with a sustained belch of cannon fire. More shot at him.

Kys ran in beside him. She had a laspistol harnessed at her waist, but she hadn't drawn it yet. She extended the heels of her palms, and four kineblades slipped out of the sheaths built into the forearms of her shirt. Each was thin, razor-sharp, twelve centimetres long, and lacked handles. She controlled them with her mind, orbiting them about her body in wide, buzzing circuits, in a figure of eight, like some lethal human orrery.

A hostile opened fire directly at her with an autopistol, cracking off four shots. Without flinching, she faced them, circling a pair of the blades so they intercepted and deflected the first two shots. The second two she bent wide with her mind, so that they sailed off harmlessly like swatted flies.

Before he could fire again, Kys pinned the hostile to the stone wall with the third kineblade.

Mathuin was firing again. 'You okay there, Kys?' he yelled over the cannon's roar.

'Fine,' she smiled. She was in her element. Dealing death in the name of the Emperor, punishing his enemies. That was all she lived for. She was a secretive being. Patience Kys was not her real name, and none of the band knew what she'd been baptised. She'd been born on Sameter, in the Helican sub, and had grown to womanhood on that filthy, brow-beaten world. Things had happened to her there, things that had changed her and made her Patience Kys, the telekine killer. She never spoke of it. The simple fact was she had faced and beaten a miserable death, and now she was paying death back, in the God-Emperor's name, with souls more deserving of annihilation.

With a jerk of her mind, she tugged the kineblade out of the pinned corpse and flew it back to join the others. They whistled as they spun, deflecting more gunfire away from her. Five more hostiles lay ahead, concealed behind mouldering pillars. With a nasal grunt, she sped the kineblades away from her. They shot like guided missiles down the terraceway, arcing around obstacles, whipping around the pillars. Four of the hostiles fell, slashed open by the hurtling blades.

The fifth she yanked out of cover with her telekinesis and shot. Now, at last, the gun was in her hands.

Inexorable as a planet moving along its given path, Ravenor floated into the gloom, passing between Kys and Mathuin as the ex-bounty hunter hosed further mayhem at the last of the hostiles on his side. Thonius ran up alongside him.

'What now?' the interrogator asked hopefully. 'At least we're out of that ghastly rain.'

Screamlight echoed and flashed down through the tower from far above, reverberating the structure to its core. Kys shuddered involuntarily. Her nose was bleeding again.

+Carl? Zeph?+

Ravenor's mind-voice was quiet, as if he too was suffering the side-effects of the psychic screams. +Rearguard, please. Make sure Kara and Harlon make it in alive.+

'But–' Thonius complained. Mathuin was already running back to the archway.

+Do as I say, Carl!+

'Yes, inquisitor,' replied Thonius. He turned and hurried after Mathuin.

+With me, please, Patience.+

Kys had just retrieved her kineblades. She held out her arms to let them slide back into her cuff-sheaths. The concentrated activity had drained her telekinetic strength, and the terrible screamlight from above had sapped her badly.

+Are you up to this?+

Kys raised her laspistol. 'I was born up for this, Gideon,' she grinned.

THE PROSPECT IS, *as most are, vague. There are no specifics. However, it is regarded as a one hundred per cent certainty by the masters of the Fratery that a daemonic abomination is about to be manifested into the material universe. This, they predict, will come to pass between the years 400 and 403.M41. Emperor protect us, it may have already happened.*

There are some details. The crucial event that triggers the manifestation will happen on Eustis Majoris, the overcrowded and dirty capital world of the Angelus subsector, within those aforementioned dates. It may, at the time, seem a minor event, but its consequences will be vast. Hundreds may die. Thousands… mayhap millions, if it is not stopped.

The daemon will take human form and walk the worlds of the Imperium undetected. It has a name. Phonetically 'SLIITE' or perhaps Slyte or Slight.

It must be stopped. Its birth must be prevented.

All I have done in my long career in service of the ordos, all I have achieved… will be as nothing if this daemon comes into being.

* * *

'IT'S GETTING A little uncomfortable out here,' Nayl remarked. A las-shot had just scored across the flesh of his upper arm, but he didn't even wince.

'Agreed,' said Kara, ejecting another spent clip onto the cobbles of the span and slamming in a fresh one.

They'd been backing steadily under fire, and now the archway was tantalisingly close.

They both ducked their heads instinctively as heavy fire ripped out of the archway behind them and peppered the landwards-end of the bridge span. Mathuin was covering them at last.

They turned and ran into cover, bullets and lasfire chasing their heels.

Inside the archway, Thonius was waving them in. Mathuin's cannon ground dry and he paused to pop out the ammo drum and slap in a fresh one from the heavy pouches around his waist.

Nayl bent in the shadows and reloaded his pistol quickly, expertly. He looked up and stared out into the torrential rain. Out there, in the dark of the storm and the swiftly falling night, he counted at least nine muzzle flashes barking their way.

'How many?' he asked.

This time, Mathuin didn't answer. He turned his stony, hard light gaze towards Kara and raised an eyebrow.

'Fifteen,' she said at once.

'Fifteen,' mused Nayl. 'That's five each.'

'Hey!' said Thonius. 'There are four of us here!'

'I know,' Nayl grinned. 'But it's still five each. Unless you intend to surprise us.'

'You little bastard,' snapped Thonius. He raised his weapon and pinked off several shots at enemy across the span.

'Hmmm…' said Nayl. 'Still fifteen.'

+Kara. Can you join us?+

'On my way, boss,' said Kara Swole. She grinned at Nayl. 'Can you deal here? I mean, now it's seven and a half each.'

'Get on,' Nayl said. He started firing. Kara dashed off into the darkness behind them.

Thonius blasted away again. They all saw a hostile on the far side of bridge, through the rain, tumble and pitch off the crag.

'There!' Thonius said triumphantly.

'Seven each then,' Mathuin remarked to Nayl.

THE DIVINE FRATERY, *as I have learned, find it particularly easy to identify in their prospects others who have dabbled in farseeing and clairvoyance. It is as if such individuals somehow illuminate their life courses by toying with the future. The bright track of one has attracted their particular attention. It is through him, and the men and women around him, that the prospect of the manifestation has come to light.*

He will cause it. Him, or one of those close to him.

That is why I have taken it upon myself to warn him.

For he is my friend. My pupil. My interrogator.

KYS HADN'T EVEN seen or sensed the cultists behind the next archway. Ravenor, gliding forward without hesitation, pulped all four of them with his chair's built-in psi-cannons.

Kys followed him, striding forward through lakes of leaking blood and mashed tissue. She was worn out. The constant screams were getting to her.

They heard footfalls behind them. Kara Swole ran into view. Kys lowered her weapon.

'You called for me?'

+Indeed I did, Kara. I can't get up there.+

Kara looked up into the gloomy rafters and beams above them.

'No problem.' She took off her coat. Beneath it, she was dressed in a simple matt-green bodyglove.

'Hey, Kar. Luck,' called Kys.

Kara smiled.

She limbered up for a moment and then leapt up into the rafters, gripping the mouldering wood and gaining momentum.

Rapidly, all her acrobat skills coming back to her, she ascended, hand over hand, leaping from beam to beam, defying the dreadful gulf beneath her.

She was getting increasingly close to the flitting source of the screamlight. Her pulse raced. Grunting, she somer-saulted again, and landed on her feet on a crossmember.

Kara stood for a moment, feeling the streaming rain slick down over her from the tower's exposed roof. She stuck out her hands for balance, the assault weapon tightly cinched close under her bosom.

There was a light above her, shining out from a stairless doorway in the shell of the tower. Faint artificial light, illu-minating the millions of raindrops as they hurtled down the empty tower shaft towards her.

'Seeing this?' she asked.

+Yes, Kara.+

'What you expected?'

+I have no idea.+

'Here goes,' she said and jumped into space, into rain-fall, into air. A hesitation, on the brink, dark depths below her. Then she seized a rotting timber beam and swung, her fingers biting deep into the damp, flaking wood.

She pivoted in the air, and flew up into the doorway, feet first.

She landed firmly, balanced, arms wide.

A figure stood before her in the ruined tower room, illuminated by a single hovering glow-globe.

'Hello Kara,' the figure said. 'It's been a long time.'

She gasped. 'Oh God-Emperor... my master...'

The man was tall, shrouded in a dark leather coat that did not quite conceal the crude augmetics supporting his frame. His head was bald, his eyes dark-rimmed. He leaned heavily on a metal staff.

Rainwater streaming off him, Inquisitor Gregor Eisen-horn gazed at her.

DOWN AT THE archway, Thonius recoiled in horror. 'I think we have a problem,' he said.

'Don't be such a pussy,' Nayl said.

'Actually, I think he might be right,' said Mathuin. 'That's not good, is it?'

Nayl craned his neck to look. Something blocky and heavy was striding towards them over the bridge span. It was metal and solid, machined striding limbs hissing steam from piston bearings. Its arms were folded against the sides of its torso like the wings of a flightless bird. Those arms, each one a heavy lascannon, began to cough and spit. Massive hydraulic absorbers soaked up the recoil.

The archway collapsed in a shower of exploding masonry. Nayl, Thonius and Mathuin fled back into the cover of the gallery behind.

'Emperor save me,' Nayl exclaimed. 'They've got a bloody dreadnought!'

RAINWATER DRIPPED OFF Eisenhorn's nose. 'Gideon? Is he with you, Kara?' he asked.

'Yes, he is,' she stammered. 'Throne, it's good to see you.'

'And you, my dear. But it's important I speak to Gideon.'

Kara nodded. 'Ware me,' she said.

Far away, down below, Ravenor heard her. Kara Swole stiffened, her eyes clouding. The wraithbone pendant at her throat glowed with a dull, ethereal light.

She wasn't Kara Swole any more. Her body was possessed by the mind of Gideon Ravenor.

'Hello, Gregor,' Kara's mouth said.

'Gideon. Well met. I was worried you wouldn't come.'

'And ignore a summons from my mentor? Phrased in Glossia? "Thorn wishes Talon ..." I was hardly going to ignore that.'

'I thought you would appreciate a taste of the old, private code,' said Eisenhorn. His frozen face failed to show the smile he was feeling.

'How could I forget it, Thorn? You drummed it into me.'

Eisenhorn nodded. 'Much effort getting here?'

Kara's lips conveyed Ravenor's words. 'Some. An effort made to kill us. Nayl is holding them off at the gateway to the tower.'

'Old Harlon, eh?' Eisenhorn said. 'Ever dependable. You've got a good man there, Gideon. A fine man. Give him my respects. And Kara too, best there is.'

'I know, Gregor.' A strangely intense expression that wasn't her own appeared on Kara's face. 'I think it's time you told me why you brought me here.'

'Yes, it is. But in person, I think. That would be best. That way you can stop subjecting Kara to that effort of puppeting. And we can be more private. I'll come down to you.'

'How? There are no stairs.'

'The same way I got up here,' Eisenhorn said. He looked upwards, into the rain hosing down through the broken roof.

'Cherubael?' he whispered.

Something nightmarish up in the strobing screamlight answered him.

ITS PITTED STEEL hull glossy with rain, the dreadnought machine strode in through the shattered archway. The booming storm threw its hulking shadow a hundred jagging directions at once with its lightning. Its massive cannon pods pumped pneumatically as they retched out streams of las-bolts. The weapons made sharp, barking squeals as they discharged, a repeating note louder than the storm.

Behind it, three dozen armed brethren of the Divine Fratery charged across the bridge span.

Stone split and fractured under the bombardment. Pillars that had stood for eons teetered and collapsed like felled trees, spraying stone shards out across the terrace flooring.

Nayl, Mathuin and Thonius retreated back into the empty inner chambers of the ruined tower. Even Mathuin's rotator couldn't so much as dent the dreadnought's armour casing.

'Someone really, really wants us dead,' Thonius said.

'Us… or the person we came here to meet,' Nayl countered. They hurried down a dim colonnade and Nayl shoved both his comrades into the cover of a side arcade as cannon fire – bright as sunbursts – sizzled down the chamber.

'Golden Throne! There's got to be something we can try!' Nayl said.

Mathuin reached into his coat pocket and pulled out three close-focus frag grenades. He held them like a market-seller would hold apples or ploins. It was just like Mathuin to bring a pocket full of explosives. He never felt properly dressed unless he was armed to the back teeth.

'Don't suppose you've got a mini-nuke in the other pocket?' asked Thonius.

'My other suit's at the cleaners,' Mathuin replied.

'They'll have to do,' said Nayl. 'We'll go with what we've got.' He looked round. They could hear the heavy clanking footfalls of the dreadnought bearing down on them, the hiss of its hydraulic pistons, the whirr of its motivators.

'They may not even crack the thing's plating,' Mathuin remarked. As well as a supply of ridiculous ordnance, Zeph Mathuin could always be relied on for copious pessimism.

'We'll have to get them close,' said Thonius.

'We?' said Nayl. He'd already taken one of the grenades and was weighing it up like a ball.

'Yes, Mr Nayl. We.' Thonius took another of the grenades, holding it between finger and thumb like it was a potentially venomous insect. He really wasn't comfortable with the physicality of fighting. Thonius could hack cogitators and archive stacks faster than any of them, and could rewrite codes that any of the rest didn't even understand. He was Ravenor's interrogator because of his considerable intellect, not his killing talents. That's why Ravenor employed the likes of Nayl and Mathuin. 'Three of us, three bombs,' Thonius stated. 'We're all in this together. I'm not going to be pulped by that thing without having a go at stopping it myself.'

Nayl looked dubiously at Mathuin.

'It's not up for debate, you vulgarians,' Thonius said snottily. 'Don't make me remind you I'm technically in charge here.'

'Oh, that would explain why we're technically nose deep in crap,' Nayl said.

A thick section of stone wall blew in nearby, hammered to fragments by withering cannon fire. The massive weight of the dreadnought crushed heat-brittled stone into dust as it stomped through the gap.

The trio began to run again, down the next terrace, trying to put some distance between them and the killing machine.

'Get ahead!' Mathuin said. 'I'll take the first pop.' Nayl nodded and grabbed hold of Thonius, who was still puzzling over his grenade, figuring out how to adjust the knurled dial to set the timer. Nayl got the interrogator into cover.

Thonius straightened his sleeves. 'If you've pulled my coat out of shape, Nayl…' he began.

Nayl glared at him.

Behind them, in the open, Mathuin primed his grenade and turned. As the dreadnought hove into view, he hurled the small, black charge.

KARA REJOINED RAVENOR and Kys like an ape, swinging down through the rafters and leaping the last few metres.

Eisenhorn descended after her. He was being carried by a grotesque figure, a human shape twisted and distended by arcane forces. The thing glowed with an eldritch inner light. Its bare limbs and torso were covered with runes and sigils. Chains dragged from its ankles.

It set Eisenhorn's heavy, cumbersome form down on the flagstones.

'Thank you, Cherubael,' he said.

The thing, its head lolling brokenly, exposed its teeth in a dreadful smile. 'That's all? I can go back now?' it said. Its voice was like sandpaper on glass. 'There are many more phantoms up there to burn.'

'Go ahead,' Eisenhorn said.

The dreadful daemonhost zoomed back aloft into the rain-swept heights of the ruin. At once, the ghastly screaming began again. Light pulsed and flashed.

Eisenhorn faced Ravenor's chair. 'The Fratery has unleashed everything they have tonight to stop me. To stop me talking to you. Daemonhosts of their own. Cherubael has been battling them. I think he's enjoying it.'

'He?' said Ravenor via his chair's voxponder. 'Last we met, you called that thing an "it", my master.'

Eisenhorn shrugged. His augmetics sighed with the gesture. 'We have reached an understanding. Does that shock you, Gideon?'

'Nothing shocks me any more,' said Ravenor.

'Good,' said Eisenhorn. He looked at Kara and Kys.

'We need a moment, Kara. If you and your friend wouldn't mind.'

'Patience Kys,' Kys said, stern and hard.

'I know who you are,' said Eisenhorn, and turned away with Ravenor. In a low voice, he began to tell his ex-pupil all he knew about the Divine Fratery.

'Kar… that's Eisenhorn?' Kys whispered to Kara as they watched the figures withdraw.

'Yes,' replied Kara. She was still rather stunned by the meeting, and Ravenor's brief waring had left her tired.

'Everything you and Harlon have said about him… I expected…'

'What?'

'Something more intimidating. He's just a broken old man. And I can't think why he consorts with a Chaos-filth thing like that host-form.'

Kara shrugged. 'I don't know about the daemonhost. He fought it and hated it for so long, and then… I dunno. Maybe he's become the radical they say. But you're wrong. About him being a broken old man. Well, he's broken and he's old… but I'd rather go up against Ravenor unarmed than ever cross Gregor Eisenhorn.'

* * *

MATHUIN'S GRENADE EXPLODED. The aim had been good, but the device had bounced oddly at the last moment and had gone off beneath the striding dreadnought. The machine paced on through the ball of fire, untroubled.

Mathuin dived for cover as the cannons began pumping again.

'Crap… my turn, I suppose,' said Nayl. He clicked the setter to four seconds, thumbed the igniter, and ran out into the hallway, bowling the grenade underarm.

Then he threw himself into shelter.

The grenade bounced once, lifted with the spin Nayl had put on it, and smacked bluntly against the front shell of the dreadnought.

It was just rebounding off when it detonated.

The dreadnought vanished in a sheet of flame that boiled down the hallway, compressed and driven by the walls and roof.

As it cleared, Thonius saw the dreadnought. Its front was scorched, but it was far, far from dead.

'Damn. Just me then,' he said.

'YOU'VE DABBLED IN farseeing,' Eisenhorn said. 'I know that. Your time spent with the eldar drew you in that direction.'

'I won't deny it,' Ravenor replied.

'That makes you bright to the Fratery,' said Eisenhorn. 'It illuminates you in the interwoven pathways of the future. That's why they located you in their prospects.'

Ravenor was quiet for a moment. 'And you've come all this way, risked all this danger… to warn me?'

'Of course.'

'I'm flattered.'

'Don't be, Gideon. You'd do the same for me.'

'I'm sure I would. But what you're telling me is… crazy.'

Eisenhorn bowed his head and ran the fingers of his right hand up and down the cold grip of his runestaff.

'Of course it sounds crazy,' he said. 'But it's true. I ask you this… if you don't believe me, why are these cultist fools trying so hard to prevent our meeting here tonight? They know it's true. They want you denied of this warning.'

'That I will trigger this manifestation? This daemon-birth?'

'You, or one close to you. The trigger point is something that happens on Eustis Majoris.'

Within his force chair, Ravenor was numb. 'I won't lie, Gregor. My current investigations focus on that world. I was en route to Eustis Majoris when I diverted to meet you here. But I have no knowledge of this *Slight*. It hasn't figured in any of my research. I can't believe that something I will do… or something one of my band will do… will–'

'Gideon, I can't believe my only ally these days is a daemonhost. Fate surprises us all.'

'So what should I do, now you've warned me? Abandon my investigations on Eustis? Shy away from that world in the hope that by avoiding it I can also avoid this prophecy?'

Eisenhorn's face was in shadow. 'Maybe you should.'

'No,' said Ravenor. 'What I should be is careful. Careful in my own actions, careful to oversee the actions of my team. If there is truth in the Fratery's prophecy, it is surely bound up in the dire conspiracy I am just now uncovering on Eustis Majoris. But I must prosecute that case. I would be failing in the duty you charged me with if I didn't. After all, the future is not set. We make it, don't we?'

'I think we do. I hope we do.'

'Gregor, when have either of us shirked from serving the Throne just because we're afraid things might go bad? We are inquisitors, we seek. We do not hide.'

Eisenhorn raised his head and let the falling rain drops patter off his upraised palm. 'Gideon, I came to warn you, nothing else. I never expected you to change your course. Now, at least, you aware of a "might be". You can be ready for it. That's all I wanted.'

Far behind them, the sound of rapid cannon-fire and dull explosions echoed through the tower.

'I think the time for conversation is over,' said Eisenhorn.

* * *

THONIUS'S POCKETS WERE not full of munitions and ordnance like Mathuin's, but he reached into them anyway.
In one, a mini-cogitator, in another, two data-slates. In
a third, a clasped leather case in which he had wrapped
his tools: files, data-pins, fine brushes, tubes of lubri-
cant, a vial of adhesive, pliers and tweezers. All the
bric-a-brac that aided him in conquering and tinkering
with cogitators and codifiers.

'Carl! Get into cover!' Nayl was yelling.

Thonius slid out the vial of adhesive and wiped the
drooling nozzle down the side of the grenade ball, waiting a moment for it to get contact-tacky.

Then, taking a deep breath, he leapt out of cover into
the face of the dreadnought and lobbed the grenade. It
hit the front casing, and adhered there, stuck fast.

Mathuin threw himself out of cover and tackled Thonius, bringing him down behind a pillar.

The grenade exploded.

'You see?' said Thonius. 'You see how *thinking* works?'

But the dreadnought wasn't finished. The blast had
split its belly plates, but it was still moving, still striding,
still firing.

Thonius shrugged. 'Okay… we're dead.'

The dreadnought suddenly stopped blasting. It faltered. A chill swept over the chamber.

Ravenor's chair slid into view, heading towards the
killer machine. With the force of his mind, he had
momentarily jammed its weapons.

Sudden frost coated the walls, Ravenor's chair and the
dreadnought. The machine tried to move. Cycling mechanisms shuddered as it attempted to clear its guns.

A tall figure strode past Ravenor, heading for the dreadnought. It held a runestaff in one hand and a drawn sword
in the other. Its robes fluttered out behind it, stiff with ice.

'Holy Terra!' exclaimed Nayl. 'Eisenhorn?'

A second before Ravenor's mental grip failed, a second
before the cannons resumed their murderous work,
Eisenhorn swung the sword – Barbarisater – and cleft the

dreadnought in two. The sword-blade ripped along the fissure Thonius's cunning grenade had put in it.

Eisenhorn turned aside and shielded his face as the dreadnought combusted.

He looked back at them all, terrible and majestic, back-lit by flames. 'Shall we?' he said.

WITH THEIR DREADNOUGHT gone, the remainder of the Fratery force fled. The warband and the two inquisitors slaughtered many as they made their escape into the storm.

Tugging one of her kineblades out of a body with her mind, Kys watched Eisenhorn ripping his way through the faltering hostiles around them.

'Now I see what you mean,' she said to Kara Swole.

'I'M DONE HERE,' Gregor Eisenhorn said. He looked back across the bride span to the tower. Screamlight was still dancing around the summit. 'Cherubael needs my help now. I should go and see how he's doing.'

'I will be vigilant,' Ravenor said.

Eisenhorn knelt and pressed his gnarled hands flat against the side of the chair.

'The Emperor go with you. I've said my piece. It's up to you now, Gideon.'

Eisenhorn rose and looked at the others. 'Mamzel Kys. Interrogator. Mr Mathuin. A pleasure meeting you.' He nodded to each of them. 'Kara?'

She smiled. 'Gregor.'

'Never a hardship seeing you. Look after Gideon for me.'

'I will.'

Eisenhorn looked at Harlon Nayl and held out a hand. Nayl clasped it with both of his.

'Harlon. Like old times.'

'Emperor protect you, Gregor.'

'I hope so,' Eisenhorn said, and walked away, back across the bridge span towards the tower where the screamlight still flashed and sparked. They knew they would not see him again.

Unless the future was not as set as it seemed.

MALINTER FELL AWAY below them, vast and silent. Nayl piloted the transport up into low orbit, flashing out signals to their ship.

Once the nav was set and automatics had taken over, he turned his chair on its pivot and looked at Ravenor.

'He wasn't the same,' he said.

+How do you mean?+

'He seemed so sane I thought he was mad.'

+Yes. I thought that too. It's hard to know whether I should believe him.+

'About what?'

+About the dangers ahead, Harlon. The risks we may take.+

'So… what do we do?'

+We carry on. We do our best. We serve the Emperor of Mankind. If what Gregor said comes to pass, we deal with it. Unless you have a better idea.'

'Not a one,' replied Nayl, turning back to study the controls.

+Good.+ sent Ravenor, and wheeled his chair around, returning to the cabin space behind where the others were gathered.

Nayl sighed and looked ahead at the turning starfields.

The future lay ahead, its back to them, saying nothing.

FOREVER LOYAL
Mitchel Scanlon

IT WAS WITH good reason they called it Hell's Marsh. A lesson Arvus Drel, former notary minoris to the planetary archives of His Excellency Governor Arbenal of the Imperial backwater Bajoris IV, had learned to his displeasure in the course of three miserable days spent within its bounds. Three days spent wearily trudging from one dismal quagmire to the next, while all the time the mud underfoot pulled treacherously at boot and ankle. Three days enduring the bites of szetze flies the size of a man's thumb. Three days of cold, damp discomfort. Hell's Marsh, indeed. Drel had cursed the whole damned place to hell with many a ragged and unhappy breath. Cursed the marsh. Cursed his companions. And, above all else, cursed that circumstance ever forced him to so foul and loathsome a place.

The notary looked behind him at the landscape as it stretched away. They had lost sight of the shuttle days ago, and he cursed that they could not have landed closer to his conjectured co-ordinates. But the treacherous swamps were too soft for the lumbering craft to settle on, and they had been forced to abandon it on the only safe section of land they could find. From then on it had been a long toil on foot. His gaze wandered up into the sky. Through the misty swarms of mosquitoes he could see Bajoris IV itself, hanging in space like a livid, blue balloon. His head spun slightly at the thought that he was no longer standing on the ground of the planet where he had spent all his life. Hell's Marsh was Bajoris's moon. It was uninhabited, dangerous and completely without value. Or so everyone thought. Never did he imagine that he would ever have had to set foot on its stinking surface. Yet here he was…

Sergeant Jarl, leader of the platoon of PDF troopers assigned to escort Drel on his mission, glanced behind him and grinned.

'Ha. Now there's a face that could sour milk, my friends. From the looks of it, I'd say the notary was beginning to wish he'd never set foot on the marsh.'

A hulking brute of a man, Jarl seemed to find gruff and sly amusement in his charge's every discomfort. And, not for the first time, Drel found himself looking at the heavy fur of the cloak around Jarl's shoulders and wishing whatever unfortunate beast it once belonged to had put up more of a fight. Still, he was enough of a diplomat to keep the thought to himself. Instead, forcing a lacklustre smile, he tried a more civil reply.

'Not at all, sergeant. Though, granted, I had hoped we would be closer to our objective by now.'

'Teh. With country like this, it is always going to be slow progress, notary,' Jarl shrugged. 'If you know a short-cut to this lost city of yours, I'm sure we'd be glad to hear it.'

Biting his lip, Drel said nothing. The sergeant's mood seemed even enough, but three days in the marsh had already led to frayed tempers, and Drel knew better than to risk provoking Jarl and his men. They were Volgars, nomadic warrior tribesmen from the planet's polar wastes, probably conscripted into the Planetary Defence Force as punishment for non-payment of tithes. As far as Drel was concerned, they were little better than barbarians, with Jarl likely some minor clan chieftain awarded sergeant's rank as a mark of his status.

Far from the civilised lifestyle he was used to, Drel was keenly aware of his isolation. He was in the company of men to whom violence was second nature, men who would think no more of killing a man than Drel would of swatting one of these damned szetze flies. And, while the Volgars might be under orders to protect his life at all costs, he would not care to see their loyalty put too strongly to the test. Not with so many quagmires hereabouts where one might dispose of an inconvenient body. And especially not if they ever learned just how much they had been misled.

'The notary has gone quiet again, Jarl. Perhaps he don't know no shortcuts. Or else he's just enjoying his walk in the marsh so much, he doesn't want it to end.'

This from another of the Volgars, Trooper Skeg, a grizzled veteran whose elaborate facial tattoos failed to disguise the spectacular ugliness of the features beneath. All the Volgars wore similar designs, their ugly Northlander faces painted in swirling blue-black masks of whorls and arches, as though touched by the fingerprint of some savage god. But in his heart of hearts, Drel was forced to admit it was not just their stench he found intimidating. Never the largest nor most forceful of men himself, he felt dwarfed by his escorts' sheer physical presence. They were men built on a bigger scale, each one brawny, broad-shouldered and bear-like, standing half a head or more taller than him. And, while he suffered and stumbled through the marsh beside them, the Volgars seemed immune to every hardship.

It was then, as they made their way down yet another muddy and overgrown trail, that it happened. One of the Volgars had turned towards him with a sardonic smile, some fresh example of barbarian wit no doubt ready on

his lips, when there came the sense of a distant discharge
and a sudden stiffening of the air. Layer by layer, in the
space of a single heartbeat, the trooper's face disappeared before Drel's horrified eyes, revealing first the wet
red musculature beneath the skin, then the glistening
white bone of the skull itself. For a moment the skull-
face stared at him with empty sockets, an idiot smile
seemingly still fixed upon its lipless mouth. The exposed
spine rose from the undamaged flesh of the trooper's
torso as though it were no more than some unwanted
suit of clothing his skeleton was ready to discard. Then,
abruptly, as though realising their mistake, flesh and
bone alike collapsed in a steaming pile of offal. Though
Drel might have screamed then, he found his horror at
the gruesome spectacle outweighed by more pressing
concerns. Spying movement in the long rushes on either
side of the trail, he was forced to entertain the unwel-
come notion that he himself might well be the next to
die.

'Ambush!'

As Jarl's men shouted hoarse and desperate warnings,
Drel saw half a dozen gaunt, machine-like figures emerge
from among the rushes. Their bodies dripped with muck
from the marsh, silent but for the eerie whisper of reed-
stems whipping through the spaces of their ribs.

The skeletal figures advanced towards them, eyes burning with ancient malice; a malice which found able
counterpoint in the sickly green death-glow emanating
from the strange weapons each machine-warrior held in
unfeeling hands. One of their weapons fired and a
trooper died an ugly death, reduced to a flailing skeleton
in the blink of an eye. Then, in a roar of obscene oaths
and battle-cries, the Volgars charged forward to meet the
advance with lasguns blazing.

Paralysed by indecision, Drel found himself briefly
alone at the eye of the storm as, all around him, fragile
flesh and unyielding metal met in uneven confrontation.
He saw a machine-warrior cut down a screaming trooper

right in front of him and for an instant the killer paused, death's head turning first one way, then the next as it cast about for a new victim. To Drel's horror, he saw the creature turn its smouldering and soulless eyes to gaze his way.

His panic-clumsy fingers scrabbled at the holster by his side as the creature advanced slowly towards him and Drel inadvertently took a step back. He abruptly realised his mistake as he felt his feet lose their purchase in the soft surface of the trail. He felt the ground slide away, the skeletal figure before him seeming to slip beneath his field of vision. It was replaced by a view of the dismal grey sky overhead as he landed on his back in the slurping mud of the marsh, the impact jarring the laspistol from his fear-slick fingers just as he finally managed to pull it free of its holster.

Caught helpless, Drel saw the machine-creature loom over him, arms raised as it lifted the axe-blade at the end of its weapon to deliver a killing blow. But the blow never came – the creature suddenly spat out a spray of broken metal as a fist-sized hole appeared in the front of its face. It stood frozen for a moment, arms still raised, the symmetry of its death-mask features abruptly ruined, as eyes like burning coals became flickering embers. Then, strangely, the cadaverous outlines of its body seemed to almost soften and fade, before, in a sudden flaring flash of gangrenous light, the machine-warrior disappeared so swiftly it was as though it had never been there at all. Drel was left blinking in amazement, staring past where the metallic figure had been to see Sergeant Jarl standing a few paces behind, a thin line of smoke rising like a question mark from the barrel of the bolt pistol in his hand.

'Well, notary, they may look like death, but it seems if a man tries hard enough they can still be made to die.'

THE ENEMY HAD BEEN destroyed. But it soon became clear the men of Sergeant Jarl's platoon had paid a heavy price. Of the thirty men who had come down the trail only half still lived. Fifteen men were dead, their lives traded dearly for six of the enemy. Assuming the skull-faced figures that had ambushed them could ever be described as having lived at all.

Once a head count had been made and the wounds of the survivors dressed, Jarl and his men set about gathering the mostly skeletal remains of their dead before performing a brief approximation of the primitive funeral rites of their northern homelands. The body of each dead trooper was tied into a foetal position with twine, their lasguns similarly tied to dead hands so they would have a weapon with which to fight the daemons that would confront them at the gates of the afterlife. Then, after some words had been said and Jarl had cut a shallow but bloody notch into his forearm in memory of each departed comrade, their huddled bodies were thrown one by one into a deep watery pit in the marsh.

Drel noticed the Volgars were careful to strip the dead of any potentially useful equipment before consigning them to the waters – even removing the power packs from their lasguns. Whether this was a sign that they believed the dead had no need of such things in the Otherworld, or simply a matter of pragmatism outweighing superstition, he could not be sure. Not that he was overly concerned with the fate of the dead Volgars either way. When it came to the question of remains, he was more interested in those of the enemy.

Or rather, the lack thereof. For like the creature Jarl had slain, each of the machine-warriors had disappeared when they suffered fatal wounds, vanishing like night-time terrors at the first touch of dawn. It was a mystery to which Drel could give no explanation. But whatever the cause, the enemy were gone, leaving the bodies of their victims and a few scraps of twisted metal as the only sign of their passing.

Holding one such fragment in his hands, Drel gazed at it with mingled horror and fascination. It was curved, marked with rectangular tooth-shaped protrusions at its base, its outer surface still stained with the patina of the marsh while the inner seemed impossibly smooth and ageless. It looked to have come from the upper jaw of the creature that had nearly killed him. Standing there with that fragment in his hands, Drel found himself wondering just how long the creature had been there, lying hidden in stagnant waters waiting to repel any intruder in the marsh. Centuries, perhaps? Even millennia? Were there others still out there, waiting patiently somewhere on the trail ahead to finish what their fellows had started?

'I'd say you owe us some answers, notary.'

It was Jarl, a dangerous edge to his voice as he spoke. He stood facing Drel, knife in one hand and blood trickling down his left arm from the fifteen fresh notches he had carved into his bicep. His men gathered behind him, glowering at Drel with faces set in hard and unforgiving lines. Looking at them, Drel realised the next few minutes might well dictate the future course of his life. Not least the immediate question of whether he would ever leave this trail alive.

'Answers, sergeant?' he replied, in what he sincerely hoped was a commanding and imperious tone. 'You have your orders. They should be enough.'

'I've lost fifteen good men, notary. All of them kinfolk, or else blood-sworn to me. Men who would've trusted me to lead them into hell. It looks like that's where I did lead them, blindly, and at your say-so. I want answers. I want to know why we came to this marsh. I want to know what those damned metal daemons were. Most of all, I want to know about this ruined city you told us you wanted to find, and what's there that could be worth my men's lives. I want to know all this now, notary. Or else I'm going to tell you where you can stick your orders. And then, I'm going to show you what you can put there with them.'

Jarl brandished his knife in front of Drel's face by way of emphasis. For his part, Drel did his best to reassure himself he could still turn this situation to his advantage. He must pick his words carefully, and, above all else, show no fear. If the Volgars smelt blood in the water, all was lost.

'What do you know of the history of this world, sergeant?' he asked. Seeing Jarl's answering sneer, he quickly continued. 'Would it surprise you to learn that thousands of years ago, in the dark days before contact was re-established with the Imperium, people lived on Hell's Marsh in much the same way as your people do now in Volgar? That they were divided into dozens of squabbling nomadic tribes who lived – and I mean no offence when I say this, sergeant – in a state of barbarism, barely comprehending that a wider galaxy even existed?'

'I will take your word for it, notary,' Jarl said, the dangerous tone still present in his voice, although for the moment, at least, he had lowered his knife. 'But what does this have to do with our mission?'

'Everything, sergeant. You see, sometime in this moon's distant prehistory, one of those feuding tribes managed to raise themselves above their rivals. They called themselves the Neand, and somewhere in what are now these marshlands they built a city; a city from which they dominated this world for close to five hundred years, at the same time demonstrating a level of technological sophistication far in advance of anyone else.'

'Phh. If these Neand of yours were so special, notary, how is it I have never heard of them?'

'Few have, sergeant. You must understand that the entire span of the rise and fall of Neand civilisation took place in a time before histories were written. Even most scholars count them as little more than myth. It was only recently, through some of our earliest written records, that it was established where their city was located. There, you have your answers. It is time we were on our way once more.'

'Hold fast, notary,' Jarl said, his eyes hard and tight with anger. 'I don't remember saying we were going anywhere. To hell with your city and your answers. I've lost fifteen men. I don't intend to lose any more!'

'I mourn for your dead, truly I do. They were heroes, each and every one of them. But to turn back now would only dishonour them. Nor would that be the worst of it. You must understand, sergeant, there are facts about the nature of our mission that I am not at liberty to disclose. Facts which, were you to hear them, would convince you instantly of its importance. But for now, let me remind you I am here at the express order of Governor Arbenal. And let me tell you, if you fail in your duty, you and your men may be jeopardising the life of our entire planet.'

'Strong words,' Jarl growled. 'Takes more than strong words though, to make a thing true.' But despite the show of anger, Drel could see the big man was starting to waver. As a barbaric warrior, he was easy prey to words like 'heroism' and 'honour,' and even as a conscript trooper, still fell prey to words like 'duty'.

'Be that as it may, search your heart for a moment and you will see the truth of what I tell you. Ask yourself: in all your years of service to the divine Emperor, have you ever fought anything like the creatures we fought here today? Ask yourself that, then tell me if you think I am lying when I tell you our world is doomed unless we complete our mission.'

Now it was Drel's turn to pause, letting the words hang in the air as the Volgars considered their weight. They were all wavering now. They looked uncomfortable, unsettled, uncertain. It was time to press home his advantage.

'I am not unaware of the sacrifices you and your men have made. Nor will I try to tell you that there may not be yet more sacrifices to come. The governor has given me wide powers in this matter, and so I offer you just reward for your bravery. Continue with me to the city and I promise that once the mission is ended I will see to it every man here is given an honourable discharge and free passage back to Volgar. And with it, fifty kilos of gold per man. Think of it: you will return to your homeland as free men and heroes. Heroes, incidentally, who will be as rich as kings. Think on that, then tell me if you still say orders be damned.'

No one answered. But, from the thoughtful gleam in each man's eyes, no answer was needed. The tide had turned. He had them now. With reason, argument, and a touch of bribery, he had won the day.

It was almost a pity that so much of it was untrue.

NOT ALL OF IT, of course. The city itself was real enough, though it was all but forgotten, lost as surely in the mists of history as it was in the mists of the marsh. But as they made under way again, Drel reassured himself that even after thousands of years some part of the city and its treasures must still remain. And he would find them. He would not countenance any thought otherwise.

Jarl and his men were quiet now; their earlier banter replaced by a sombre watchfulness as they continued down the trail. The ambush by the 'metal daemons', as Jarl called them, had shaken the troopers badly, and Drel realised it was almost a miracle he had persuaded them to continue at all. A miracle of greed over superstition.

No, not just greed. It was his promise of free passage back to Volgar that had clinched it. One did not need to be a barbarian to see these men longed to return to their homes with every fibre of their being. And now he had seen that weakness in them he would remember it. Given the events of the expedition thus far, he had every reason to believe it was a lever he might have to use again.

They paused as the trooper on point raised his hand to beckon caution. With ears straining at every sound they stood motionless for a moment, barely daring even to breathe. But there was only the oppressive ever-present noise of the marsh: the cries of distant birds, the buzz and hum of insects, the sound of marsh waters lapping gently against the muddy bank of the trail. Then, seemingly satisfied, the trooper on point signalled the advance once more. Drel realised their progress would be slow now; for all their bullish bravado, Jarl and his men were spooked, jumping at shadows and pausing at the slightest uncertain sound. They must be close to the city by now, close enough that the Volgars' newfound caution could only add a day to their journey at most. And he could afford to wait a day longer. He had already waited his entire life.

Of course, it was only recently he had even realised he had been waiting at all. It was not so unusual for a man in his position to know discontentment. He had served the governors of Bajoris IV for nearly thirty years, a nameless bureaucratic cog in the service of a succession of distant uncaring masters. And what had been his reward for those years of dedication? At the age of forty-three he had risen as far as he was going to as notary minoris to the planetary archives – a glorified librarian – while all around him, men barely more literate than Jarl were raised above him by virtue of contacts and influence he did not have. Was it really so surprising he had grown unhappy with his lot? And when in the course of cataloguing some of the oldest records in the archives he had found the papyrus scroll, was it surprising his thoughts had turned immediately to how he could make this remarkable discovery work for him?

The scroll was over four thousand years old: so fragile he had needed to use forceps to handle it. Misfiled by one of Drel's predecessors, it had lain gathering dust for centuries, until, seeing it, Drel had recognised its importance at once. As he read the scroll, he realised his entire life up to that point had been spent marking time until he found it.

The scroll contained a treatise by the sage Terodotus, outlining a brief history of the Neand. Written centuries after their downfall, it told of how, with the aid of their technology, the Neand had drained part of the marsh and built their city to be the hub of a burgeoning moon-wide empire. At the same time, Terodotus wrote that the Neand were also a deeply religious people, whose lives were structured around regular rituals of praise and

thanksgiving dedicated to their unnamed god – a god
whose benevolence they held responsible for all their tri-
umphs. In the name of their god, the Neand dominated
Hell's Marsh (although it wasn't called that then) for centuries. But, for all their achievements, even they could not
endure forever. Under weight of war with jealous tribal
rivals, the boundaries of the Neand Empire were slowly
pushed back until only the city in the marsh remained.
Then, the waters of the marsh rose once more and the
Neand found even their last stronghold threatened,
though, finally, it was neither war nor waters, but religion
that sealed their fate. In the wake of some form of religious schism, the guardians of the Neand's faith turned
on their fellow city-dwellers, slaughtering every man,
woman and child in a single terrifying night of blood-
shed. Their city was slowly forgotten as it was gradually
swallowed by the rising marsh. *Sic transit gloria mundi*, as
Terodotus put it in the Old High Gothic dialect of his
time.

So pass away the glories of this world.

But whatever wider parable the ancient sage had hoped
to teach with his history of the Neand was lost on Arvus
Drel. Instead, the tale of their city and its marvels awakened a desire he thought he had made peace with years
ago. A desire for wealth, power and all the finer things. A
desire for everything in his life that he had so far gone
without. A desire awakened by a single, simple word.

Archeotech.

Before he had even finished reading the scroll, Arvus
Drel found himself considering the resources at his disposal. With information as to the possible location of a
vast treasure trove of archeotech at his fingertips, it was
not a question of whether he would go after it.

It was only a question of how.

'You REALISE, THIS is highly irregular,' Captain Vlix had said,
glancing up from the sheaf of papers on his desk to look
sourly at Arvus Drel. 'First you come here demanding I give

you a platoon of men and a shuttle. Now you say I can't even vox my superiors for approval?'

'As I said before, captain,' Drel replied, doing his best to imitate the smooth arrogance of an envoy on an important mission, 'this is a matter requiring more than the usual discretion. You will see it is all laid out plainly in the orders I have given you.'

'The orders. Yes...' Vlix's voice trailed off as his gaze returned to the papers on his desk. For long minutes he studied them, but Drel felt no great fear at the scrutiny. The signatures, Governor Arbenal's seal, even the paper's embossed watermark, were all quite genuine. As notary minoris to the planetary archives, he had access to countless such official documents. It had only been a matter of finding a suitable template and, making use of a previously unknown talent for forgery, creating some small alterations. Then, armed with his fraudulent papers, he had sought passage to an isolated PDF outpost to acquire the troops he needed to put his plans into motion.

'Corporal Drinn, bring me the duty roster.'

At last, despairing of finding any fault in them, the captain abandoned his inspection of the papers to press a stud on the vox-com at his desk. Then, as a corporal hurried from a nearby anteroom with a heavy logbook in his hands, Vlix took it from him and began leafing through the pages with a pained expression.

'You must understand,' he said, 'at an outpost like this, manpower is limited.'

'All the same, captain, I feel confident you will put every resource at my disposal,' Drel replied, the smugly condescending tone in his voice letting the captain know he expected nothing less.

'As you wish,' Vlix said, eyes returning to the pages of the roster before rising again with a subtle gleam. 'Now, as to those men you wanted, I do believe I may have found some suitable candidates.'

Abruptly, Captain Vlix stood up, absent-mindedly buttoning his uniform jacket as he strode from the office

with Drel trailing behind him. There was a definite spring
in the captain's step now, almost as though something he
had seen in the roster had given him a new lease of life,
a change that Drel could not help but view with a certain
foreboding.

Following Vlix through the cramped corridors of the
command post, Drel began to hear the voices of dozens
of shouting, cheering men. As they stepped into the
parade ground outside, he saw the source of the noise: a
crowd of at least fifty troopers gathered in the centre of
the parade ground, standing in a ring around some
unseen spectacle. Seeing his commanding officer's
approach, a harried lieutenant gave up his attempts to
restore order to turn and smartly salute the captain.

'It's Sergeant Jarl, sir,' the lieutenant said, his voice helpless. 'He is demonstrating unarmed combat techniques to
some of the men.'

Following in the captain's wake as he pushed his way
through the cheering throng, Drel saw that at least half the
men in the crowd were Volgar Irregulars. He saw money
changing hands as odds were adjusted, other men squabbling, even coming to blows. Then, Vlix reached the inner
circle of the crowd, and Drel saw what had caused all the
excitement.

In the open space at the centre of the crowd, two men
were fighting. One was quite possibly the biggest man
Drel had ever seen: a tattoo-faced, top-knotted Volgar
primitive wearing a heavy fur cloak with sergeant's stripes
branded on his shoulder. He was unarmed. Although the
other man – a uniformed local PDF trooper of less extraordinary build – was armed with a bayonet on the end of
his lasgun, there was no question the Volgar had the
advantage. Jabbing desperately with his weapon, it was
all the trooper could do to keep the big man away. Suddenly, the trooper thrust too far and the Volgar caught
hold of the lasgun barrel with one meaty hand. For a
moment the two men struggled for possession of the
weapon, though in truth the trooper was the only one

struggling. At last, growing bored with the game, the giant used his grip on the lasgun to pull the trooper towards him, simultaneously raising his knee to make crushing contact with his opponent's groin. With a high-pitched scream the trooper bent double, his face striking one of the Volgar's raised elbows before collapsing to the ground as all around the other Volgars whooped in triumph.

'Sergeant Jarl!' Vlix yelled.

As the Volgars fell into sullen silence, Drel despaired inwardly as he understood the reason for the spring he had seen in the captain's step earlier. Evidently it was in Vlix's mind to kill two snakes with one stone. He was going to give Drel the one group of men in his command he would be glad to see the back of – the Volgars. As he saw Jarl turn to grudgingly salute his commander before walking towards them, Drel realised the captain's cunning might still work to his advantage. He noticed Jarl could not resist giving one last kick to the head of his fallen opponent before walking away.

Yes, thought Drel. On reflection, this is exactly the quality of man I need.

'AND I TELL you it is suicide!' Crouching beside him within the cover of a tall stand of reeds, Jarl's voice was an urgent whisper. And, as much as it would have suited his purpose to argue otherwise, privately Drel was forced to admit the sergeant might well be right.

Six days had passed since their meeting on the parade ground. And now, the day after the ambush on the trail, they had finally reached the ruins of the city in the marsh. Little of its former glories remained. From the occasional weathered outcrop of rock bearing the faint outlines of what once must have been exquisite carvings, Drel could see the majority of its buildings were submerged in the mud of the marsh beneath their feet. All that was left above the waterline were the monumental ruins before them – ruins of the great temple that had once dominated the city from a low hill at its centre. But even that had not escaped unscathed. Time and the elements had done their worst, leaving the temple and its surrounding walls in an alarming state of disrepair. Everywhere, eroded stonework seemed ready to collapse under the weight of time; to enter the temple at all was to risk being buried under a landslide of rubble. But it was not the perilous state of the place's masonry that had raised Jarl's ire. For all the carelessness of its ruin, the temple compound had not been left unguarded. At regular intervals, along every section of its crumbling outer gates and walls, stood more of the sinister machine-creatures that had ambushed them earlier.

'I count a dozen at least,' Jarl whispered. 'That's twice as many as before, and they killed half my men. So I say to hell with your gold and promises. The only thing attacking that damned place would get us is dead!'

For perhaps the first time in years, Drel found himself without a ready answer. Jarl was right: whatever small numerical advantage the troopers possessed was easily outweighed by the sheer fearsomeness of the guardians which, even now, patrolled the wall ramparts or else stood motionless, with unblinking eyes trained on the landscape about them. Any hopes he had harboured that the creatures who had ambushed them on the trail might be the last of their kind were cruelly dashed. As matters stood, an assault on the temple could have only one outcome.

Watching them as they went about their duties, Drel pondered the nature of his enemy. They certainly seemed like machines: he found it impossible to believe they were essentially alive, as he was. But if they were machines, who had made them? Had the Neand created them to guard their city, leaving the sentries to stand unceasing at their posts long after their masters were as dust? There was no clear answer, but as an educated man Drel refused to be defeated. All things could be laid bare by reason, he told himself. And, if he had never seen the like of these machines before, then perhaps it was a question of considering when he had seen or heard of anything similar.

His first thoughts were of things he had heard of but never seen: the God-Machines of the Adeptus Titanicus, and the servitor creations of the Adeptus Mechanicus. But he quickly abandoned them; the Titans were giants, while the servitors of the tech-priests were said to be a fusion of machine and once-living flesh – neither remotely like the skeletal figures guarding the city. But the machine-creatures' eerily precise and methodical movements put him in mind of something else. Years ago, a merchant eager to win favour had purchased a set of life-sized clockwork automata shaped to look like marching guardsmen, and had gifted them to Governor Arbenal. They had been remarkably ingenious, attached to runners set in a circular grooved track. Once activated, the guardsmen would march round and round until the reserves of energy stored in their springs were exhausted. At first delighted, the governor had put them on display in his palace foyer, where Drel had seen them during his infrequent visits to the palace.

Drel had always found something hideous in the mechanical figures' blank imitation of life, and he'd been pleased when, finally growing tired of his gift, the governor had ordered the automata put into storage. But now, watching the temple walls, Drel saw something that made him think perhaps the machine-creatures and those automata were not so unalike.

From his vantage among the reeds, Drel saw a small piece of ageing wall rampart crumble beneath the feet of the metal warrior above it. Caught off-balance, the creature stood awkwardly on one leg for a moment, only to be doomed by its slowness of wit as, suddenly, the whole section of wall on which it stood collapsed, throwing the metal biped violently to the ground in a shower of toppling masonry. Crushed among fallen debris at the foot of the wall, it tried to free itself, impotently writhing its limbs, reminiscent of the struggles of an insect caught in molasses. Then, abruptly, its strength failing at last, the creature disappeared in a flash of ghastly green light. But what seemed extraordinary to Drel was the fact the other machine-creatures did not at any point go to help their fallen brother, or even turn their eyes to glance its way. And it occurred to him: what if the machine-creatures were just automata? More complex and sophisticated than the marching guardsmen perhaps, but still machines, with all a machine's limitations. What if they were only acting according to pre-defined instructions and incapable of responding to any situation unforeseen by their makers? If that were the case, it might be just the edge he needed. His mind made up, Drel turned to Jarl beside him, to give the crouched and glowering Volgar a confident smile.

'Suicide, sergeant? Not at all. I assure you, not only will we breach those temple gates, but we will live to tell the tale of it to our grandchildren afterwards.'

THERE WERE FURTHER arguments, of course. But eventually even the most unimaginative of the Volgars were forced to admit his plan had merit. Then, after several hours scouring the marsh for suitable materials and applying the native skills that had probably stood them in good stead in their primitive homelands, the Volgars came to him with an acceptable facsimile of the device he had asked them to build.

It was a handcart of sorts, mounted on rough-carved wooden wheels and designed to be pushed towards its destination. Held together with reed-stem ropes and wooden dowels, with hand-rails set wide enough apart for three men to push it at once and a makeshift wooden hoarding to shield them, it looked every bit the flimsy scratch-built device it was. All the same, Drel was sure it would serve his purpose well enough.

'Now!' yelled Jarl.

From their hiding places among the reeds, the troopers opened up with their lasguns, concentrating their fire on the machine-creatures standing on the ramparts above the temple's dilapidated gates. The Volgars' marksmanship was poor, but still the machine-warriors seemed taken aback by the sudden withering fusillade of fire. Then, before the enemy could regain the initiative, a trio of Volgars emerged from the reeds to push the lumbering handcart towards the temple gates.

Watching them straining every sinew to move their recalcitrant burden through the mud, Drel began to believe his plan might work. As he had predicted, only the four guards nearest the gates had responded to the attack, the others standing motionless at their posts as though nothing was amiss. But then, he saw one of the gate-guards fire its weapon, a crackling beam of energy reducing the hoarding on top of the handcart to ash. Another of the creatures fired twice more, the first beam passing harmlessly over the heads of the handcart's crew. But with the second beam the creature found its range, flaying the flesh from a screaming crewman in an instant. Seeing it, Drel felt icy doubts clutch at his heart: if the machines thought to fire at the cart itself, the assault would be over. But the enemy seemed to lack the wit to shoot at anything other than the crew, while the remaining crewmen were careful to keep their heads down as the air above them boiled with virid fire. Then at last Drel saw the handcart finally reach the gates.

'Now, Jarl! Now!' he yelled as, seeing four machine-creatures sally forth to defend the gates, the handcart crew abandoned their burden and turned to run.

'Not until my men are clear,' Jarl rumbled back. He gripped a small black cylinder that was dwarfed in one giant fist. For a moment Drel feared loyalty might ruin everything. The machine-creatures at the gate decided the issue for them as they cut down the fleeing troopers in mid-stride. Then, eyes dark with hatred, Jarl pressed the stud of the remote detonator in his hand and the handcart exploded.

It had taken every grenade and scrap of explosive the Volgars had, but Drel could not help but feel satisfied as the handcart's cargo detonated, enveloping the machine-creatures and the gate in a blinding flash of fire. He found himself even more satisfied when the smoke cleared to reveal splintered gates yawning open on broken hinges and no sign of any surviving guards.

'For Volgar!' Jarl screamed, as he rose from among the reeds and started for the shattered gates. 'And for the honour of our dead!'

Taking up their sergeant's cry, the remaining Volgars charged forward with him. Racing to keep up, Drel marvelled at the success of his plan. Even with the gates ruptured and their comrades destroyed, the remaining machine-warriors on other parts of the wall showed no sign of taking action. It was as he thought – each machine-warrior was detailed to guard its own section of wall and no other. With the sentries guarding the gates gone, and judging by the reaction of the others, he and the screaming horde of Volgars might as well have been ghosts.

After reaching the sheltering arc of the all but nonexistent gates, the Volgars paused long enough for Drel to catch up.

'Where to now, notary?' Jarl asked.

'The grey pyramid-shaped structure just ahead of us,' Drel panted, still out of breath. 'The main building of the temple. That is where the ancients would have kept most of their archeo... ah, the materials which are the object of our mission.'

If Jarl noticed the slip of the tongue, he gave no sign of it. Instead, turning to face his men, he said: 'You heard him. We go in two files and we go slow. Keep your wits sharp and your lasguns ready.'

Slowly then, eyes nervously scanning the ruined buildings either side for tell-tale movement, they advanced into the temple courtyard. Their objective, a squat and ugly pyramid with great stone steps running up its face, stood perhaps three hundred paces away at the centre of the temple complex. But with the sepulchral silence of that place restored, to Drel they seemed the longest steps he had ever taken. This was a place of the dead, where every shadow seemed to harbour hidden danger and the air hung heavy with menace. But he had come too far to turn back. Even with every nerve in his body urging him to run and never look back, he refused to be dissuaded.

He was so close now. He need only walk between the double row of crown-sized silver domes marking out the pathway to the temple, and everything he had ever dreamed of would be in his hands. Power, riches, respect; he need only keep walking and it all would be his. As they made their way down the pathway, Drel saw one of the silver domes start to rise from the mud. It was then that he realised the magnitude of his error.

With nightmare slowness, two dozen machine-warriors rose from the ground on either side of them. A trooper screamed in pain, the sound dying abruptly as the fleshy apparatus birthing it was scourged from vacant bones. Another man died, lasgun falling unfired from skeletal hands as a bile-green light stripped them of their flesh. Then another, and another, and yet another. But, already running, Arvus Drel was not there to see it.

He ran for his life. He bounded up the steps of the pyramid in a dozen fear-crazed steps, his boots slipping and sliding under him. On reaching the doorway just below its apex, Drel felt his heart skip a beat as the door held fast. Jarl suddenly appeared beside him, putting a shoulder against it to force the screeching portal open. Darting inside, Drel dimly realised the surviving Volgars were right behind him. But he was past caring. He was running for his life, and, if Jarl had not grabbed him then and slammed him hard against the wall, he might never have stopped.

'You brought us here, Emperor damn you! Now tell us how to escape!' Jarl screamed. Behind, his men did their best to barricade the door by piling ancient funeral urns and reliquaries against it like so many sandbags. Jarl slapped him, hard enough to rattle his teeth. For a moment, Drel just stared dumbly back. Then, in a sudden burst of fevered insight, he saw the answer.

'The holy-of-holies!' he said, speaking quickly for fear Jarl might hit him again. 'Don't you see? For the machine-creatures to be guarding this temple it must be important to them in some way. There must be something here that is valuable. Something left by the Neand. Something they would not want to see damaged. And where better to keep something of value than in the most sacred place in the temple – the holy-of-holies? That is where we should make our stand!'

Jarl stood brooding on his words for a moment. Then, abruptly, the decision was made for him, as the temple door disintegrated and the machine-creatures outside began to pick their way through a sea of upturned urns and reliquaries towards them.

'We go then,' Jarl said, pushing Drel before him. 'But you had better find this place quick, notary, or I'll kill you myself.'

Drel needed no prompting. With Jarl and the Volgars following he ran down the corridor, the clanging echoes of metal feet behind them telling him the machine-warriors had not given up the pursuit. Now and then, Drel heard a Volgar scream. But he did not look back. He just kept on running, hopelessly lost, through a labyrinth of ancient marbled halls that led him deeper and deeper within the earth. He ran past rooms full of all manner of extraordinary things: hieroglyphic obelisks, strange machines, the mummified remains of creatures seemingly saurian in origin, artefacts which would once have excited in him great awe and interest, but now could only ignore. He had run past such treasures. Run past glory. Run past riches. Run past ambition. With sudden desperate despair, Drel turned a corner to see the massive bulk of a stone door before him and realised he could run no farther.

'You try the door, I'll hold them back!'

It was Jarl, now his only living companion, a glimpse of white bone peering out through the ruptured flesh of his forearm where the beam of one of the machine-creatures' weapons had caught him. The other troopers were dead, fleshless skeletons lying haphazardly along the path they had taken like a thread, leading back to the beginning of the labyrinth. But Jarl refused to go so easy into the night. Turning towards the relentless phalanx of approaching metal-warriors, he fired his laspistol with a scream of defiance. The las-bolts found their mark: two machine-creatures fell, then abruptly vanished. But there were so many now, marching remorselessly towards them with steps as sure and certain and inevitable as death.

Facing the door, Drel saw nine indecipherable sigils embossed at its centre, arranged like a code-pad in three rows of three. Lacking any better option he pressed them at random, hoping by desperate chance to stumble on the correct combination. A hopeless task. But suprisingly, with an awful grinding of stone against stone, the door suddenly slid open. Amazed, Drel immediately stepped into the room beyond as the door began to close behind him. He heard Jarl's voice and, turning, saw the sergeant throw his now-empty pistol at the enemy and start to run towards him. But it was too late, the door was all but shut between them. His last sight of Jarl through the diminishing gap of the doorway was the sergeant's imploring face as the metal hands of the machine-creatures reached out for him.

'The door, notary!' Jarl screamed. 'Stop it! Sweet Emperor, don't let it close!'

But Drel did nothing.

JUDGING BY THE DURATION of the screams, it took Jarl a long time to die. Long before they stopped, however, Drel had abandoned whatever polite interest in the sergeant's fate he might once have maintained. Calm now that the impassable bulwark of the stone door stood between him and Jarl's killers, he had already turned to inspect his newfound refuge.

He found himself in a vaulted room, fifteen paces wide and twice as many long. Facing him, the smoothly lustrous black stone of the far wall was blank, while the long granite walls on either side were covered in the same hieroglyphs he had seen elsewhere in the temple. On a small dais at the centre of the room there stood a lectern. Its flat, obsidian top was etched with the imprint of a three-fingered claw. Otherwise, the room was empty; though he quickly found his eyes drawn to an artful mosaic set into the middle of one of the hieroglyphic walls.

It depicted a smiling, golden figure, standing with hands held open in a welcoming gesture. Although human in proportions, the figure was obviously not human, possessing an elongated head and heavy downward-arching horns, with an elliptical groove set into the long expanse of its forehead. It could only be the Neand's god. But while clearly intended as an object of veneration, Drel could not help but see something malevolent in the knowing curve of the figure's smile. Perhaps it was the cunning artistry of the mosaic, but wherever he walked in the room the eyes of the smiling god seemed to follow. The gaze was unsettling; almost as though the Neand's god had looked deep into his soul and saw something there to amuse it.

He noticed a more familiar script hidden among the hieroglyphs and realised some of the words on the wall were written in an archaic form of Old High Gothic dialect. Words which, slowly, haltingly, he began to translate. Standing in that ancient chamber, he saw the secret history of the Neand and their city unfold before him.

The Neand had not built this city; that was the first revelation. Millennia ago the Neand's nomadic ancestors had come and found a ruined city buried in the mud. The city was full to the brim with all manner of wondrous alien technologies, and littered with the mummified remains of an unknown race of sentient saurians, apparently native to the moon. Deciphering the hieroglyphs, the Neand had learned the saurians had founded the city aeons earlier, at the instruction of a benevolent god who had come to them from the stars. This star-god had given the saurians all their technology, asking in return only that they prove themselves worthy of his gifts. He told them he was a god who expected strength in all things. If his people were worthy, they would prosper in his absence. Then, promising to return sometime in the future to judge their labours, the star-god left them.

That the extinct saurians had not prospered was readily apparent. But refusing to read any omen in the failures of others, the Neand had settled in the city, mastering the technologies they found there to rebuild the city to its former glories. In the centuries that followed, they worshipped the saurians' god as their own, confident that when he returned he would be pleased to see how well the newcomers had used his gifts. Nor did their worship end there. The Neand also gave praise to the slumbering machine-servants the star-god had left behind; machines called necrons, said to rest in a black stone monolith deep beneath the temple...

A black stone monolith.

With a start, Drel paused in his reading to look with fearful eyes at the black stone wall at the far end of the room. Could it be the outer wall of the monolith written of in the Neand accounts? Gazing at it he felt a shiver of apprehension, afraid at any moment a hidden panel might open and machine-creatures emerge to kill him. But the stone of the wall was still and silent.

No, he told himself. If that was the monolith they would have come for me already. It is just a wall like any other, carved of a curiously lustrous stone perhaps, but no more sinister than the granite walls either side. But for all his own reassurances he could not escape a feeling of foreboding. Then, as much to distract his thoughts as anything else, he began to read what was written on the walls once more.

But the greatest gift the smiling god had left his people had not been the city, its technologies, or even the sleeping necrons. Even though the star-god had told the saurians he expected them to show strength at all times, still he understood that inevitably they would face moments of weakness. And so he left a summoning device behind, in the shape of an obsidian-topped lectern – the same lectern in the room where Drel now stood. He promised that, come their darkest hour, one of them need only place a hand upon the device and the servants of their god would awaken to answer the call.

Come their darkest hour.

From what was written on the walls, it was clear the Neand took this promise as the final proof of their new-found god's benevolence. To them it was a covenant, a sacred contact upon which their entire civilisation was founded. And so, when after centuries of dominance they found themselves hemmed in by enemies and fighting a losing battle with the marsh, a momentous decision was reached. A delegation of priests was sent into the summoning chamber to put a hand upon the lectern and call their god's servants to them. And there, the records of the Neand abruptly ended.

Their darkest hour.

To Drel there seemed more questions here than answers. If the Neand summoned their god's servants, how was it their entire civilisation came to be destroyed? And if these servants – these necrons – allowed the Neand's ancestors easy access to the marsh millennia ago, why today had they treated Drel and the Volgars as invaders? And then there was the matter of the saurians. Surely they would have seen the coming of whatever disaster engulfed them and turned to their god's servants for aid? It made no sense., until he remembered the scroll he had seen in the planetary archives, and how the ancient sage Terodotus had written the Neand were slaughtered by 'the guardians of their faith'. There was a similar Old High Gothic phrase written on these walls, but inadvertently Drel had given it a different translation. The same words which meant 'the guardians of their faith' could have another meaning.

The servants of their god!

With sudden insight he finally understood. The Neand had summoned their god's servants, just as the saurians must have aeons earlier. Only for both races to learn that when the necrons were awakened they did not bring aid. They brought judgment. For, having summoned the necrons, the peoples of the city had demonstrated weakness. And by showing weakness they had failed the star-god who, from the first, had told them just what manner of deity he was.

A god who expected strength in all things.

Staring at the smiling face of the figure on the mosaic before him, Drel could not help but shudder at the thought of a god who would leave such a bitter 'gift' for his people, knowing that one day, no matter how hard they struggled, they would succumb to the temptation to use the summoning device and then be destroyed. It was almost as though all of it – the rise and fall of the Neand civilisation and that of the saurians before them – had all been some dark and sinister game for their god's amusement.

Gazing at the god in the mosaic, Drel found himself hating the haughty curve of those sickle-bladed lips. It was as though the figure was laughing at him. Then, a revelation hit him that pushed all thoughts of the Neand, the saurians, and their laughing god aside. Glancing at the solid seamless walls of the wider room around him, Arvus Drel came to a sudden and frantic realisation.

He was trapped.

TIME PASSED. It passed at first with pleading, then screaming, then at the last with long ragged breaths. Then, when the dead eyes of Arvus Drel could no longer see it, a doorway opened.

For an instant, the black stone of the wall at the end of the summoning chamber seemed to shift almost imperceptibly, before a whole section of it rose to reveal something like a vertically hanging pool of bile-green waters. Ripples spread and played across its surface, the green taint growing ever more vivid. Then, the waters of the pool seemed to coalesce as dark shadows appeared within them. Finally, a skeletal metal form broke the surface as, one by one, the guardians stepped from the monolith into the chamber.

They stood there for long moments, death-skull faces turning slowly, deliberately, to scan the room's interior with burning eyes. There, they saw a body lying beside the door at the other side of the room, fingers reduced to blood-encrusted stumps as their owner had desperately tried to claw his way through solid granite. Sure now that any danger of damage being inflicted on the delicate mechanisms of the summoning chamber had passed, the guardians collected the body and dragged it from the temple. This body once had a name. Once it was Arvus Drel, former notary minoris to the planetary archives of His Excellency Governor Arbenal. But the guardians did not care. To them it was simply the body of an intruder from one of the races who had already failed the test of the city. An intruder, killed by a need for food and water which they no longer shared. A body to be dragged outside and discarded to the muddy embrace of the marsh with its fellow invaders, like all the thousands of others who had come to the city before them. Then, with their duties for the moment done, the guardians returned to the monolith to sleep once more.

To sleep and to wait.

Perhaps, in time, more intruders would come from the failed races and the guardians would be awakened to drive them from the marsh once more. Perhaps, in time, a new race would evolve here and come to the marsh to see the city and the gifts their god had left for them. Their civilisation might even flourish for a time. Until, inevitably, one day they would come to the summoning chamber to put a hand upon the lectern and their god's servants would awaken to destroy them. Perhaps one day, even their god himself might return. But his servants, the necrons, did not care. Regardless of whether he returned or not, they would continue to serve him. However much time passed, they would continue to wait. Whatever might come, they would never falter. While other races rose and fell, planets died, stars were extinguished, they would endure. It was the one sure and certain thing among the restless maelstrom of Eternity. Eternally steadfast. Unendingly patient. Faithful beyond death.

ELUCIDIUM

Simon Spurrier

Excerpt One:
Opening passage, *'Primacii: Claviculus Matri'*

WE ARE THE *unclean*.

We are reviled (so they say). We are despicable and pestilent and abominable. We are known as 'thing', as 'freak', as 'heretic'. The derision is as tedious as it is endless.

Is there truth in their words?

Am I, then, a freak? By their standards, yes. And if 'heresy' lies in considering their atrophied carrion-god detestable then yes, I suppose I qualify there also. Mine is a higher calling.

But am I a 'thing'? Am I but an object to be culled, a flawed specimen to be dissected and terminated? Am I, then, unimportant?

No. No, against that charge at least I will defend myself. I am a child of the Mother's divine will. They may cast rocks and aspersions and labels upon me all they wish. It will do them little good.

Behold: The Great Sky Mother approaches. Blessed be.

* * *

THE LATCHCRAFT TOUCHED down on the icefield with dignified relief, unsettling a compact torus of snow and pistoning at its jointed landing legs. A thin gurgle of vapour – little more than ethereal spittle – undulated vertically from its warm engines, lost to the flurrying weather.

Its descent from the orbit-platform – ice-studded winches guiding it ponderously along the guide-chord like some rappelling invader – had been excruciatingly slow. Buffeted violently by atmospheric whimsy, sent spiralling around the axis of the cable with every contradictory gale and snow-filled gust, only the craft's gyroscopes – newly blessed by a trio of tech-priests – had allowed its passengers to retain any semblance of formality in their bearing. They disembarked with varying degrees of concealed nausea, green faces closed and rigid, unwilling to betray their obvious discomfort: a gaggle of merchants and pilgrims, clutching at their belongings with white knuckled possessiveness, peering sullenly across the bulging citydome.

A man – of sorts – lurked in a nearby doorframe, breath steaming beneath the shadows of his cowl. Notably tall with a thickset build betrayed by the movements of his robes, his ogreish stature was moderated only by the perpetual hunch with which he carried himself. His name was G'hait, and as he watched the dissipating crowd of passengers he couldn't help but wonder abstractly upon what strange sights they'd seen, what distant worlds they'd returned from, what marvels and horrors lurked above the opaque snow clouds that blanketed the sky.

Garial-Fall was a world without sunlight.

Oh, there was *light*, of a kind: a wan diffusion of halfhearted brightness that murdered every shadow and obstructed any view of the stars. But there was no sense of solar direction, no sunrise or sunset: only a gradual waxing or waning of the blanketlight to distinguish between day and night. In its wisdom the Plureaucracy of the Hive Primus (shoehorned, no doubt, by the Imperial

Governor) had commissioned from the Adeptus Mechanicus a geostationary orbit-platform, its battered solar cells drawing energy from the distant sun, feeding it by means of the guide-cables into the power-hungry hivedome below. In one fell swoop the tech-priests had provided Garial-Fall with energy, a strategic weapons platform and a stardock. Only the latchcraft, with their uncomfortable descents through the cloud layer, marred the smooth running of an otherwise efficient system.

One of the merchants, running short of restraint, vomited noisily across the snow at his feet, melting a splatter-work pattern into the frost. G'hait rolled his eyes and returned his gaze to the steaming vessel, its two final passengers disembarking silently from a private cabin on the starboard face.

The first was tall, wearing an acolyte's robe. Like G'hait the figure's head was hidden beneath a sackcloth cowl, threadbare symbols and scriptures embroidered around its hem. What little movement the robe betrayed revealed a certain wiriness to the figure's physiology; a thinness and scarcity of movement that could easily be confused with undernourishment or uncertainty. G'hait was not so easily fooled: he recognised the calculated movements of a warrior, every motion executed with efficiency and slow grace. The figure collected a few items of light luggage and stood silently, awaiting the command of its companion.

Dressed from head to toe in robes of Imperial purple, neck ringed with a mantle of hawk feathers and platinum baubles, leaning without a trace of infirmity upon an obsidian staff, Cardinal Ebrehem Arkannis was an impressive sight. Before G'hait could even step from the doorway the Cardinal's aquiline features were twisting in his direction, raptor eyes flashing with arctic intelligence.

'There you are...' he tutted. 'So much for the grand welcoming committee.' His voice seemed to puncture the wind, rustling uncomfortably across the air. 'Out you come.' A thin finger crooked, drawing G'hait from the shadows.

He stepped into the squalling snow with a nod, suppressing his distaste at the Cardinal's attention; inspected like a grox-stud at the agriquarter livestock auctions.

'I take it you were expecting me?'

He nodded.

'Then lead the way, child.'

G'hait worked his jaw, thoughtful. The nascent sense of unease troubled him: so instinctive was his predatory confidence that to find himself awestruck by a stranger was a… challenging sensation. But then, G'hait had always been cursed by the need to consider; the compunction to overanalyse and over think every situation. He frowned and remembered the advice of his master: to obey without thought, and to be thankful in so doing.

Drawing his robes tight against the cold, waving the two figures after him, he turned and stalked through the frosted bulkhead, entering the ancient and rambling lens of the citydome. The Cardinal and his tall companion followed wordlessly behind, their movements punctuated only by the rhythmic striking of the obsidian staff against the icy floor.

GARIAL-FALL, LIKE SO many Ultima segmentum colony worlds, owed much of its existence to the forbidden enterprise of ancient technologies. Some forgotten society – in some forgotten millennium – had erected the heatdome to protect the city within, stretching its languid camber like some glutinous bubble, ossified and pitted by time. Beneath its intricate surface, striated by chattering logic engines and grinding gears, the city clustered in a haphazard confusion of tiers and stacks, substantially warmer (albeit still uncomfortably cold, by human standards) than the ice wastes beyond.

At the exit from the port G'hait hired a rickshaw, barking directions at the half-sentient servitor that drew it. Its legs and arms pistoned and hissed as they took the strain, grossly thickened by metallic cords to take the weight of its passengers. G'hait steered the moronic creature across gantries and plungestreets, rising through ghettoes and trade quarters, stepping aboard steam-driven elevators and dodging rattling tramways. The diffused light of the sky, made febrile by the scarlet tint of the dome, was bolstered throughout the city by gaslights and hovering illuminators: an ugly blend of cadmium taints and tungsten stains. G'hait's companions regarded their environs in silence – skirting the Heatsink with its decorative gang totems; bisecting the Foildom and its well guarded excavations; passing the foundations of the towering Apex Block where the Plureaucracy met each day.

The rickshaw delivered them to the icy plain at the heart of the central plaza, pausing in the frozen shadows of its single, brooding structure. The Cathedral was typical: a swollen façade of jutting pylons and steeples, meticulous frescoes and jagged ornamentation scattered like acne across its bulk. It stood isolated, bulkily dressed stallholders and hawkers peddling their wares raucously around it.

In stolen glances G'hait's impressions of the Cardinal had grown, absorbing his etched features, his hatchet-like nose, his bloodless lips, his etiolated pate. More than anything his eyes set him apart, deeply shadowed beneath prominent brows, they nonetheless contrived to *glow*, catching the light in strange ways.

G'hait scowled in the darkness of his robe, thinking: We don't need you, you smug bastard. We were doing fine on our own.

WITHIN, TO G'HAIT's mind, the Cathedral was unremarkable. A buttressed stronghold of ostentatious architectural filigree, intricate frescoes, decadent gold and silver ornamentation and regularly re-dyed tapestries. Glorious, gaudy and pompous: G'hait barely even glanced inside as he diverted to the small stairwell at the Cathedral's leftmost periphery.

Beneath, the structure's true design was manifest.

Through archways and down stairs, past buried cloisters with an air of carefully arranged antiquity, below

lost treasuries of antediluvian relics and walkways thick
with synthesised cobwebs – the Cathedral bared its can-
cerous guts and the infestation that had taken root
there. It *festered*.

Guided by machinations and grand designs beyond the
ken of a mere maelignaci, the Anointed Congregation of
the Celestial Womb met in shadowfasted chambers and
rough hewn cells, whispering and praying together,
chanting with quiet solemnity and spreading, always
spreading, the Good News.

THE COUNCIL WAS waiting.

G'hait shuffled – in as much as a figure of his enormity
could shuffle – into the Chamber of Voices with a glance
across the throng. His master, Primacii Magus Kreista,
stood at one end of the semicircle, betraying not a flutter
of recognition at the entrance of his preferred acolyte.
G'hait admonished himself for having expected any.

Beyond the primacii magi stood a waiting rank of
favoured maelignacis of all generations, cowled and
robed appropriately, and at either edge of the chamber –
where the wan luminescence of stolen illuminators failed
to penetrate – the suggestive rustling of a purii brood
marred the shadows.

Foremost, though arranged artfully to one side so as
not to detract attention from the magi, massive and corpulent upon its wheeled platform, the Broodfather lolled
with animal stupidity, mewling and salivating. Great wattles of sagging flesh – segmented and wormlike –
gathered beneath its limbs, splattered by the oleaginous
secretions of its maw. A swatch of maroon silk, embroidered with the New Dawn iconography favoured
throughout the underchurch, was secured carefully across
its bulk, disguising the intricacies of its obesity. Thus
cloaked – cocooned like some truculent grub – it
thrashed and gurgled in a psychic torpor, made soporific
by the mental spoor of its flock. Its head was a brachy-
cephalic contusion of wrinkled flesh and cartilage, slack

with age and flecked with spittle, bristling nonetheless with stiletto fangs and recurved canines. It hissed and hummed, utterly moronic, ignored resolutely by all those present.

A congregation, G'hait mused, unlike any other.

'Elucidium Magus Arkannis.' he announced, gesturing the Cardinal within.

Arkannis, followed by his silent attendant, crossed the threshold into the cavern, movements predatory – a coiled ice-serpent nuzzling through snow, homing upon its prey.

If the council had hoped to intimidate their visitor, if they had hoped to temper his authority with a display of solidarity and solemnity, regarding his entrance with collective disapproval; if they had hoped in some way to visibly manifest their physical majority, measuring it deprecatingly against his solitude – then they failed.

He reached the centre of the chamber, and he smiled.

'There will be changes.' he said.

ACROSS THE CITY, in the blackened alleyways of the Heatsink, a figure thumbed an activation rune on the grip of a power maul and spat on the ground.

'The way I look at it,' he said, 'you kids got no *respect* for your elders.'

'N-no law against that...' The breathless reply appeared to filter from a disarrayed heap of litter at the bulky man's feet; upon closer inspection resolving into a body, curled in foetal pain, bruises intumescing on cheeks and brows, nose ebbing with a gentle stream of blood. It groaned.

The looming giant, light catching dully on its segmented plates of black armour and the dome of an ebony faceplate, shook its head and tutted slowly, like a cog tooth jumping its sockets. '*I'll* decide what's against the law, kid, not you.'

The power maul flared phosphor-blue, stitching a lightning-strike glare across the alley and throwing its shambling architecture, its detritus-strewn base and its pair of occupants into sharp relief. Shadows crawled across walls, flickering in time with the mace's irregular current.

It arced vertically, dragging the shadows with it, and when it connected with the crumpled figure's skull it sizzled sharply, spitting a bright fountain of sparks and detonating the shrieking head like a ripe fruit. Fragments of splintered bone and gobbets of brain matter sheared outwards, pooling and mixing with a thick soup of cranial fluids. The wielder of the maul scowled, deactivating the weapon with a sigh, irritated by the moist splattering across its armour.

Another figure, similarly dressed in midnight-black armour, stepped from a connecting alleyway. It saluted.

'Marshall. Heard a discharge – you need any help?'

The first figure shook its head, kicking the headless wreck at his feet. 'Negative. I caught up with the pickpocket, that's all.'

The new arrival nudged the corpse with a booted foot, grin smearing across the visible portions of his face. 'Self defence, right, Marshall?'

'Heh. You know it, deputy.' The man glanced at an auspex display mounted on his wrist and swore.

'Problem, Marshall?'

'I'm running late. Got an appointment with the Plureaucracy.'

'Serious...?'

'Nothing to it. The pompous bastards couldn't find their arses with both hands, let alone pin me for anything worth a damn.'

'You in trouble, Marshall?'

'Ha! Vigilators are here to keep the peace and uphold the Emperor's law, deputy. We do not bow to the tastes of fat politicians. Remember that.' He nudged the corpse again with his foot, spitting into the slick of blood and brain on the floor. 'Get a team to clean up this mess.'

'Yes sir. And good luck with the Plureaucracy, sir.'

Marshall Delacroix shook the loose blood from his power maul, stamping into the dark knot of streets that surrounded the imposing Apex Block.

'Vigilators make their own luck, Deputy.'

SPLENDID AND TERRIBLE, Arkannis's gaze raked across the gathering. He grinned, he blinked, and he spoke.

'I represent the Elucidium.' he said.

His voice held its audience awestruck, forgoing the practicalities of sound and resonating instead somewhere *within*; sinking claws and pincers into the mind itself.

'Think of me as a… a wayfarer. A trailblazer, if you will. I go ahead of her, preparing her way, and She is forever at my heel.'

Arkannis turned his gaze – more potent than the barrel of any weapon – and fixated the semicircle of primacii magi. Even those wearing expressions of unconcealed disdain seemed spellbound: brows accreting with crystal concentration, eyes misting with the strength of the words. G'hait, watching with a hammering heart from the doorway, felt the air turn greasy once more. Psychic puissance unsettled the staleness of the chamber.

'Finally,' the Cardinal trilled, beaming with what little warmth his cold features could generate. 'Finally, She is upon us. Her hour is at hand.

'The Great Sky Mother is Coming. Blessed be!'

'Blessed be!' the congregation echoed. In that instant, in that unthinking response to his proffered litany, the gathering silently bestowed upon Arkannis all the seniority he would need. He seized control of the Underchurch without so much as a confrontation, just as he had known he would.

The assurance – the *certainty* of his authority – was palpable, and as he talked and talked and talked G'hait felt it filling his mind like a drug.

THE CARDINAL OUTLINED the Plan. He admonished the listeners for their laxity, but praised their resolve. He detailed the days that would follow. He wielded his oration with the skill and grace of a swordsman, earning respect before demanding results, beguiling them before commanding them.

He told them how the Blessed Liberation would arise, how they must contribute to its success, where they must be stationed and in what numbers, with what provisions and equipment... He allowed no margin for uncertainty or alternative: he told them, and they believed.

Even the purii, their understanding of language dissolved upon a froth of base instincts, seemed roused by the address, hissing from their shadows and drawing soft fingers across crystalline carapaces, chittering in the gloom. G'hait was glad of the pall of shade concealing them – at once prideful and revolted by his heritage.

Only the Broodfather, the swollen patriarch of the Underchurch, went unaffected by the newcomer's words. It merely flexed and mewled, too glutted by the psychic feast its congregation unwittingly provided to react with intelligence.

Secret and parasitic, lurking with malevolent hunger beneath the frosted streets of the Garial-Fall hivedome, the cult of the Celestial Womb rustled and flexed, fingering weapons and gnarled talons with a growing murmur of accord at Arkannis's words.

Presently the crowd dissolved, orders received.

Excerpt Two:
Section II ('That You May Know Us'), '*Primacii*: Claviculus Matri'

WE ARE AN *uncanny breed, by the standards of humanity. Our ancestry is our life, and our life is forfeit. We give it willingly in the name of the Mother, and in so doing assure our place at her side.*

If we must die, let us die. If we must suffer, let us suffer.

The Skymother will endure. Always.

She hurls her seeds before her, harbingers of her arrival, couriers of her celestial design. She sows. She spawns.

A man, then, or woman, is seeded. Their friends, their peers, their colleagues; they would call it 'infection', if they knew. The host is tainted.

He or she is contagii, favoured with the flesh seed. Still human – largely – yet simplified. Distilled by the desire to serve. The Celestial-Womb gifts its carriers with Purpose – an endowment impossible to the withered Carrion God.

The host breeds. He takes a woman, or she takes a man. Gripped by instincts they cannot hope to understand they are united; purified by the simplicity of their urges. To nest. To reproduce. To multiply. Their child is not human.

We are an uncanny breed, yes.

We are a race of eugenic coalescence. Ours is the realm of amalgam: of blend, of segue, of mix. Neither this nor that, we are divine mongrels.

Hybrids, all.

'IT WAS YOU. You invited him here, didn't you? I checked the transmission records.'

'I never sought to hide it. I could have done.'

To G'hait the voices seemed strained; just one part of the psychic exchange that filled the room. Archmagus Jezaheal – first among the Cult's magi – stabbed out towards Magus Kreista with an angry finger and pursed her bloodless lips. Her single braid of hair – an ebony cascade from an otherwise depilated skull – dragged across the jade mantle covering her shoulders.

'You forgot yourself, Kreista.' she spat, furious. 'This was not your decision to make.'

'I forgot nothing.' Kreista said, voice slow and controlled. 'I simply feared that without my intervention the decision would go unmade.'

'Meaning what?'

The man sighed, shoulders stooped. 'Meaning that the inadequacies of our operation are painfully obvious. I have neither taste nor time for disobedience but... I won't condone wilful ignorance. The council closets away our failures, pretending there are none. I couldn't let it continue, archmagus. I made this decision to aid us, not to undermine your authority. I have no regard for such things.'

G'hait lurked massively at one end of his master's private suite, carefully veneering his interest in the voices across the room. The two magi faced each other, framed with an unhealthy cast from the sputtering coal stove in the corner.

G'hait had served as Kreista's personal attendant since his infancy had finished. In as much as he was in the practice of bestowing his respect upon individuals rather than the Underchurch as an aggregate, he owed much of it to his master. The wizened man was an uncharacteristically pragmatic primacii, desiring in his attendants intelligence and edification as well as brute aggression. In every other maelignaci of the congregation the seeds of creative intelligence were muted; replaced by a servile subjugation and obedience to the goals of the community, guided by the psionic resonances of the Council.

To them, G'hait thought, he must seem freakish. The product of teratosis, of genetic imperfection, of embryonic mutation. In him the human side of his ancestry had conspired to leave his mind capable of imagination and disobedience, of reactions beyond the biological criteria of instinct. That he had not been terminated as soon as his individuality manifested itself was due to Kreista, who held the values of uniqueness – normally the remit of the primacii magi alone – in high esteem.

In Kreista's service G'hait had – against the rules of the church – learned to decipher and craft the spidery characters that formed text: and even to master the rudiments of Underchurch scriptology. He owed his master a great deal.

Jezaheal, her lip curling with irritation, hissed. 'This is insubordination! I should have you flogged!'

Despite the woman's seniority, G'hait felt bunched chords stirring beneath the irregular musculature of his shoulders. His obedience to the Underchurch and its

primacii council was without question, but he would tolerate no harm to his master.

'Do what you will,' Kreista replied, waving a dismissive
hand. 'It's too late. He's here now. All this venom won't
change a thing.'

G'hait allowed his muscles to relax. Even separated by
the smoggy breadth of the room, he could see that Jezaheal was defeated. Her shoulders slumped with bad
grace.

'Then I hope you're proud,' she spat, half-hearted.
'You've invited a stranger into our congregation – mother
alone knows what shadows he brings with him. He could
be a spy, for all that we know.'

'His reputation precedes him, archmagus.'

'You think that matters? You're a fool, Kreista.'

'He's no spy! The Elucidium are our allies! Why don't
you see it?'

'All I see is a fop, dressed in the… the peacock robes of
the Withered God!'

The tiny hairs at the nape of G'hait's neck, a vestigial
gift from his human parents, bristled coldly. Even as he
turned to investigate the discomfort a sharp voice was
speaking over his shoulder. He tensed.

'Then you are not looking hard enough.' said the Cardinal, sweeping into the musty cell with hawkish features
set and robes dragging, like some limaceous trail, on the
flagstones.

Jezaheal rallied magnificently. 'Arkannis,' she said,
voice cold. 'It does not suit such an… *honoured* guest to
resort to eavesdropping…'

The Cardinal smiled, icy features curling in an almost
convincing parody of mirth. 'Oh, archmagus, I assure
you… Had I the inclination I could eavesdrop on your
conversation from *orbit.*' His eyes flashed. 'Alas, I am here
to speak with Magus Kreista, not to pander to your neu-
roses.'

The archmagus hissed, her knuckles clenching at her
sides. 'You need to learn some respect.' Her manner put

G'hait in mind of a cat, arching its back in grandiose outrage at some perceived threat. '*I* am the senior magus
here.'

'And you, my good woman, need to learn when you are
outgunned.'

Across the room G'hait watched Jezaheal's expression
cooling, becoming an ice cold lance of fury. 'Is that so?'
she whispered.

G'hait saw what she was doing a split second too late
to brace himself.

The air surged around her, a shivering blast of psionic
disruption that lurched outwards from the gaunt
woman's eyes, filling the chamber. G'hait staggered
against the doorframe, momentarily stunned, blinking
lights from his eyes. Even Kreista rocked in his spot,
moaning quietly in his throat.

The Cardinal, who had absorbed the brunt of the petulant assault without betraying so much as a flinch,
chuckled lightly.

'Good,' he said, in the manner of a doting parent con-
gratulating their child. G'hait half expected him to pat the
astonished archmagus on her head. 'I'm gratified that the
primaciis of this world still practice the *Vocis Susurra*… All
too many of the Mother's magi allow the Arts to go
unlearned.'

Jezaheal all but snarled at the patronisation, stalking for
the doorway with her pallid cheeks burning. G'hait, despite
his astonishment at the mental barrage, suppressed a smile
at her humiliation. The threat to flog his master still rankled.

She swept past him, nose in the air.

'Archmagus…' the Cardinal said, moments before she
crossed the threshold.

She spun on her heel, struggling to summon the appro-
priate ire. 'What?'

'Fops – even those that are dressed as peacocks – are
given free rein to travel amongst the unenlightened. You
might remember that, next time you skulk through your
tunnels like a worm.'

'You d–'

'That is all.' The Cardinal's voice allowed no room for disobedience.

Primacii Archmagus Jezaheal strode from the room, dismissed like a lowly contagii.

'Well,' Kreista allowed himself to sink into a padded seat at his desk, old features crumpling in arthritic gratitude at the support. He stroked his hircine beard with a thoughtful rhythm, regarding Arkannis shrewdly. 'Well, well.'

'It is my understanding,' the Cardinal said, returning the old primacii's gaze with an amused twinkle, 'that I have you to thank for the invitation to this world.'

'You do.'

'Tell me... What made you contact my order?'

Kreista pursed his lips, considering his answer. A gnarled finger extended towards G'hait, surprising him from his silent reverie.

'Acolyte...' he said, voice thick. 'Where are your manners? Fetch the Cardinal a chair.'

G'hait scurried to comply, struggling to reconcile his distrust of the gaudy stranger with a burgeoning respect for his obvious talents. The memory of the archmagus's exit, disgrace and venom shrouding her features, was too delicious to ignore.

THE APEX-BLOCK, so named for its position beneath the zenith of the citydome, was a pillared assortment of offices, administrative strata, tiered arrays of Arbites precincts and, surmounting it all like some whitewashed mushroom, the colossal bulk of the Plureaucracium.

Somewhere deep within its cloistered perimeter, drenched with the splatterings of icemelt from the dome, the Torus Room resonated with the pompous conjecture of the Elect-Plureaucrats. Wide and round, steeped on every side into a bowl-like depression, the room seemed to emit an almost palpable sense of sloth; lined by comfortable recliner benches and inflate mats. Its decadent comfort, dotted with bowls of fruit and sweetmeats, stood confined within alabaster walls and archways, overseen by ceiling frescoes of Imperial heroes and villains.

Meeting daily, the wheezing mussitation of the Plureaucrats provided Garial-Fall with its policies and its problems; endlessly debating moot issues as their supposed inferiors, the whips and adepts, scurried about them in the pursuit of progress. Little of any great value was ever decided in the stagnant warmth of the Torus Room, but the citizenry of the hivedome remained fiercely proud of their administration, gracefully overlooking the 'final say' authority of the Imperium-appointed Governor, who chaired the debates on the public's behalf – and executed the *true* administration of his planet in private.

Today's debate was far from extraordinary – a three-bench sub-party languidly petitioning the Plureaucracy for funds to maintain their skein of the orbit-platform's tether cables – and those 'crats not actually asleep lounged with an air of soporific contentment, like ruddy-cheeked hogs recovering from a meal. Even the speaker, chubby digits curled together, seemed to struggle against bleary-eyed lippitude, stumbling over words and wheezing after every sentence. The Plureauracracy basked happily in its own ineffectual laziness, just as it had always done.

Above them, via mildewed gantries and frosted mezzanines that dribbled icicles with frozen incontinence, on the highest roof plateau of the building, a squad of vigilators patrolled with the mechanical disinterest of those who are neither expecting nor afraid of trouble, muttering unfunny anecdotes to one another and fiddling with the triggerheads of their power mauls. If any of them had noticed the mobile shadow that crept stealthily towards them, detaching from the gloom of the chimneystack forest – which they did not – they might have remarked upon its almost supernatural silence, its spectral movements, its implausible speed.

The first of the lawmen felt an icy breath across his throat, flourishing in sudden warmth with a sharp, bewildering tug. He was dead before he could even cry out, jugular fluids smearing in horrific, beautiful patterns across the ice.

The vigilators died, one by one, and when it was finished with them the shadow that had danced through them like mist, fingers sliding with razor precision across sinews and bones, dejointing and eviscerating, twirled happily at the centre of a splatterwork spiral; a circle of heaped bodies and lubricious gore that steamed upon the ice and ran in snaking rivulets across the rooftop.

Its cloak gradually settled around it, unsoiled by even a single droplet of blood, and the figure murmured its satisfied nonsense into the astonished night and slid back into the shadows.

'THE HIVE SECUNDUS is four days north of here. It's not like the City-dome. It's…. it's what you might call a *typical* hive. Sticks from the ice like a dagger, all twisted metal and rock. An ugly thing.

'I was born into the Underchurch there and served it all my life… And in all that time, in all those hard years, only one thing remained constant.

'*Struggle.*'

Magus Kreista sat back with a sigh, eyeing the sputtering coal stove with a preoccupied distance. His audience – the hawk-like Cardinal, stooped and raptor-like in his own chair – regarded him with hooded intensity, every movement and inflection noted and stored. Arkannis, in turn, was himself studied: pondered over abstractly by G'hait, lurking as convention demanded at the periphery of the cell's lit area.

Kreista continued with a slow breath, absently tapping at the tirchwood stanchions of his seat.

'More than anything else, I struggled against *hierarchy*. To my mind the Council had become a Gerontocracy, too glutted by its own self-importance to notice its inadequacies.

Efficiency fell prey to ceremony, efficacy was lost behind religious dogma. They couldn't understand that a custom first conceived two centuries ago might now be ineffectual, or superfluous. I struggled to contemporise the Underchurch of the Hive Secundus, and failed.'

G'hait studied the listening Cardinal's face. He was watching Kreista's hand, G'hait saw, *tap-tap-tapping* at his armrest. The old primacii didn't notice the razor attention applied to his mannerisms, too lost in his narrative.

'There was an inquisitor in our midst.

'My entreaties to the Council to review our security policies had gone ignored, my interrogation of new recruits dismissed as overzealous... The servants of the Carrion God spotted our weakness and took advantage.

'I don't know who the inquisitor was posing as. A lowly contagii, a maelignaci. Who knows? One morning I went to inspect a sleeper cell in the upper-hive, and by my return in the evening the Underchurch was slaughtered. Blown apart, shot to hell. A mess, Cardinal. A royal mess.'

The old man's jaw tightened, clenching down on the sadness his voice couldn't hope to disguise. G'hait – long familiar with his master's tale – nonetheless felt his muscles bunch in anger at the genocide.

'I spent a week as an outlaw... The underhive was thick with rumours: Inquisitorial purges, whole families being burnt at the stake. Hysteria gripping the entire city, slaughtering what few shreds of the Mother's congregation remained.

'I considered my position. It was useless to stay – I could see that. I wouldn't have lasted another week. I resolved to travel to the Hive Primus, carrying news of the defeat, in the hopes that I could save the Underchurch here from the same fate.

'My acceptance here was... slow to come, but I fought hard and claimed my place on the Council. And now... now, as the great Sky Mother *finally* approaches...

'I see it all happening again.'

For the first time since he'd begun his narration, Magus Kreista tore his eyes from the dancing flames and met Arkannis's stare.

'The Underchurch here is failing, Cardinal. Contagii cells go for weeks without report, the maelignaci are under-trained and under-equipped, and the purii… They're allowed to roam at will throughout the tunnels. How long before one is spotted in the city above? How long before our inadequacies are exposed and the Mother's church crumbles here, just like in the second hive?

'You understand, Cardinal – I couldn't allow that to happen.'

Arkannis pursed his lips and, with a sort of slow exactitude that rendered every movement full of importance, said: 'Go on.'

'When I was ordained as a magus, here in the Hive Primus, I was granted access to the library; the gathered knowledge of centuries. I sifted through records expecting to find no more than the writings of long-dead magi, the… the nostalgic clutter of the years.

'Instead I found letters. Astropathic transcriptions, encoded and sealed, dispatched from *other worlds*. Hundreds of them, stacked one upon another, covered in dust. They went back a decade, by my estimate. Maybe more.

'Not *one* had been opened.'

Kreista fidgeted, his old frame afflicted by some inner anxiety. G'hait allowed his eyes to wander from the Cardinal's rigid form to that of his master, troubled by the wizened figure's growing frailty.

'You have to understand – as far as I knew, we were *alone*. In all the… the sickness and decay of the Imperium, Garial-Fall, I thought, was the only refuge of the Mother's faithful. To discover that someone, somewhere out there, *knew* of us…. it… it was beyond my comprehension. I suppose I can't blame the Council for ignoring the communiqués. We've grown used to our secrecy, insulated from the world by our own suspicions and fears. My entreaties to contact your order were flatly refused.

'The Council didn't want the help that the Elucidium offered. They cited a lack of knowledge, sowed suspicion, denied the explanations that the letters contained.

'I listened to their prattling with a hollow heart, seeing again the... the *intractability* that claimed the Hive Secundus. So I went ahead and contacted the Elucidium anyway, and now here you are.'

G'hait shifted his weight from one leg to the other, uncomfortable at the tension.

'Mm,' said the Cardinal finally, cradling his fingers beneath his chin with a slow, reptilian smile. 'Here I am.'

'Cardinal.... I have to know: are there really *others*? Other churches? Other congregations on other worlds?'

The Cardinal's smile spread, betraying a flash of immaculate ivory beneath his bloodless lips. Slowly, effortlessly commanding the attention of both individuals that watched him, Elucidium Magus Arkannis leaned forwards, features openly amused.

'More,' he said, 'than you could ever imagine.'

G'hait felt his head spinning, struggling to maintain the instinctive suspicion he felt towards the outsider; all the while conducting himself with the rigid disinterest expected of his lowly caste.

'Your acolyte there,' the Cardinal said to Kreista, jerking a dismissive thumb towards G'hait (who hissed at the sudden attention), 'is unconvinced. Or, rather, he feels that he *should* be unconvinced. Distrust has been drilled into him, like all the others. I can feel it, oozing from him like sweat from his pores.' He licked his lips absently, glancing directly at G'hait with a brief smile.

'You were right to contact me when you did, Magus Kreista. Your congregation is stagnating. The Elucidium make it their personal mission to provide solutions in these circumstances. A brave man will stand alone to face any challenge, but... it takes a wise man to seek the aid of others.

'The Elucidium cherish the wise, Kreista.'

The Cardinal cupped his hand into a loose pocket on the cuff of his robes, withdrawing a finely detailed brooch of silver and platinum. Folded into its iridescent surfaces were the ghostly images of intertwined serpents; a knot of perfect symmetry without beginning or end. The Cardinal flipped it over, admiring its intricate faces. 'Should you wish it,' he said, not taking his eyes from the bauble, 'there is an unfilled position aboard my vessel. As Elucidium it is ever my lot in life to move ahead of the Great Mother, never dawdling to greet her arrival. When I leave this world, magus, as Her shadow falls across its horizons, you would be welcomed into our order.' He proffered the brooch with a smile, pale eyes twinkling, spare hand indicating an identical trinket pinned discreetly amongst the ecclesiastical medallions and ostentatious gewgaws of his costume. 'Should you wish it, of course.'

Kreista took the jewel thoughtfully, ridged eyebrows bunching in surprise. 'Y-you honour me, Cardinal.' he said, voice quiet. 'I am merely a primacii…'

Arkannis grinned, teeth flashing again. 'So was I.' He pursed his lips, eyes flicking to the dancing firelight. 'Kreista, the Elucidium is a… a disparate society. An institution of individuals. Upon each of us is placed two responsibilities: to aid the Mother's faithful wherever we find them, and to recruit those who may serve our order in the years ahead. I believe you are such a one.'

Kreista bowed his head, face flushed with pride.

They each stood, sensing the meeting drawing to an end. Kreista inclined his head respectfully, still shaken by the enormity of what he'd learned. G'hait regarded his master from the shadows with a mixture of feelings, glad that his master's wisdom had been recognised but alarmed at the Cardinal's invitation. He tried to tell himself that his anxiety was based upon a distrust of the Elucidium, and concern at his master falling foul of their tricks. But inside, he knew, his apprehension was the product of selfishness: he couldn't bear for his mentor to leave him behind.

Returning from his thoughts, G'hait was astonished to find the Cardinal staring directly at him, head tilted to one side.

'I have one final favour to ask, magus…' the Cardinal said, turning back to the wizened primacii.

'Anything, my lord.'

'Your acolyte. I should like to borrow him.'

Excerpt Three:
Passage, Volume III ('Angels and Abominations), '*Primacii*: Claviculus Matri'

LET ME SPEAK *of humans.*
We must acknowledge at all times their regard for us. We are the stuff of their nightmares. We are their shadow gargoyles, their bogey-men. They hate us with the collected bile of millennia, and yet we must understand that their hate is merely a product.

It comes not from their hearts nor their minds, but from their god. It is a product of that which separates us from them with more polarity, more obviousness than any mere physical difference: their faith.

Their belief is a thing of nails and whips, of cords and chains – binding them, punishing them, driving them to acts of martyrdom and abasement. It makes them small.

It is an illusion. A sham-mindset of efficiency that degrades and crumbles upon closer inspection. It hides a labyrinth-gut of doubt, a meandering-bowel of hypocrisy, an imperfect and flawed tumour of hollowness and prejudice that sits and ferments in a soup of blood and shit. Faith is their crutch. Their support. It is a scaffold that they erect with morbid exactitude around their fragile minds, a safety net to catch them when they fall.

We will always be stronger than them, because we do not need their faith.

Theirs is the domain of belief, of hoping for that which cannot be seen nor felt, of pissing away the strength in their souls

*upon whimsy and chance. We do not believe, we children of
the Mother. We know.*

*We need believe in her no more than we need believe in the
sky, or the ground, or the air that we breathe. She simply 'is'.*

And she is drawing nearer. Always.

THE SENSATION OF helplessness was not something that
G'hait relished. Thick cords of chain, matte-black with
gunmetal joists and finger-pinioning handsockets, locked
him in an aspect of eternal supplication; head bowed,
shoulders hunched, every footstep a metallic percussion
as the shackles around his ankles pulled taut. His heavy
cowl slipped across his forehead, and thus blinded he
was forced to flick his head spasmodically to clear his
vision, grumbling.

'You look like you've been stabbed in the arse,' the Cardinal said, poking him in the back with his staff. 'Hunch
over more. You're playing a prisoner, child – you could at
least look a little miserable.'

G'hait huffed loudly, too irritated by the ignominy of
his role to act the penitent captive. Still, remembering
that he'd promised his master to serve the Cardinal with
the utmost obedience, he arched his spine further still,
pantomiming the uncomfortable gait of some withered
hunchback. The Cardinal inspected him with an imperious eye, nodding once.

'Much better. Now… You understand the plan?'

G'hait scowled. 'No,' he said, 'I told you. I don't know
a bloody thing.'

'Such hostility…' Arkannis stroked his chin, amused.
'Allow me to rephrase, child: do you understand your role
in the plan?'

'I'm to do as I'm told.'

'Perfect.'

'And it's 'G'hait'.'

'Excuse me?'

'My name. It's G'hait. You keep calling me "child".
You're not that much older than me, I reckon.'

Another lightning smile, tugging uneasily at G'hait's confidence.

'Tell me…' The Cardinal leaned forwards, genuinely interested, 'do you take the same tone with your master? Is respect so undervalued on this world?'

G'hait refused to be cowed by the piercing eyes, pushing all his distrust and suspicion to the forefront of his mind. 'No,' he said, frowning. 'But you're not from this world, are you? And you're not my master.'

Arkannis leaned back, smile spreading. Again G'hait felt his confidence wobble; the brief stab of uncertainty. For a moment he saw himself as a precocious infant, toying with some chimera-serpent that would hold off striking at him only so long as it amused it. There was venom beneath those arctic eyes, and it froze him to his spot without effort, draining away every last droplet of his assurance.

But it was a fleeting thing, an ephemeral slash of insecurity that was hastily resolved, guzzled up by the racial confidence that was thick in his genes.

'No,' the Cardinal said, teeth again flashing their electric grin. 'I'm not from here. But you are still, I'm afraid, merely a child. I'm older than I look. Come.'

He took a step forwards, arranging his robes with all the ceremony of a hawk preening its feathers, and left the small warehouse – connected remotely to the network of tunnels beneath the city – where he and G'hait had lurked. G'hait stumbled after him, staggering against the impediment of the heavy fetters.

Night came to the hivedome not as the cessation of light and the dominion of darkness, but as a stark polarisation of colour. With the ruby tint of the dome extinguished only the lurid illuminator lamps remained, smearing their infectious yellow pall across every surface, twisting gradients and curves into hard edges of highlight and shadow. Worse, the garish riot of blinking tones and oscillating spectrums that fronted the beatklubs contrived to add their tinted leprosy to the night: rendering every hurrying figure in flat tungsten obscenity, their thick coats and padded jerkins striated by a chessboard of purples and blues and greens.

G'hait sniffed, ignoring the sights and enjoying a lungful of the sharp, cold air, unstagnated by years of subterranean filtration like that of the Underchurch. He wished he could come to the surface more often.

'Ah,' the Cardinal said, staring away from him into the shadows. 'There you are. Take him, please.'

A cluster of forms quit the darkness in a gaggle, descending on G'hait before he could even register their appearance. Gaslight caught at gunmetal stocks and muzzles, picking out the simple grey fabric of military greatcoats and helmets. Storm troopers, G'hait realised, alarms ringing in his mind. Loyal servants of the Withered God.

He staggered backwards with a hiss, mind reeling, berating his idiocy in trusting the Cardinal. 'Bastard!' he shouted, a great glut of anger bubbling in his chest. 'Imperial bastard!'

On instinct, lights flashing in his mind, he ratcheted open his jaw, unhinging the concealed array of razor canines that lurked within with a mechanical clatter. His secondary tongue – a prehensile spear ridged with hooks and barbs – stretched taut. He snarled at the onrushing guards, body and soul fizzing with feral desperation.

'Hey,' said a voice at his back. 'Look around.'

A hellgun stock – wielded like a club by the foremost amongst the second group of troopers, who had crept up on him from behind – struck him with all the finesse of a descending mallet, spinning him in his place and dropping him to the ground.

A calm voice, lost somewhere in the nebula of pain-mist and fury, asked: 'Good. You brought the cage, I trust?'

'Of course, my lord.'

G'hait struggled to sit upright, snarling.

'Watch him,' the voice said, its amused drawl burning in G'hait's mind. 'I assure you, he's quite the rogue.'

The gun-stock loomed over his face again, still bloody from the first strike, and when it came down G'hait tumbled out of consciousness into the welcome murk of sleep.

THE NOCTURNAL BUSINESS of Garial-Fall – an endless human mantra of tragedy and triumph at any other time – was that night marred by a low uncertainty: a discordant note that went unnoticed by the citizens whose lives it bordered, like a familiar tune played a half-key too low. The Brownian motion of revellers and drunkards, whores and gigolos, slouching gang-scum and petty criminals: in and around it all something dark moved and festered, some subtle evanescence of behaviour that spread, like an invisible ripple, across the city.

Cowled figures hurried, alone and in groups, through alleyways thick with shadow. Staggering narc-junkies paused in their moronic undulations to dip in and out of apparently random doorways, then resumed their senseless tottering as if nothing had happened. Here a posse of juves checked the relative desertion of a particular street before ferrying heavy crates from one warehouse to another; elsewhere a richly dressed businessman clumsily fell against a platinum whore, surreptitiously transferring a clutch of parchments in the process.

All across the hivedome an industry of secrecy and conspiracy proliferated, and if any regular citizen suspected a thing it was immediately dismissed as just another underhand deal; another shady business transaction; another borderline illegality in a city that had grown accustomed to corruption and laxity years before.

Silent and secret, disguised behind the myriad idiosyncrasies and insanities of hivecity life, the Mother's congregation slunk from their holes and made their preparations in earnest, filled with divine purpose.

G'HAIT STRUGGLED BACK to awareness with a violence bordering on insanity. Like a child impatient for its own

birth he ripped howling from the cool shade of his
dreams, every muscle tightening, every neurone burning
in hunger for revenge. In the sludge of his ancestral memories he found a surfeit of predatory instincts and
reactions, and even before the fog of sleep had cleared
from his eyes the identity of his intended prey had crystallised in his mind.

Betrayer. Enemy. Arkannis.

He screamed and howled and shook, eyes bulging, his
betrayal as insidious as any tumour, spreading frills of
malignancy throughout his thoughts. Gripped by hostility, his senses swarmed with impressions: a kaleidoscope
of images, sounds and smells, each and every one focused
upon identifying and obliterating his target.

On every side of him shallow auditoria slanted
upwards like the walls of some civilised crater, the tor-
pidity of the air and the languid circulation of dust
characterising the chamber's obvious ancientness. From
every quarter, rows and columns of inquisitive faces bore
down upon him; withered features whose lifeless skin
seemed perfectly indigenous to this archaic environment:
a product of its own stagnancy.

G'hait at first mistook his audience for statues, or
corpses in the grip of rigor mortis: grotesque homunculi
arranged to some morbid design, curled eyebrows
bunched together, dust settling on their musty robes. But
no; as his senses blossomed their combined odour
assailed him – the unmistakable stench of human assem-
blage, with all its overtones of sweat and decay, flatulence
and halitosis, expensive scent-effervescents and all the
untidy detritus of recent meals.

Besides, with his every movement – snarling and flexing
as he was – the crowd would jump almost imperceptibly,
darting worried glances from side to side, unable to maintain their imperious disposition in the face of such
immediate rage. They were scared of him, then. Good.

Of more pressing urgency, however, was the growing
obviousness of his own ineffectuality. His muscles

boiled, impelling limbs to lash out with talons extended, gashing and slicing, splitting sinews and dejointing these geriatric meatsacks; letting the monster inside run riot, delighting in the butchery... He could see it in his mind, could almost taste the iron tang of blood-mist hanging in the air, could almost hear the aborted screams of his victims.

But, no. He was immobile. Locked in a rib-like cage of adamantium pinions and restraints, arms squeezed so tight to his chest that every breath grated his elbows against his sides and every surge of adrenaline was vented uselessly against his metal prison. Worse still, his screams were muffled – reduced to little more than the petulant bleatings of a fractious lamb. The metallic tang of a fat steel-wool gag filled his mouth, bundled tightly beneath his canines, confining the barbed extrusions of his tongue. He cursed and snarled uselessly; colourful invective lost to the meaningless prattlings that were all he could manage.

He was a specimen. A Mother-damned exhibit.

As the last cloying smog of unconsciousness was borne away by waking awareness, he realised where he was. Even as a child of the Underchurch, raised by a community far removed from that of the hivedome itself, he had heard of the Torus Room. The Plureaucracy, demonised by generations of his peers, were symbols of all that G'hait had come to despise: the ineffectuality, the pettiness and hypocrisy, the bloated elitism and decadence of rank. The blind faith. The cruelty. He found himself a captive of the very enemies he'd been taught since birth to hate and fear, and as their multifaceted attention drilled into him from every angle his yowls and impotent furies abated, leaving him surly and silent; an insect regarded through a lens by a higher order of authority.

'If you've quite finished?' a familiar voice trilled into the silence.

G'hait stiffened, recognising immediately the sardonic drawl of the Cardinal. His purple robes rustled into view from one side, hairless pate catching at the bright spot-lights that lit the floor of the auditorium. He was altered subtly: the ivory complexion characteristic of primaciis and maelignacis alike gone, replaced with a warmer hue of skin, far more human in appearance. G'hait curled his lip, sickened that he had been deceived by a thing so sim-ple as a layer of makeup.

A ten-strong squad of guardsmen, those same who had immobilised him, G'hait assumed, stood at precise inter-vals around the inner perimeter of the chamber. Arkannis stalked across the marbled floor with the practiced non-chalance of a showman; an exhibitionist providing a spectacle for his excited audience.

G'hait was smart enough to stay silent, refusing them the satisfaction of a further tantrum. Inside, where even the incisive attention of the plureaucrats couldn't pene-trate, he shrieked and committed bloody murder upon the smug features of his betrayer.

'As I was saying,' Arkannis said, addressing the withered politicians with a sharp smile, 'my investigations have yielded results of a most concerning nature...

'As a Cardinal it is the least pleasant of my holy duties to tend to the sanctity of my own flock. I came to this world, sirs, in response to matters that might otherwise be considered unimportant. Inconsistencies in the administration of the Cathedral, difficulty in collecting funds, poor attendance at sermons, that sort of thing.

'Sirs, I have served the most beloved Emperor – praise be upon him – for longer than I can remember. This pat-tern of degradation and corruption is familiar to me. I've witnessed it too often in the past to ignore it now. I came here, gentlemen, in the hope that my suspicions would prove unfounded; that I could dismiss my concerns as symptoms of paranoia or zeal.

'Alas, my fears were confirmed.'

At this the gaudy figure spun on his heel and stalked towards G'hait's cage, thin fingers reaching to grasp through the bars. It took every last part of G'hait's willpower to suppress the surge of rage at the Cardinal's proximity; biting down on the nascent banshee howl of fury that would, he knew, achieve nothing more than an exacerbation of his own sense of helplessness. He experienced the contact of the Cardinal's fingers against the fabric of his robes at an almost atomic level, glaring with as much malignancy as he could muster at the man's aquiline features.

Arkannis tugged at the robes, surprising him: his strength was unexpected. The cowl ripped, clearing G'hait's shoulders and exposing his head in its entirety to the glare of the Torus Room.

The plureaucrats, predictably, gasped.

G'hait allowed himself to imagine their impressions of his physiology, correctly concluding that, to them – to their blinkered and unchallenging view of what comprised normalcy – he must appear to be nothing less than a monster. The concept amused and depressed him at once: it would never occur to them that he regarded their moist biology in the same light.

His head, elongated and sleekened compared to their own, sloped upwards from his acute brows in a series of gnarled ridges, culminating in a wide frill of cartilaginous growths, like ossified scales from some deep sea leviathan. His hairless scalp, uniformly etiolated to the same wan shade as his hands and legs, segued in unsettling patterns with the bony crown of chitin that locked the base of his skull to the hunching plates of his back. There, where his simple jerkin revealed his shoulders, the spiny joints of his secondary limbs were revealed – thus far concealed carefully in grooves of overlapping keratin that segmented as he moved. He scissored the talons of his secret arms, earning another disgusted and terrified hiss from the audience.

It was his face, he supposed, that bothered them the most. Beneath his lugubrious brows, and despite the almost albinoesque complexion of his skin, he was just like them. A symmetrical and well formed human face with a fine nose, proud jawline and prominent cheekbones, rounded by smoothly structured lips. He smiled at them, imagining their disgust.

In him they could see themselves. Humanity, purity, innocence: however they chose to define the essence of their own being. In G'hait they saw it contaminated, mutated; infected by the taint of xenogeny. His monstrousness was all the more pronounced for its familiarity.

'Behold.' said Arkannis, gesturing expansively towards him, nodding into the crowd. 'The heresy that festers beneath your noses.'

SOMETHING WITHOUT OBVIOUS shape, bundled extrusions hinted-at beneath its voluminous shroud, as dark as the void, coiled its way between long deserted ventilation grilles and miasmic waste outlets that sputtered and gurgled into the silence.

Here, between mildewed building struts and grille floor divisions left organic and sagging by years of rust, the only sounds were the hollow retorts of the pipeways, resonating endlessly along kilometres of ducting and ventilation. Fat bundles of cables bulged and drooped listlessly; electrical hernias breaching the diaphragmatic walls of their plastic channels. Silent vermin, their blackpearl eyes twinkling in the gloom, darted to clear the pathway of the unformed shade that drifted, wraithlike, through their petty kingdoms.

And finally, its haphazard route complete, the shape sagged gratefully into a steam-fissure recess, methodically tensing and slackening each of its muscles in turn, avoiding the cramps that threatened to overwhelm it.

Here, at least, there was sound. A tinny parody of voices, corrupted by the unkind acoustic of the tight crawlspace, wended its way upwards from the bright chamber beneath.

The figure settled for the wait, passing the time by casually skewering and skinning those foolish vermin bold enough to approach.

'THAT'S QUITE ENOUGH of the dramatic gestures, thank you Cardinal.' A resonant voice divorced itself from the clamour of the Torus Room, incidentally forcing the scared Plureaucrats into silence. G'hait, increasingly uncomfortable within the confines of his cage, noted a tall man, ostentatiously dressed in Imperial finery, standing at the centre of the front row. The figure gestured distastefully in his direction. 'What's the meaning of this... abomination, Cardinal?'

'Ah, Governor Ansev.' Arkannis smiled, the mirthless grin that G'hait was beginning to associate with irritation flashing across his face. 'An explanation. Yes, of course.

'In as much as I possess any expertise in these matters – which is to say, not a great deal – I believe you are looking at a genestealer hybrid of the third generation.'

At the mention of the word 'genestealer' the room erupted in hissed litanies and mumbled prayers, horrified expulsions of breath and terrified curses. G'hait regarded their horror with predatory interest despite his own fears and furies, bewildered by their recognition of the term. He'd never heard the phrase before and was confused by its association with his self. What, he wondered, were 'genestealers' – and if indeed the nomenclature did apply to his race, how had these ineffectual fops come to hear of their existence before?

'You have proof to back this claim?' the Governor said from his seat, face ashen and voice tight.

'The evidence of your own eyes, Governor,' Arkannis replied. 'You've seen the xenogen archive material, I trust? The specimen-dissections from the wreck *Harbinger*, which passed through this sector two centuries ago? The similarities in physiology are striking, even to the layman without knowledge of xenobiology. Then, of course, there's the matter of the Hive Secundus... I understand a

genestealer cult was uncovered and purged there some
decades ago. Is it really so implausible that the tendrils of
the Great Devourer have penetrated this city also?'

By now the murmuring was reaching an almost
cacophonic level, fearful voices running together. The
Governor, fiddling with an ornamented case of 'bac
sticks, rounded on the crowd with a snarl. 'Be silent, con-
found you!'

G'hait worried at the bitter gag with his coiled tongue
and waited, hungry for even the slightest opportunity to
escape, to turn this disaster to his advantage, to do anything. He was scared – for himself and for his church –
and it was a sensation that didn't sit easily in his gut.
Mentally he recited catechisms to the Mother, appealing
for the comforting certainty of her love that had been present in every aspect of his life thus far.

'You will forgive me, Cardinal,' the Governor said,
standing with his features closed and serious, the faux
pomposity of his syntax entirely failing to disguise his
distrust, 'if I seem... incredulous. There are, to my mind,
inconsistencies in your words. Details that do not seem
to add up. Perhaps you might address them?'

'Oh?'

'Under what circumstance, I wonder, would a Cardinal
of the Ecclesiarchy take it upon himself to investigate an
abomination so grievous? A man of such stature could
hardly claim ignorance of the correct procedures, in these
situations.'

'Make your point, Governor.'

'As I understand it, Cardinal, the blessed Inquisition
are more than adept at investigations of this nature; certainly it was they who delivered the Hive Secundus from
its infection – and yet you consider yourself sufficiently
qualified to do their job for them? You arrive here in our
midst, unannounced like some rogue trader, bringing
with you your caged freak and your tall tales – hinting at
a knowledge of xenobiology, no less! Hardly the behaviour of a holy man, in my experience. An individual of

your wisdom, Cardinal – if indeed that's what you are – can surely appreciate my bewilderment.'

G'hait studied Arkannis's face, struggling to decipher the emotions that his wry smile concealed. Its meaning remained opaque. Besides, G'hait considered the Governor's questions entirely pertinent: Arkannis's actions thus far had not been those of an Imperial Cardinal, and his profound psychic talents only served to make his appointment in such a role even more unlikely.

Who or what, then, was he?

'My congratulations, Governor,' Arkannis said, the smile spreading wider still. 'Your wisdom is a credit to this world.'

Moving again with slow ceremony, he raised his right hand, fingers fanned, to the audience. A peristaltic ripple moved across the crowd, heads craning downwards, eager to see whatever bauble he displayed. A thick silver ring on his centre finger, surmounted by a ruby that glimmered like a perfect droplet of blood, snagged at the auditorium lights. Arkannis muttered a word beneath his breath, clenching his fist then opening it again.

The ring flickered, pulsing with some inner life. And then, to a hushed chorus of hisses and gasps, it blossomed: radiating a dazzling stream of light directly upwards, flaring at the dust in long ruby-red motes. A shape formed within the light stream; an effervescent illusion that held every person in the auditorium spellbound, that elicited a wave of mouths hanging agape, of low moans of recognition, of perfect and undiluted authority.

Even G'hait recognised the symbol, stomach turning over as the magnitude of Arkannis's betrayal became manifest.

It hung aloft, rotating around its vertical axis with solemn magnificence: a silver-black quadrilateral, bisected horizontally with three sharp slashes of blackness.

A serif-bearing 'I', thrice struck-through, surmounted at its centre by an ivory skull.

'I am Inquisitor Arkannis of the Ordo Xenos,' the Cardinal said. 'And my authority will be questioned no further.'

Excerpt Four:
Interior passage, Volume II ('Angels and Abominations'), '*Primacii*: Claviculus Matri'

OF THE ORDERS *of the Mother's children.*

The lowliest and most numerous are the contagii: the infected. They are the blessed meat-puppets of the congregation, gifted with the freedom that comes with service. When they accept the Kiss, when their imperfect flesh is laced with the Mother's legacy, they taste divinity. Influence, power, wisdom: these are the goals of the contagii.

The second order are the maelignaci: in whom the Mother's flesh is a birthright, a gift of a shared lineage. Those of the first generation, the sons and daughters of contagii, are animals. I will not glorify their idiocy, nor condemn it. They are unsullied by the distraction of intelligence, their worth measured in procreation and destruction. They are the Mother's engines of war and vessels of multiplication, lumbering and moronic, executing their orders without callousness nor cruelty. Their existences are brief; filled by the exigence of combat and breeding. They burn brightly, and are gone.

Their children, hybrids of the second generation, are the truest of predators. The whimsy of the lineage is manifest in them – a culture of unique specimen and unpredictable bearing, with no two alike. They can be selectively bred; their parents studded like prize livestock to exploit a particular trait. Speed, strength, aggressiveness. These are the virtues of the second children.

And the third generation. The truest of hybrids.

They are the children in whom the defences of the human genetype are all but overcome. The Mother's fleshgift may operate to whatever design it chooses, spared the erratic successes and failures of eugenic inconsistency. Their bodies are carefully formed, their minds developed to favour obedience and cunning, their spirits strong. They are the praetorians of the Mother's will, and in her name they serve and grow mighty.

'YOUR CITY IS compromised. Your security is shattered. Your purity undone. The seeds of heresy and rebellion have flourished in the shade of your laxity, and we must pray to Him-on-the-Throne that this discovery does not come too late.'

Arkannis paused, basking in the attention of the combined Plureaucracy. He wet his lips slowly, taking time to run his shrewd gaze across the rows of transfixed faces.

'Answer me now, men of Garial-Fall. Will you place yourselves beneath the jurisdiction of the Ordo Xenos? Will you do as I tell you, when I tell, how I tell you? Will you obey me, in the certainty that to do otherwise would amount to your destruction?

'Tell me. Tell me now.'

Silence draped itself across the gathering, a velvet shroud that bristled along every spine and raised gooseflesh bumps across every fat inch of flesh. Even G'hait, listening as his blood roared for butchery and carnage, felt the power behind Arkannis's words.

The Governor stood, face pale.

'We are yours to command, my lord inquisitor.'

Arkannis smiled, and as his teeth twinkled like a constellation of daggers the pale skin of G'hait's knuckles began to bleed, thinning and splitting at the sheer fury with which he clenched his fists.

'Good.' Arkannis said, pursing his lips. 'Which of you speaks for the security resources of this city?'

A rotund man stood, sweating visibly through brightly coloured robes, their ludicrous blotches of pattern – perhaps in deference to his role – arranged in a gaudy imitation of militaristic camouflage. He squirmed, putting G'hait in mind of nothing more than a maggot, writhing at the tip of a hook. 'N-Nylem Versel, my lord.'

'And your post?'

'Chairman. Uh, c-chairman of the primary sub-committee for the Provision of Civilian and Military Defence.'

The newly-revealed inquisitor cocked an eyebrow, shaking his head. '"Primary sub-committee?"' he parroted, voice sharp with scorn.

The plureaucrat wilted beneath the glare, lip trembling, nodding maniacally.

'It's no wonder your world is infected, sir.' Arkannis's disdain was merciless, forcing Versel back into his seat. 'You pampered fools were too busy voting to notice the adders nesting beneath your fat arses.'

Hot indignation filled the auditorium, its stagnant dustmotes gyrating with a new tension and urgency.

'Is there no one here that speaks for your military?' Arkannis snarled, brows knotting together.

'Aye,' said a voice.

A grizzled man stood at the periphery of a minor bench, scarred features and lean frame entirely incongruous with those corpulent figures that shared his row. He nodded professionally to Arkannis: one equal greeting another.

'You're no politician, I think…' Arkannis said, smiling.

'I'm Marshall Delacroix of the vigilators, Commander of the Precinct.' His voice, in keeping with his appearance, seemed casual to the point of slackness: clipped of the pompous formality with which the Plureaucracy conducted itself. G'hait thought he looked like a man perpetually angry with the world but unable to discern why.

'Do you make a habit of listening-in on the administrative nonsense of fat men, Marshall?'

'No, sir. I don't. I was summoned to answer charges of brutality, as it happens. Some of your 'fat men' aren't too keen on my methods, if you catch my drift. Not that they've got the authority to stop me.'

One or two of the politicians muttered disgustedly beneath their breaths, until the vacuum-like tension of the room compelled them to silence.

'How very fortunate for the pair of us, marshall.' Arkannis's gimlet eyes twinkled. 'Tell me – how far does your jurisdiction extend?'

The marshall cracked his knuckles pointedly, cruel mouth spreading into a sneer. 'Technically? As far as you want it to. Local customs don't give me much say over the PDF, but in theory I could commandeer the lot.'

'Mm. I need a General, Delacroix. I need someone to follow my orders. Someone with authority over every military resource.'

Delacroix's sneer spread even further. 'Then I'm your man, sir.'

Governor Ansev blustered to his feet, waving his wad of notes and files like some dishevelled fan. 'This is ridiculous, Arkannis! You can't hand over the armed forces of the entire hive to him! The man's a psychopa-'

'Governor,' the inquisitor's interjection silenced the incensed official, robbing him of every trace of his indignation. 'A moment ago you sanctioned my absolute authority over every resource at your disposal. Your objections are too late.

'Sit down and shut up, or I'll have you ejected.'

The Governor sank into his seat, mouth opening and closing in wordless astonishment. G'hait was put in mind of a fish, drowning in the air.

'Congratulations, Marshall. As of now you are Commander-in-chief of the combined vigilator and Defence forces of Garial-Fall. Your first act will be to declare a state of martial law. Impose a curfew, if you must. Keep citizens off the street and civil disorder to a minimum. Impress upon them the… urgency of the situation. Use whatever means are necessary.'

Delacroix's smile, already a crooked feline grin, spread further still.

'As you command, my lord.'

'Good. Spread the word. I want every enforcer, every PDF sergeant, every plebeian grunt and gunner to know:

from this moment we are at war. There is a community of evil thriving at the heart of this city, and I intend to crush it. Utterly.

'There will be a Command briefing. Every officer of rank lieutenant or above to be included. See to it that there are no absentees. I will address them in…' Arkannis glanced at a gold timepiece suspended from one sleeve of his robe, 'four hours.'

'Where?'

'I assume you have a control bunker at the precinct?'

Delacroix nodded, staggered at the speed with which his promotion had unfolded, unnerved by the utter assurance of the inquisitor's orders.

'Then be on your way. I dare say you have a great deal to prepare.'

Delacroix quit the chamber at a half-run, the vast frescoed doorways booming closed behind him, lifting a thin layer of dust from their moulded surfaces.

'Well,' said Arkannis into the silence, beaming. 'That was easy enough.'

THE QUIESCENT PRESENCE trembled then tensed, thin limbs pausing in their grisly pastime. A semi-disembowelled rat was tossed aside, gelatinous innards trailing behind.

The shape peered from its alcove warily, slender talons gripping at either edge of the damp ducting that enclosed it, lifting itself clear like some horrendous larva, quitting its cocoon.

Nearby, thick with decades of dust and mould, a sturdy grille punched slatted lines of light into the crawlspace; parallel bars of warm luminescence, bleeding up from the chamber below.

In its mind, through brutalised and dissected layers of alien contemplation and abstraction, past thick boundaries of utter insanity, it could feel its master calling to it. The tiny, impotent voice at the pit of its brain that struggled to disobey, that railed against the psionic commands that gripped it, was drowned.

The creature placed a hooked claw against the grille's bars and, filled with the anticipation of action, tugged.

G'HAIT TRIED TO flex a limb, suppressing the insidious cramps that crept across his muscles. The cage constricted him on all sides, imprinting its lattice of coarse bars onto his exposed flesh, a chequerboard of bruises that quickly flared blue and purple against his albino skin.

Despite the pain he kept his eyes fixed squarely upon Arkannis, sick with hatred that no number of venomous glares nor bestial snarls could hope to assuage. The so-called 'Cardinal' stood beaming at the silent audience, resolutely ignoring his captive, all the rigid formality that he'd displayed moments before suddenly and startlingly surrendered – lost the very instant that Marshall Delacroix had left the chamber. To G'hait's mind his posture and bearing now was that of an excitable child; happily awaiting some forthcoming spectacle.

The Imperial Governor, losing patience with the protracted silence, stood with an audible sigh, exasperation palpable in his voice. 'Inquisitor – what exactly are you intending to do?'

Arkannis rolled his eyes. 'Governor, I'm growing a little bored of your outbursts. I told you to be silent.'

'But–'

'*Sit.*' The word resonated beyond the material plane, thick with psionic puissance, rippling and alive in the air. On every side of the auditorium those plureaucrats who were half standing to discuss matters quietly with their neighbours, or who sprawled too far from the vertical, or who knelt in the footwells of their benches in prayer, collapsed into their seats with a startled yelp. Like an expanding ring of movement the gathered politicians found themselves compelled to sit bolt upright, unable to disobey the mental command that ripped at their very brains. Even the guards, standing upright at the periphery of the chamber, collapsed to the ground like boneless meat, sitting cross-legged for a moment before clambering to their feet, confused. To G'hait the psionic command was a torture, impelling his cramped legs to fold away, forcing him to push himself harder still against bars that refused to bend or break.

Arkannis, watching the madness with a wry smile, chuckled to himself. 'Oops.'

And then a noise filled the Torus Room – a sharp squeal that plucked moans of terror from the gathering, slowly rising in volume.

'E-emperor preserve!' the Governor burbled, eyes locked upwards. 'What is it?'

'That,' said Arkannis, not bothering to crane his neck with the rest of the crowd, 'is the sound of adamantium tearing. There's something almost… primal about it, don't you think?'

'Guards!' the Governor squealed, terrified.

'Yes… Yes, that's a good idea.' Arkannis smiled. 'Guards – prepare yourselves.'

The ten storm troopers racked their hellguns with a succession of mechanical clatters, planting themselves firmly in sturdy firing positions. Not one of them said a word, or tilted the muzzles of their weapons upwards to track the source of the keening noise.

G'hait's mind reeled, lost in a web of confusion. He was certain that he was missing something, some piece of this puzzle; but all his focus was bent upon anger at the Cardinal's betrayal, blinding him. The need to understand – itself a product of his unique and freakish biology – was crushed; buried beneath a landslide of rage.

And then Arkannis winked at him.

And then a ventilation duct high above the auditorium collapsed and dropped, like a gunmetal corpse with its spine severed.

And something followed it down.

And the world went mad.

* * *

SOMEWHERE, AT THE back of its spinning mind, the insane creature registered the sounds of gunfire. Percussive and ugly, the rhythmic pounding of hellgun shells reverberated across the air, as tangible to the creature's hypersensitive skin as repeated blows of a hammer.

It crooned delightedly to itself, already detecting the unmistakable stink of blood, spreading wide its limbs like some rappelling spider, plunging vertically from the ruptured vent. It landed on its feet – of course – and smiled. And kept on smiling.

Obese meat-things shrieked and burbled before it, or else froze with dinner plate eyes and mouths gaping. It articulated its limbs without effort or conscious thought; razor blurs of dark skin and exoskeletal chitin, silent and impossible to track.

The head of a nearby preymorsel – its fat wattles quivering as it screamed – fell from its attendant neck, an expression of intense confusion spreading across its jugulated face. Carnage, silent and precise, rippled across the throng; robed in black and impossible to define. Here an arm was sheared at its elbow; a perfect incision that swept a porous plateau across muscle, sinew and bone. There a set of intestines were released from the tight confines of their abdominal prison, springing forth with elastic joy to tumble and collect across the floor.

The creature danced through the crowd like a laughing god, humming and giggling to itself, and wherever it passed men died before their minds even registered the presence of their deranged killer.

G'HAIT WATCHED IT all unfold with slow horror and mounting confusion, adrift on a sea of nonsensical events and contradictory impressions. The screams rose to an almost unbearable pitch, eclipsed only by the relentless hellgun salvoes, stalling his whirligig thought process before it even began.

Like vultures lurking at the periphery of some exquisite execution, the storm troopers that perched at the rim of the auditorium bowl gunned down any bustling plureau-crat that dared approach. Despite the roaring weapons the politicians fled ever upwards, porcine eyes wide and limbs scrabbling across the steep tiers of seating. Bright fabrics ripped and singed, fluids splattered with explosive momentum, sheared and punctured bodies flopped and toppled backwards, crushing their neighbours, shards of bone and jewellery tumbling in their wake.

And behind them, fuelling their terror, provoking their clumsy, comical ascent, a storm cloud boiled through their midst. Somewhere at its heart was a figure – G'hait's darting vision could discern that much – but its features and shape were beyond even his ability to perceive. As it knifed its grisly way through the throng, flipping and ducking around geyser-gouts of arterial spray and dis-sected flesh, G'hait recognised the funereal shroud of the Cardinal's attendant – the wiry figure who'd accompa-nied Arkannis from off-world. He remembered noting the warrior's stance, the disciplined movements, the aura of control.

The transformation was breathtaking. The figure had become a god of knives, a scalpel-jester; an incision-dervish that parted musclecords like water and hewed bone like soft wood. A swell of carnage billowed out-wards in concentric rings, a scarlet mandala that blossomed to incorporate every bench, every marbled expanse, every shredded body. A set of disembodied fin-gers flittered through the air, striking at G'hait's cage with a series of sharp, ballistic crackles. He barely noticed, spellbound by the devastation.

'She's enjoying herself…' a dry voice said, near enough to G'hait's ear to startle him. He twisted his head as much as the cage would allow to find Arkannis standing close, regarding the frenzied butchery with a quiet smile. A lace-like trail of blood, gusted from some impossible-to-follow incision elsewhere in the Torus Room, painted itself across his face in a delicate ruby stripe. 'Hmm,' was his only reaction.

G'hait, unable to speak, thought: she?

'Oh yes,' Arkannis said, unprompted, withdrawing a silk kerchief from a pocket and elegantly wiping at the bloodsmear. 'Her name is Trikara. She's quite the artist.'

An eyeball tumbled past Arkannis, ocular nerve orbiting like some frenzied lassoo. 'Mind you...' he said, leaning in towards G'hait with a conspiratorial smirk, 'she does rather tend to show off.'

The stink of blood and gunsmoke invaded G'hait's senses, firing instinctive reactions buried deep in his genes, drawing tendrils of saliva across his gag-bound chin and tensing his cramped muscles still further.

'I shouldn't try fighting it, child,' Arkannis said, regarding him with lidded eyes. 'It's in your blood. One can't escape their lineage.'

G'hait thought: You're reading my mind...

The Cardinal chuckled, like a parent amused by the naivety of their child. 'You've only just worked that out?'

Bastard! You betrayed the Mother!

'Did I? Did I really? Perhaps you'd care to look again.'

G'hait glanced away from the frost-toned irises, astonished by the devastation that, scant moments since the assault had begun, already littered the room. It seemed like some callous whirlwind, composed of a thousand spinning razorblades, had swept through the Torus Room. Few plureaucrats remained alive now, fleeing and tumbling in disarray as the blurred assassin closed upon them.

'It seems to me,' Arkannis said, ignoring the few remaining screams, 'that I haven't betrayed the Mother at all.'

G'hait's mind spun, exhausted and bewildered. The thought surged at the centre of his brain, impossible to conceal: *I don't understand!*

'Alas,' Arkannis sighed, brows dipped in a passable imitation of sympathy, 'understanding is overrated. Today, with your help, we have obliterated the mightiest of the Mother's enemies and instigated the downfall of all others.'

With my help? You caged me… I haven't done anything!

'Oh, but you have. You remember my good friend Marshall Delacroix? When the news reaches him that the entire administration of his world has been found thus – slain, ripped to shreds by some wild animal…. how do you think he'll react? He'll remember the snarling beast that was presented to the Plureaucracy, and he'll draw an entirely inaccurate conclusion…'

H-he'll think that I broke free… He'll think that I did this!

'Very good, G'hait. You aren't as stupid as I feared. Yes, Marshall Delacroix, newly-promoted General of the Garial-Fall defence force, whose colourful records credit him with a history of overreaction and overzealousness, will spread the word that a cult of vicious heretics, able to break through adamantium and overcome an entire squad of storm troopers, has blossomed at the heart of his world. He'll impose his wretched martial law and he'll come down on criminals and curfew-breakers like a shower of boulders… I've met men like him before, G'hait. They think that panic can be bottled-up, corked like some rare vintage. It can't. The harder you repress it, the stronger it becomes.

'Our friend Delacroix, believing all that he heard in this room today, and burning with power and vengeance, will sow the seeds of discord and unrest far more effectively than you or I ever could. When the Mother's faithful flock rises up, it will be to find a population already in disarray, stamped underfoot by a martial regime, terrified of shadows and begrudging the tyrants who are supposed to be protecting them. What better circumstances could exist for the rebellion?'

But Delacroix will be prepared! He'll attack the church!

'Those were not my orders to him, G'hait. You heard what I said. I told him to organise a command briefing, remember?'

But…

'Tell me, child. How else could we – the Mother's faithful children – have conspired to collect every ranking officer amongst our enemy in one place, at one time?'

G'hait almost gagged, appalled and awestruck at the depth of the deception, forming an impossible conclusion: *You knew he'd be here today... It was no coincidence at all...*

'Very good. There are no coincidences in my work. I checked the Plureacracy's schedule from off-world, weeks ago, and timed my arrival to coincide with the marshall's hearing. Simple.'

And what is your work, 'Cardinal'?

Arkannis's face straightened, wry smile annihilated. He stared directly at G'hait, leaving no room in the hybrid's mind for doubt or uncertainty, filling all of his consciousness with the penetrating depths of his eyes. 'I am Elucidium,' he said, and, lifting a key from a chord at his belt, unlocked the cage that held G'hait prisoner.

IN ITS LAIR, lounging with vapid obesity upon a palette of decaying meats, splattered with the coagulated resin of its own spittle, the patriarch stiffened.

Its nonsensical gurgling faltered; the spasmodic rotations of its tiny porcine eyes resolved with something like focus, and, as the three contagii selected to clean and tend to the grotesque messiah milled in empty-minded confusion, it straightened.

Frills of atrophied flesh, segmented and creased by centuries of flaccidity, gathered and hung like waterlogged carcass-meat, dislodging the slime of sweat and dead skin that puddled across the shifting behemoth. Flakes of eroded cartilage – little more than sawdust shards of pallid and brittle chitin – rained from its pied carapace like a fine snow. It flexed the humanoid hands of its secondary limbs, knuckles crackling like dry timber, ossified talon nails clicking together.

Never before in living memory had the corpulent gargoyle appeared anything other than vegetative. To the congregation its existence was iconic rather than practical: an avatar of the Mother around whom to centre their worship and respect. It was an idol: as insensible and incommunicable as the stylised statues of the humans' Emperor, carved in alabaster and ivory in the Cathedral above.

The patriarch was a glyph; a symbol; a focus of worship. Nothing more. It had ever been thus.

But not so now.

It squatted enormously on its haunches, regarding and flexing its limbs with mute fascination – a child achieving self awareness for the first time. The recurved hooks of its principal limbs, long sickle claws with glistening muscle cords at their bases, scissored with a slow rasp, cutting edges playing across one another musically.

The contagii, not understanding this new situation and lacking the relevant orders to confront it, seemed to switch off, gazing vacantly into nothingness in the absence of other regulation.

The purii had no such idiocy. Out from the shadows they slunk, scuttling from myriad tunnels and drains, long arms and wicked talons extended in some horrific parody of human celebration, summoned by the awakening of their strongest, most ancient brother.

Sensing the burgeoning excitement of its congregation, plucked from its comatose insensibility by the surge of focus and anticipation that they generated, the patriarch awoke to preside over the eve of his flock's long awaited rebellion.

G'HAIT'S BODY MOVED independently of his mind, surging with a burst of animal frenzy that bypassed his intellect and fed instead upon the most feral of his instincts. Before his senses were even fully engaged and he could register the opening of his cage, his hands were locked around Arkannis's throat, his secondary claw-limbs poised to incise across the man's exposed neck. He pounced like some venomous reptile, pushing his enemy onto the ground and straddling his chest, tensing for the blow that would open the so-called Cardinal's jugular in a glorious, beautiful fountain.

'Maelignaci,' Arkannis said from beneath him, voice tight, face betraying not a hint of fear or anger at the assault. 'Wait.'

G'hait ripped the gag from his own face with a spasmic swipe of a claw, not caring for the long gash he scored into his own flesh in so doing. He spat the balled wad of steel-gauze with relish, ratcheting his jaw to relieve its ache.

'You die, inquisitor!' he snarled, lost in the storms of his own mind, claws raised above his head.

'I'm no inquisitor, child. You know that.'

'You're a liar!'

Arkannis smiled. 'There are two reasons,' he said, 'that you will not kill me. The first is that I am not lying. I've just ordered the genocide of an Imperial administration, G'hait. Use your brain.'

'I saw the ring! T-the symbol of the Inquisition!' His certainty wobbled dangerously, threatened by too many unanswered questions, too much confusion.

'A souvenir. I've killed more of the Inquisition's holy fools than I can remember. They part with their little trinkets with poor grace, in my experience.'

'That's... Y-you expect me to believe you now? You think I'm an idiot?'

'No, child. Quite the reverse... Which brings me to the second reason that you won't kill me.'

'Oh yes?'

'Oh yes. Because you'll be dead before you move an inch.'

A sharp pressure against his throat – not hard but... insistent – registered vaguely at the back of G'hait's mind. Distantly, as though it were happening in another world, he noticed that the shrieks and screams of the Plureau-cracy had been silenced. A hand gripped his shoulder with mock familiarity, tightening the razor contact beneath his chin.

Arkannis's grin widened further. 'G'hait, meet Trikara. Trikara, this is G'hait.'

The thing behind him hissed and giggled beneath its breath, airy tones vaguely feminine in their delirious cadence. The sniggering wasn't helping G'hait's confidence – or his concentration.

'Now,' said Arkannis, apparently unaware of the ignobility of his position, prone against the marble. 'You are a maelignaci of unusual intelligence, G'hait. I suggest you use your brain.'

'But… I don't…'

'You don't understand – yes, we've established that.' Another smile lit the pinioned face. G'hait fought the urge to cut it in half. 'But consider the evidence. In one fell swoop, with no more cost than your damaged pride, I've created the exact set of circumstances that your ineffectual little congregation should have established years ago. I've undermined the stability of this city, I've sliced off its fat head, and I've forced the long arms of its military into a trap…

'And now you, G'hait, want to kill me because I made you stand in a cage? Not quite the selfless devotion I'd expect of the Mother's faithful, boy.'

G'hait felt his cheeks burning, hating the grinning figure. 'So why me? And why not tell me what you planned?'

'Because I needed a reaction. I needed a convincing little monster.'

G'hait scowled, still not understanding. Arkannis rolled his eyes.

'Outrage, G'hait. I needed outrage. I needed someone to scream and shriek like a beast. All that… that betrayal and fury that you're clinging to so nicely… I wanted it boiling out from every pore. You've seen the other maelignacis of the Underchurch. Empty-headed things, G'hait. Puppets. They lack your spirit.'

'You needed me as an alibi.'

'Quite. The slightest hint that you trusted me… that we were allies… would have ruined everything.' He chuckled. 'No hard feelings, eh?'

G'hait glared at him, hatred sputtering and beginning to die, swallowing his bruised pride with a conscientious effort. His sense of betrayal was nothing compared to the Mother's duty.

'You have proof for all this?' he snarled, the last few traces of ire bubbling tenaciously in his guts.

Arkannis smiled indulgently, cold eyes flashing. 'Consider this, child: I could have had you terminated at any point. I still could, at that. And yet here you are, alive and angry and ugly. Hardly the work of a betrayer, I dare say… Besides… There's the evidence of your own eyes. Look around.'

For the first time since the extraordinary conversation began, G'hait slid his eyes away from the recumbent Cardinal and surveyed the devastation. The figure behind him, still pressing its scalpel-like claw against the all-too-human skin of his throat, giggled into the silence.

Bodies lay like ruined sculptures, intermingling, their fat joints coagulating across the marble. Disembodied hands sprouted like wan saplings, clutching lifelessly at the air. Decorticated faces grinned from lipless mouths, eyeballs lolling with lifeless intensity amongst the liberated mess of intestinal trauma. On all sides the Torus Room had become an obscenity: an artwork of such glorious viciousness and aesthetic perversion that even G'hait, burdened as he was by human inadequacies like revulsion and fear, could not help but be impressed in the feral pit of his mind. Only the storm troopers, guns finally lowered, remained standing; grey uniforms macerated with patches of blood and flesh.

Arkannis watched G'hait absorb it all, and with only the merest flicker of attention silently ordered his murderous companion to release her grip. G'hait staggered upright, too stunned to speak, and the Cardinal stood before him with a sweep of violet fabric.

Still reeling, G'hait allowed his wandering attention to fall upon the figure that Arkannis had called 'Trikara', not sure what to expect. That she was lithe and athletic beneath

the cloak was entirely expected, yet still her fragile form –
so thin that to G'hait she appeared little more than some
skin-hung skeleton, emaciated to the point of brittleness –
drew a hiss of surprise from his throat. Clad in a textureless
ebony bodysuit, stitched crudely with black wire to accom-
modate the extraordinary length of her limbs, her
movements were like oil shifting across rocks; like the subtle play of darkness at the heart of overlapping shadows.

Her hands caught immediately at G'hait's attention, if
only for their sheer incongruity: beside the lissom blackness
of her wardrobe they seemed at once monstrous and elegant: flesh so pale it was almost white, calcifying and
segueing with the ridged plates of chitin particular to his
race. Long segmented digits, like the legs of some ivory crustacean, ended in hooked claws like scythe-blades, slick with
blood and gore. They retracted into the insectile fingers with
a wet rasp, eliciting another giggle from their owner.

Her face, even more than her butcher's claws, astonished G'hait. Perched imperiously upon a swanlike neck,
it was composed with an almost feline aesthetic: eyes
wide and tilted, nose merely a fine ridge, cheekbones
extraordinarily prominent, mouth little more than a tiny
underscore. Even the dimpled crests of cartilage above
her brow, characteristic of the Mother's taint, couldn't
destroy the exotic allure of the face, its skin almost lumi-
nous. Her ears, arching proudly from beneath a shock of
jet black hair, tapered upwards into long, languid points.

She dribbled and giggled, instantly destroying what
brief beauty – no matter how alien it might have been –
she possessed. Extending a long finger towards the random heaps of cooling meat that had so recently been the
Plureacracy of the Hivedome, she caught G'hait's eye and
snickered like a flirtatious adolescent, drawing a moist
tongue across her lips. Something moaned.

'Ah…' Arkannis said from behind him, amused. 'A gift
for you, G'hait. I think Trika' must like you.'

It was the Governor, and he was dead. Almost.

* * *

Excerpt Five:
Interior passage, Volume II ('Angels and Abominations'),
'*Primacii*: Claviculus Matri'

THE FIRST ORDER *are my brethren, the primacii: scions of the
fourth generation.*

*In our biology the lineage reaches its zenith, withdrawing its
eccentricities and crudities to the inside, working its labile craft
upon the mind, the soul, the anima. We, of all the Mother's
flock, are best able to create, to innovate, to imagine. We, who
have tasted sentience and promised its heady gifts to the service of Her godhead: we are truly the most blessed of her
children.*

*The primacii are bred with a disposition towards gauntness
and intellectualism; our minds are honed to an incisive edge,
our tastes and pleasures unbridled by the Mother's credence.
We may exercise our intellects in whatever way we see fit, shep-
herding the entirety of the Mother's flock towards that most
divine, most perfect, most profound conclusion:*

Her ascendancy.

She comes; blessed be!

THE RETURN TO the cool tunnels of the Underchurch filled
G'hait with more relief than he could have imagined. Still
reeling from the unexpected events of the evening, his
head pounded with the thoughts and sensations that
were his particular disability. As he followed Arkannis
and Trikara through the wending catacombs, the muffled
scurrying from resin-coated shadows around him broadcast the attention of other maelignaci; lumbering and
moronic or sleek and vicious, they regarded his passage
with disinterest that – he fooled himself into thinking –
bordered on disdain. In truth they were no more interested in him than in anything: servile only to the direct
orders of the Council.

He would never be like them; spared the complexity
and grief that came with sentience. Theirs was an animal-
istic simplicity, an utter devotion and supplication to the

Mother's will (channelled, the council regularly crowed, through the primacii) that G'hait found himself envying.

The memory of Governor Ansev's execution (mewling like vermin through G'hait's thoughts, the thick sinews of his elbows and knees sliced and raw) filled G'hait with guilty satisfaction. A gift, Arkannis had called it. A gift to help him vent the anger and rage that had accreted in his mind like a tumour, dizzying his thoughts and tripping his senses. He was astonished at the speed with which events had darkened, trapping him at the heart of some impossible and complex ruse. A magus posing as an inquisitor posing as a Cardinal; G'hait had relished the opportunity to divorce himself from the confusion, lost in a haze of a bloodlust.

Briefly he'd tasted the feral simplicity of his brethren. Briefly he'd allowed the monster out of its emotive cage, stampeding through the frail shell of abstraction and intelligence that was his particular weakness. Briefly he'd tasted what it meant to be maelignaci, true and sincere and unsullied, rather than a mere Mother-damned freak with the mind of a human.

Briefly he'd tasted slaughter, and when he'd looked down at his work, at his claws slick and sticky with human blood, at the shredded jelly-flesh that was all that remained of Governor Ansev, he'd exalted in the sheer animal obviousness of it.

It didn't last, of course. How could it? Within moments the tangle of hopes and dreams was re-established, the complexities and deceptions of pride and trust and sentiment reformed, the illusory ganglia of emotion suffused itself again through his brain like some tentacled predator. And now, an hour later, thick with the blunt stink of drying blood, he walked again through the Mother's congregation as a pariah, a monstrositiy, a freak.

His feelings towards the purple-robed Cardinal too were difficult to classify. In some dark corner of his mind he couldn't deny that a core of resentment still burned, but he'd long ago learned that such sentiments were symptomatic of his anomaly, and fought hard to ignore it. Surrounding it, confused and effervescent, a nebula of trust and distrust circulated; skeins of impressionable awe and distaste, of astonishment. He admired the cunning of the 'inquisitor' ruse, appreciated the circuitous logic of Arkannis's deception but – above all else – struggled to reconcile his regard for the man's motives. Cardinal, inquisitor, magus: which was the true Arkannis?

G'hait remained a step behind his companions, equally as awestruck by Trikara – once again hooded and cowled – as her master. He'd asked the question that had burned through him upon seeing her, of course, back in the charnel house ruin of the Torus Room:

'What is she?'

Arkannis had blinked, face filling with the sort of slow indulgent smile that again had G'hait anticipating some untrustworthy half truth, some questionable response. 'Have you heard,' the man said, 'of the eldar?'

G'hait had not. The Cardinal's dizzying explanation had left him clutching at what few ideological solidities remained in his life. To discover so late that humanity were not the only race amongst the Mother's enemies, that indeed there were myriad civilisations and cultures scattered throughout the stars, that they were just as powerful and fearful as one another – each as cruel, as blinkered, as hostile to the simple affections and devotions of the Mother's church… G'hait had felt, briefly, as though he were falling.

'The Mother's seed, G'hait, is sown amongst every race. You think the taint is confined to the soft-meat of humanity? You think the Mother's Chosen don't flourish eloewhere?'

'W-what?'

'Eldar, ork, tau, hrud… The contagii are an adaptable breed, child.'

'I don't und–'

'Trikara is maelignaci, like you.'

'B-but… But her ancestors weren't human?'

Another smile, at that; acknowledgment of a correct answer. 'Very good…' Arkannis had pursed his lips, regarding Trikara with a frosty intensity as she'd dribbled and giggled nearby. 'Sadly,' he said, 'Eldar biology is rather less… crude… than that of humanity. The taint requires many more generations to achieve the primacii mutation. By which time, typically, the hybrid community has been discovered and purged. The eldar are nothing if not vigilant.

'I found Trikara by chance in the course of my travels. She's of the fifteenth or sixteenth generation, as far as I can tell. Heh – utterly insane of course, but quite devastating, I think you'll agree. And she does what she's told. The eldar mind is a strange thing, G'hait… Brilliant, sharp, multifaceted… but easily broken. Like a fake diamond.'

With that Arkannis had snapped from whatever trance-like introspection he'd entertained and, clicking his fingers impatiently, had ordered the squad of storm troopers into the centre of the Torus Room.

'Contagii,' he'd explained in response to G'hait's oblique stare, peeling a gasmask from one typically vacant, empty-eyed face in demonstration. 'I had the Council place them in my care. Think of them as sacrificial lambs.'

Without so much as a spoken command Trikara had blurred in her place; a succession of fleeting impressions scattered in jigsaw patterns across G'hait's vision. Here he glimpsed a limb, there a claw, there a flashing smile or twinkling eye. And then there was nothing but meat, and red mist, and Trikara's giggle.

'It will seem as though there was a firefight,' Arkannis said, surveying the scene with a shrewd eye. 'They'll find bodies with bullet-wounds and assume the troopers were panicking, firing wild. Trying to kill an enemy that – heh – dodged their bullets and cut them to shreds. They're always blind to the most obvious explanations, these humans.'

G'hait had looked around and seen, with a realisation that churned from his steel-capped boots to the crown of his ossified skull like a great bloody wave, crashing against his consciousness, that he was one of only three beings alive in a room of diced, disjointed meat. He wasn't sure how it had made him feel, and when Arkannis led him and Trikara away into the stagnant night of the city, he couldn't deny that a part of him, some dark feral piece that lived despite his sentient curse, yearned to remain in the abattoir playground.

Now, back in the cool of the Underchurch, such abstractions seemed distant and ethereal, eclipsed behind the reality of the resinous dips and alcoves of the tunnelways. Arkannis's stride, measured in the rhythmic striking of his staff, carried G'hait and his companions deep into the private chambers of the primacii council; past the cell of his master and onwards, inexorably approaching the cullised doorway into the personal domain of Archmagus Jezahael.

MARTIAL LAW CAME to Garial-Fall with all the discretion of a steel boot, administered with calculated violence entirely sanctioned by its wearer. Marshall Delacroix and his cadre of advisors authorised long-repealed excesses of control and repression, enforcing a hastily fabricated curfew in the pursuit of civilian containment.

It didn't work.

Delacroix's operation had been characteristically unsubtle. Charged with preparing his city for a potential war he'd stoked the population's fears with an almost arrogant disdain: proclaiming his remit via media tubes and broadcast pavilions, booming from public announcement speakers, glaring down with grizzled menace from viewscreens and news-auspexes alike. Evil was abroad, he'd warned. Heretics and seditionists – a nest of killers in the city's midst. He'd assumed, perhaps, that his charges would respond with a docility born of their fear: submitting gratefully to a police-administration determined to provide them with security and deliverance.

His understanding of human nature was entirely naïve.

Even as sleek Arbites tanks clawed their way from underground depots, pintle turrets swivelling with slow malevolence, the first riots sparked in the Heatsink. Erupting with apparent spontaneity (although perhaps, had they paused to consider, the rioters might recall cowled figures moving amongst the throng, whispering urgently and chanting their anger into the night), they accumulated quickly. Crowds accreted in xanthic-yellow streets, the beatklubs emptied their surly patrons into the city like a tide of braying wolves, and citizens made sick and angry with fear howled their indignation – demanding protection, liberation, freedom.

An hour after the first stone was hurled, as steamcarts were overturned and the plush hovcars of rich merchants set alight, as the bedraggled masses of the Slumquarters added their voices to the mob, as shop fronts were shattered all along the central strasse of the well-to-do Foildom and the reaction to Delacroix's pronouncements spread to encompass every locality within the city's lenticular cover, the first shots were fired.

Faced with a mass of angry rioters, backed into a walled culvert by the press of shouting, terrified bodies, a vigilator enforcement squad surrendered their power mauls and instead brought their shotguns to bear. The first volley – aimed deliberately low at their conscientious sergeant's command – shredded the knees and shins of the foremost rioters, dropping them in a tangle of broken bone. They thrashed and moaned in puddles of their own blood, shivering, too stunned to register the damage to their bodies. For a moment the crowd was arrested in its advance, drawing a single collective breath of horror and outrage. For a moment it might have gone either way.

Then the rioters surged forwards howling, the vigilators tilted their shotguns upwards, and the city was filled with thunder and blood.

ARCHMAGUS JEZAHAEL MADE no attempt to disguise her displeasure at Arkannis's visit. Entering her chambers both uninvited and unannounced, with Trikara and G'hait in tow, his arrival was as imperious and flamboyant as G'hait had come to expect.

'Ah, primacii!' he declared, smiling broadly, bowing with a mock flourish. 'Do excuse my intrusion, won't you – I'd hoped to discuss a… sensitive matter. I trust I'm not interrupting anything important?'

Jezahael arched an eyebrow, indicating the scraps of parchment and flickering auspex littering her desk.

'I'm completing the plans for your premature uprising, as it happens. If I'm to be sidelined by my own congregation in favour of a stranger, I at least have the right to arbitrate his movements.' She sneered. 'So no, nothing important.'

Arkannis waved a hand with genial dismissal. 'Of course, of course… But, tell me: what use are plans when events are already in motion?'

Her icy demeanour faltered, confusion fleeting across her features. 'What?'

'Oh, come now. Surely you were aware?'

'Aware of what?"

'That the uprising is already underway…'

'Y-you…. What? It can't be…'

'I assure you it is.'

'But… but it's too soon! Mother damn you, Arkannis – you've only been here one day and already you've undone years of pla–'

'Alas, the Mother waits for no one. A reason to celebrate, surely?'

'No! I-I mean, yes – yes, of course we should celebrate her arrival, but we're not ready! We haven't even begun to infiltrate the administration! It takes time! It's too soon!'

G'hait, watching Arkannis's face closely, felt the air thicken. The Cardinal's hawkish smile dwindled and died, leaving only his stark glower, burning into Jezahael with razor malevolence.

'Your leadership of this church is no longer required,' he said, icy voice entirely bereft of its previous sardonic trace.

Jezahael's astonishment bordered almost on the ridiculous – hissing and reddening with a disbelief impossible to confine. G'hait felt his blood burn, glutted with adrenaline at the Cardinal's extraordinary proclamation.

'W-what do… who…' The archmagus was reduced to spluttering breathlessly, searching for words. 'How dare you!'

'I dare,' Arkannis said, 'because I am Elucidium. I answer not to you, nor your church, nor your peers. I answer to the Mother alone, and in her name I say you are a failure, an embarrassment, an unnecessary resource.'

For an instant G'hait thought Jezahael might strike the Cardinal, drawing herself up with feline bluster and drawing back her lips, a feral mannerism he would normally expect from the purii, not their supposedly 'civilised' masters.

But her attack, if indeed it was pending, never came.

A single sound – like an expulsion of breath – filled the room. Even as the unmistakable scent of ozone wrapped itself around G'hait's senses, tinged with the tang of blood, Jezahael was crumpling to the ground, face set in an astonished rictus of confusion, eyes crossed in a dying attempt to focus upon the neat hole in the centre of her forehead – where a solitary wisp of smoke preceded a thick spout of cranial gore. She collapsed in disarray, sludgelike fluids pattering heavily across flagstones. She jerked twice, grunting spastically, and was still.

Arkannis replaced the ornate laspistol in a holster-pocket within his robe and hemmed, satisfied, beneath his breath. G'hait struggled against waves of astonishment, as if wading in a heavy stream, desperate to react.

'Wh… You… She's…'

Arkannis turned to him, face blank. 'G'hait,' he said, utterly calm, 'I need you to trust me.'

G'hait's mind spun. He wondered if anything would ever seem real, or solid, or stable again. Honesty seemed the best policy. He spluttered: 'But I don't!'

'Listen to me, child. This is for the best. The congregation needs a figurehead, a… a rallying point, if you like. Jezahael can be far more valuable to her church dead than she ever could in life. Every new endeavour needs its sacrifice, G'hait. Trust me.'

'I can't! I don't know who you are! I don't know anything any more!'

Arkannis almost smiled. 'You know…' he said, quietly, 'I don't believe I've ever come across a maelignaci quite like you before..'

'How can I trust you? You just… You killed the archmagus!'

'Yes. She was an inefficient fool.'

'She was still the archmagus!'

'G'hait – to whom are you loyal?'

'Wh–?'

'To whom?'

'To the Mother!'

'Good. Who else?'

'To the Underchurch!'

'Excellent. Who else?'

'T-to my master…'

'Magus Kreista?'

'Yes.'

Arkannis nodded, smiling. 'Yes… Yes, extraordinary. An independent-minded maelignaci, no less. Able to form its own loyalties, its own suspicions… Fascinating.'

'Stop it! Stop talking about me!'

'G'hait, be calm. In each of your loyalties this act is justified. In the Mother's name, the archmagus was weak. To the Underchurch she was a poor leader, stalling its progress. And surely you haven't failed to notice her contentions with your – ha – beloved master? Your loyalty does you credit…'

'Y-you still killed her… oh Mother… I-I…'

'Just trust me, G'hait.' the Cardinal's voice, briefly, became emotive: almost warm in its request. 'For a few hours, that's all I ask. Until then you remain in my service, as your master commanded you. He told you to be obedient, G'hait, you remember? So, you will hold your tongue. Is that clear?'

So subtly that G'hait immediately doubted its relevance, Trikara brushed against him. For a split second he was certain that one exquisite claw, with a clumsiness entirely out of keeping with all that he had seen of her previously, drew itself lightly across his chest; like a razor breath of wind. The movement seemed innocent – the random gesture of a deranged mind, but when G'hait returned his gaze to Arkannis, the Cardinal's shrewd stare told him everything he needed to know.

He thought: A warning, then.

'I'll hold my tongue,' he croaked, boiling within.

'Good. Now – go to your master. Tell him I have need of you a while longer. Tell him I'll address the Council within the hour.'

G'hait turned on his heel and strode away.

'G'hait,' the voice followed him. 'Be quick. We have a meeting to attend.'

HIS MASTER'S CHAMBERS were empty.

The silence of the dingy room gave G'hait a sense of profound wrongness, and only by casting back his mind could he discover its source: he realised with a start that as long as he'd known Magus Kreista the wizened primacii had never, to his knowledge, left this low febrile cell; except to attend the Council's occasional meetings and MindChoir ceremonies. It was Kreista's home, G'hait knew, and the ancient man belonged to it as fully as he did the Underchurch itself.

In this room G'hait had been taught to read. Here he'd gripped an inky stylus with awkward fingers, growing in confidence and assurance with each inelegantly scribbled character. Here he'd been taught the sacred scriptures, had digested the catechisms of the Mother's faith, had absorbed the holy texts central to his beliefs.

Here he'd learned to respect his mentor, to place his trust in a magus who recognised some purpose in him where others saw only biological monstrosity and freak-ishness. Here he'd learn to bequeath upon his master a portion of loyalty that was, he realised now with a guilty jolt, greater than that with which he regarded his Church, his people, his legacy. Were his priorities then irretrievably corrupted?

Did he care?

And now his master was not here. At his moment of cri-sis, as his world overflowed with confusions and horrors, as the purple-shrouded stranger that had entered his life systematically destroyed each and every thing he held dear; at that moment, when he'd needed his master more than ever to provide stability in his time of chaos – he found himself alone.

'P-primacii?' he mumbled from his customary position of guardianship by the door. Only the empty silence of the room greeted him.

As he left he paused at the next chamber door along the spittle-walled corridor, brusquely informing its inhabi-tant – some Council primacii whose name he neither knew nor cared to learn – of Arkannis's orders.

There would be a Council meeting inside the hour, whether Kreista's disappearance was resolved or not.

Excerpt Six:
Passage, Volume IV ('The Carrion God'), *'Primacii*: Clav-iculus Matri'

HATE THEM.

Hate the unblessed, the unshriven, the untouched. Hate them for their cruelty, hate them for their dismissal, hate them for their ignorance. Hate them for their god.

Hate them because, be you primacii or maelignaci or Con-
tagii, you may guarantee this, reader:

They hate you.

Content yourself thus, noble hybrid: they will learn. At some
time, be it near or far, they will learn their folly. They will
embrace the Mother as she fills their world, and she will peer
upon them and say: 'You are too late.'

To all things she comes, and to all things she delivers obliv-
ion.

Only her faithful children will be gathered to her side, there
to bask for eternity. We welcome the death she brings, for it
speeds our union with her Godhead!

I feel it in my blood, I feel her call, I feel her approach.

And so shall it be.

MARSHALL DELACROIX ENTERED the briefing room of the
Central Precinct in sullen idiotropy, struggling to concentrate on the sharp ringing of his footsteps rather than
dwell on the news he'd just received. The communiqué –
its short text abrupt and cryptic but given undeniable
authenticity by the security code at its head – felt as
though it would burn a hole in his pocket. He fingered it
anxiously; as if to double check its reality.

The room – a claustrophobic environment even at the
best of times – was busier than he'd ever seen it. Assembled commanders of no less than five PDF regiments
jostled nervously with tacticians, savant servitors, all
manner of support staff and comms-operatives, vigilator
luminaries and his own grim-faced aides. Hard lighting
scribbled unflattering highlights across cheekbones and
brows, dropping perplexed gazes into impenetrable
shadow, underlining lips with hard, unbroken slashes of
shade. The combined military might of Garial-Fall
regarded Delacroix in mute expectation, blank faced and
nervous; every head twisting to follow his arrival. He
swallowed, throat dry.

'Gentlemen.' he said, startled by the volume of his own
voice. 'We have a situation.'

A grimfaced general in the front row replied archly, voice thick with cynicism. 'I think that's a given, Delacroix. We heard your announcements. It's a warzone out there, by the Throne...' The man's crooked bionic eye snapped its iris open and closed. 'What's this all about?'

'Everything I said in the announcements is true.'

The general's incredulity bubbled in his voice. 'Xenogens on Garial-Fall, eh? I had no idea you were an enthusiast of the ridiculous.'

A nervous gust of laughter rippled across the throng.

Delacroix's lip curled. He didn't number diplomacy amongst his strengths and frankly lacked the patience for discussion. His fingers clenched at his side, grasping subconsciously for the power maul that was typically holstered there. 'So ridiculous,' he snarled, 'that the Imperial Governor and all the Plureaucracy are dead. Killed by a warpshit alien.'

The silence exploded, exclamations of horror puncturing the air on all sides.

'Dead!'

'..mperor's tears!'

'..o who's in charge? What's going to...'

'..man's obviously taken leave of his sen...'

'Xenogens...'

'...don't believe a pissing word of...'

Delacroix snatched a small controlbox from a cowering aide and stabbed at the switch on its surface. An ancient projector – coiled circuitry looping with arterial complexity around brass gauges and lens controls – came to life with a dry rustle. The indignant crowd, yowling in disbelief, turned as one to regard the image thus projected.

'Oh...' a voice said.

'You're looking,' Delacroix hissed, 'at a forensic slate-pict taken in the Torus Room an hour ago.'

Exact details, were difficult to distinguish, so elaborate was the arrangement of forms represented. Despite the unevenness of the depicted elements – composed with whimsical artistry in disturbing whorls and geometrical arrangements that dragged at the eye, calling it to absorb every horrific touch, every abattoir flourish – it maintained nonetheless a sense of unity; a universal aspect that married every facet together: its colour.

It was red.

'Skinned,' Delacroix said, answering the group's unspoken question. 'Every last one of them.'

'God-Emperor have mercy...'

Someone near the back vomited with as much discretion as the tight confines allowed.

'Three hours before the... before that was discovered, I was in the Torus Room.' Delacroix sighed, torn between a natural dislike of attention and a secret enjoyment of the captivation of his audience. 'We were presented with a xenogen specimen by a... a man called Arkannis. He claimed to belong to the Holy Inquisition.'

'The Inquisition, here?' the fearful hiss worked its way amongst the crowd; the mere mention of that dreaded organisation inspiring almost that same awe and fear as had the news of the xenogen threat itself.

'He told me to gather you all together. He said he'd lead us. He said we should be ready for a fight...'

A young PDF lieutenant gestured in horror at the screen. 'How can we fight that? W-where's this inquisitor now?'

Delacroix felt bile in his throat. He hadn't worked out how to present this part yet.

'Not here.' he said, sighing. 'He won't be leading us anywhere.' He pushed a hand into his pocket and pulled out the note, its incontrovertible code marking its header. 'I received this five minutes ago. It's from... well, from another inquisitor, also here on Garial-Fall.'

'Another one?'

'Isn't one enough?'

'They'll bring the Emperor's wrath down o–'

'Quiet.' Delacroix fought for the right words. 'It says... It says that Arkannis is a fraud. It says he's planning a trap.'

'W-what?'

'A trap? What kind?'

'I don't know. Message doesn't say.'

'It's a fake!'

'It's not a fake, by the Throne! Listen – it was sent from a public callbooth using a security code so high that my comms-servitor overheated and shut down. It's genuine. No doubt.'

'Then–'

'Look,' Delacroix said, wrestling with the hubbub, 'whatever's going on here we need to move carefully. I was appointed to command this rabble and I inten–'

'You! On the word of a fraud? Ha!'

'I intend to do so! I've issued orders to my men. Zero tolerance. Our priority must be civilian control!'

'You can't control them, you fool!' the stone faced general dipped his brows in anger, waggling a fat finger. 'They're too busy panicking at your Throne-damned announcements!'

Delacroix felt a vein throbbing in his temple, temper shredding like a rush of water. Everything seemed to be spiralling out of his grasp.

'They will be controlled, Emperor's Grace, or they'll suffer the consequences! I can't fight a war when the streets are full of peasants!'

'He's right, you know.'

Silence settled.

The new voice – somehow contriving to override the throng of hurled invective despite its serenity – belonged to a figure leaning calmly in the doorway. Heads craned.

'You!' Delacroix hissed.

'Me,' said Cardinal Arkannis, a faint smile playing across his earthworm lips. 'How charming to see you again, marshall. I see the meeting I requested is right on time.'

'Y-you should be dead.'

'Oh?'

'You were in the Torus Room!'

'Ah... that.'

'That! A-and the letter!' Delacroix brandished the communiqué like a weapon, utterly out of his depth. 'It says you're a fraud! It says you're with the enemy!'

'Does it? Does it indeed?' Arkannis pursed his lips. For a moment Delacroix thought the man's cold façade had been punctured, so intense was his expression. He remained, nonetheless, utterly unconcerned with the marshall's growing air of confrontation. 'How very fascinating.'

Delacroix glared at him in disbelief, grizzled features turning almost purple. 'You don't deny it?'

'Should I?'

'You die!' A pistol was in Delacroix's hand before any of his astonished comrades could react. Acquainted for too long with the comforts of command, the sudden promise of violence left many of them startled; hissing in fear. Not so the marshall, whose finger closed on the trigger without so much as a doubt passing his mind.

Arkannis tutted, eyes flashing. 'Put it down, you silly man.'

The gun clattered noisily to the floor, discharging with an angry boom and the insect-whine of a ricochet, its spastic course culminating in a thudding impact into the rockcrete ceiling. The marshall was left agog; staring in silent befuddlement at his own rebellious fingers.

'Wh... how...'

'Quiet. Gentlemen, my name is Arkannis. As our good friend the marshall has already ascertained, I'm not here to help you.'

'How did you get in here? I... I posted guards.'

'Yes... I'm afraid they had a falling-out with some of my colleagues.'

The grim-faced PDF general, mustering his dignity with far more aplomb than Delacroix, pushed his way to the front and regarded Arkannis with a scowl, voice almost – but not entirely – concealing its quaver.

'Listen. Look here. What do you want?'

Arkannis seemed surprised by the question. 'Want? Oh, nothing. Nothing at all.' He smiled. 'I just came to pay my respects to the dead.'

'The...?'

'Enough talk, gentlemen. I'd like to introduce you to some friends of mine.'

The door pushed open behind him, something hard and sharp scraping along its exterior surface with a velvet gride. The silence thickened. Hunched and slow, prowling, a trio of shapes slunk with tiger grace into the chamber.

Stalking on doubled-kneed legs, each step a birdlike jolt of controlled energy, their entry seemed to suck the very light from the room; warping every shadow around coiled, alien carapaces, knotting around uneven spines and ridges of bone. Their arms, two on either side of each insectile thorax, pistoned in time with each step, uppermost raptor claws scissoring together, secondary extremities – perversions of human hands and fingers – clutching the air. In jointed gaps between cartilaginous claws, segmented flesh glistened with a sticky film of moisture. Their heads, hung low against bony shoulders, seemed by contrast smooth and organic: flesh so pale it was almost translucent, stretched across a constellation of purple capillaries – like the skin of a waterlogged corpse. Tiny porcine eyes glared beneath knotted brows, surmounted upon a prominent jaw thick with needle teeth.

'These are purii,' Arkannis said conversationally, regarding their slinking forms with an arched brow, exoskeletal frills and chords deepened and roughened by the unkind shadows. 'You would call them "genestealers," though they aren't in the business of theft. Not the most scintillating of conversationalists, I'll give you that, but they're loyal enough. In their own way.'

The creatures hissed together, a sussurant chorus of malevolence that seemed to quiver the air itself. Time stretched; extending with the elastic precision of grasping limbs; tentacles of some cold-coiled leviathan. Cowled in shadow and almost silent, the predators approached their cowering preythings hungrily, beady eyes focused and sharp, stooped shoulders bobbing. The foremost amongst them, old flesh pitted with whorls of colour and bony protrusions, twisted its chorded neck towards Arkannis, rasping a low murmur of enquiry.

'Be about your business.' the Cardinal said.

G'HAIT LISTENED FROM outside the door, lurking in the gloom of the hallway with Trikara, willing himself not to listen to her deranged gibbering. A small group of vigilator sentries – previously guardians of the heavy bulkhead through which Arkannis and his... 'companions' had passed – lay at his feet. Mostly.

In truth G'hait's regard for his purestrain cousins was becoming increasingly indefinable. The rush of recognition and genetic pride he felt at their presence was tempered always by a spasm of disgust; a nameless horror at his association with such 'otherness' that left him stunned by their mannerisms and movements.

He'd never seen them outside the spittle-resin context of the Underchurch before. Returning from the fruitless search for his master, the discovery of Arkannis awaiting him with a brood of slinking, hissing beasts... it had stunned him to silence. The Cardinal had merely grinned wider at his reaction.

And now here they were. Entombed (or so it felt) at the heart of the Central Precinct, its obsidian towers and impregnable walls pressing in like unkind ribs, constricting his confidence, asphyxiating his ability to think. To be so deep within enemy territory, to be conducting such missions with the nonchalance characteristic of Cardinal Arkannis; it left G'hait dizzy.

And then the sounds began from the next room, and his thoughts were cleaved in two. Wet noises, mostly, but now and then the dry splintering of bone would pronounce itself; the garish creak of tensioned bodies that, succumbing to whatever murderous pressures assaulted them, sang their popping-corn chorus into the air.

Someone, startling G'hait from his fascinated audience, summoned the presence of mind to scream – a desperate shriek of such raw emotion that it transcended any boundary of language and rushed, like electricity, through his senses. It was aborted almost immediately; its arrest coinciding with a great scrabbling at the door, spiralling downwards from an unearthly howl to a far more mundane gurgle, bubble-flecked and lugubrious, surmounted by a pathetic thump – as of a wet mass tumbling to the ground. G'hait shuddered – but whether through discomfort or desire he couldn't tell.

It lasted one minute. One minute of quiet, if frantic, noises. Of silken snips and zip-like slices, of mute struggling and fluid disruption. And then, silence. And then just the moist pattering of working jaws, of tongues lapping greedily at pooled liquid; of hungry predators reaping the harvest of a successful hunt.

Arkannis stepped into the hallway with a nod.

'Well,' he said. 'That's that, then.'

THE CALL WAS unavoidable now. Pushing consciousness through long dormant neurones, spasming and twitching its way across vast slabs of coiled medulla, colossal lobes of intestinal meat, counter-veined and cross-arteried.

Somewhere at the peak of this electric barrage – this maelstrom of thought, crystallised within its brainmeat vessel – a curved cylinder of moist flesh, itself striated by convulsing polyps, flexed and heaved. Its elaborate structure reticulated, absorbing from the very air a matted tangle of psionic residues; each and every one growing in focus, in aggression; in unity.

Across Garial-Fall the children of the Underchurch rushed about their secret business, hearts racing with racial anticipation, filled with the excitement of pending ascension. The uprising was imminent. They could taste it. They could feel it on the air.

And their patriarch – no longer moronic, no longer vapid and obese upon its rotten palette – listened to their unified chorus with relish, muscles eager, eyes focused.

It listened and feasted on the unwitting call of its brood, and in so doing channelled its meandering waveform out and away; out into the endless void, where a swarm of intricate shapes ploughed a furrow across the vacuum, slouching ever nearer.

EVEN TO G'HAIT, unfamiliar with their cerebral idiosyncrasies, the primacii council were manifestly in a state of anxiety. They shuffled and fidgeted in their places, their aura of psionic intensity fluctuating, as if uncertain. They had congregated as instructed to await Arkannis's arrival, and as the Cardinal and his companions stalked into the Chamber of Voices G'hait could predict the cause of their agitation.

'Friends,' Arkannis greeted them with a flourish, then peered left and right with a frown, as if seeking a face amongst the crowd. 'Where is Archmagus Jezahael?'

G'hait looked at the ground, keeping his thoughts blank.

Magus Kreista cleared his throat, brows dipped. 'The archmagus is dead,' he said, jaw clenching. 'Murdered in her office.'

Arkannis absorbed this information with convincing astonishment, kneading at his chin. The Council regarded him with thinly-veiled suspicion.

'I see…' Arkannis said, nodding. 'Yes. Yes, it all makes sense.' He sighed. 'I had hoped to avoid this but… no, my hand has been forced. Friends, there is an inquisitor in our midst.

A whispered exchange flittered through the magi, quickly dissipating.

Arkannis went on. 'This traitor, this servant of the Carrion God… Twice he's attempted to wound us. I shan't allow a third injury.'

Kreista's eyes narrowed. 'Twice?'

'Oh yes… In the first instance he has stolen from us Magus Jezahael; a finer and more courageous servant of the Mother we would be hard pressed to find. Let us give thanks for her life, and pray that her soul rests with the Mother. Blessed be.'

The phrase brought its equal echo from the Council – clear and strong despite their uncertainty. 'Blessed be.'

Arkannis drew a breath and continued, not slowing. 'The traitor is also guilty of alerting our enemies to our plans. With the ascendance so near at hand, an intelligence leak could be nothing short of disastrous.'

A young magus at the edge of the Council, an intricate tattoo dissecting her pale brow, spoke up: 'And you know this how? Forgive us, magus, but the time has come for some proof of your assertions.'

'Am I then doubted?'

'You are unfamiliar, which is much the same thing. In your short time on our world you've affected more change and upheaval than… than any of us can recall before. At present these changes appear to be bearing fruit – and so you receive our thanks. But don't make the mistake of considering yourself above suspicion, Cardinal. You are a stranger, after all.'

'And there you betray your ignorance, my young friend.' Arkannis smiled. 'Oh, please, do not be offended. You – none of you – have travelled between worlds. You've not seen what the Inquisition can do. You've not learned its tricks.'

'We fail to see how this is releva–'

'They are devious, magus. The inquisitors of the Emperor's Throne are cunning creatures, not to be underestimated. Do not fear the unknown, in seeking their work. Fear that which is familiar. That which is closest to you. That which seems above suspicion.'

'You have a culprit, then?'

'I have. I'd hoped his actions might condemn him rather than having to go through all this tedious melodrama, but…' He shrugged.

The Council exchanged glances. G'hait frowned, watching Arkannis closely. The Cardinal's thin lips broke into another smile.

'Magus Kreista,' he said, 'I should like to hear your excuses.'

G'hait felt a rush of angry adrenaline in his mind, even as the Council turned as one to regard his master. Unable to repress the venom, he blurted a furious 'No!', drawing startled glances from the primaciis.

Arkannis glanced at him for a split second, annoyed. 'Be quiet.'

Something twisted, like a knife, in his mind. His mouth wouldn't open.

The Council returned their astonished gazes to Magus Kreista, who in the brief interim had moved some small distance from their group.

He was holding a laspistol.

He was aiming it at the Council.

'Now's as good as time as any, I suppose.' He said.

Something dark and ugly broke in G'hait's mind.

THE ELEGANCE OF the orbit-platform, its fluted towers and sweeping archways rotating with lazy grace against the procellous cloudcover of Garial-Fall, was reduced somewhat by the haphazard components of its construction. Solar cells plundered from ancient hulks glittered with a broken incandescence, baroque viewing towers and stout lance arrays jibbed with mangled asymmetry from unexpected pits and tiers. It was a cobbled mansion, pirouetting vastly above the world that was its anchor, tethers snaking away through miles of atmosphere to find the hivedome below.

Arcane devices, twitching across the platform's upper surfaces, paused briefly in their exertions; realigning upon a distant locale according to their disinterested logic engines. Something had been discovered.

In a red-lit control bunker within, squashed into a seat riddled with mechanical paraphernalia, Tech-priest

Acolyte Teriqol felt something unexpected flit across his mind. The logic-engine interface, squeezing raw data into his memory, spiked with a warning tone. He sat upright with a small gasp, frowning behind cable-strewn brows.

'Commander?' he called, voice quavering. 'Commander Larkan?'

A junior communications officer slouched over, picking his way between servitors and tech-priests, equally as engaged in their observations. He sniffed. 'What is it, acolyte?'

'I need to speak to the commander.'

'He's not here. What have you got?'

'Sir – with respect… This is a command-level observation. The Anima machina has imposed a classification level.'

The officer sighed. His eyes seemed glazed.

'Acolyte, the commander left to attend a meeting on the surface two hours ago. We haven't been able to raise him since. How urgent is this… "command-level observation"?'

'Utmost, sir.'

'Then you'll have to make do with me. I'm the highest ranking officer, for now.'

Acolyte Teriqol twitched, weighing his options through mechanically enhanced thought paths. Eventually a decision arose and he nodded, copper wiring bouncing like hair around his temples.

'The long-range scanners have an inbound contact, sir. There are no arrivals scheduled.'

The officer raised an eyebrow. 'Can you get an ID?'

'No.'

The man bit a nail, fidgeting. 'Probably nothing. There was another one two days ago, wasn't there? An unannounced Ecclesiarchy shuttle, if memory serves.'

'Yes, sir. But this is… This contact is different. Larger. Multiple objects.'

The officer's eyes narrowed.

'A fleet?'

'Probably sir, yes. It seems… well. It's bigger than anything I've ever seen.'

The officer nodded. 'What's the ETA of the contact, acolyte?'

'Sir… At present speed… Early morning. Ten hours, maybe less.'

'You haven't told anyone else about this?'

'No sir. Of course n–'

'Good. You know, I didn't really believe it, when I was told. But it's true. She's coming. She's finally coming. Blessed be.'

The petty officer drew a knife from his belt and lurched towards Tariqol, eyes empty.

'I'D BE VERY surprised if you're not armed, Arkannis. Let's see it.'

Kreista's gun held the Cardinal firmly in his place. Very slowly, face blank, he reached into a pocket and removed the ornate laspistol.

'Kick it towards me,' Kreista said. 'Don't try anything clever. I've seen it all before.'

Arkannis appeared to consider for a moment, regarding the intricate weapon in his palm. Kreista arrested any thoughts of rebellion pointedly, arming his gun with a cold clatter. Arkannis nodded and placed the laspistol on the floor, kicking it daintily towards his enemy.

G'hait, watching as though from another world, wanted to scream.

He wanted Kreista to deny that he was an inquisitor.

He wanted his master to put down the gun, to diffuse the situation, to prove his innocence.

He wanted Arkannis to say that it was all a misunderstanding, that everything was going according to plan, that there were no inquisitors on Garial-Fall.

He wanted someone to explain what was going on. To decode the confusion in his mind. To unlace the layer upon layer of bluff and double bluff that he'd been exposed to since Arkannis arrived.

He wanted his master to tell him everything would be alright.

He wanted to run and rip and tear his way through the world.

He wanted to understand.

None of it happened.

The Council stood like a gaggle of geese, white skin and tall necks rigid with fear. Kreista half smiled, bowing with a mock flourish.

'You might as well know.' He said. 'My true name is Ariale. I'm an Inquisitor of the Ordo Xenos.'

He silenced the Council's uproar with a vague wave of his weapon. They floundered, indignant and betrayed.

Arkannis was not so easily cowed, standing apart from the others with eyebrows knotted. He tutted. 'It was you, then. The inquisitor in the Hive Secundus. You pulled the same trick there, didn't you?'

Ariale chuckled. 'Very good. But the, ha, trick is rather older than that. I've purged more of your Mother's sordid little congregations than I can remember. Always from the inside. Like cancer.'

'Nobody suspected? Nobody tasted the...' (Arkannis almost spat the word) 'humanity in your mind?'

'Of course not. I learned how you primaciis think years ago. I've seen dissections, Arkannis. I've tortured a hundred magi to an early grave, and extracted every secret they had to give. I assure you my mind is perfectly safe from the likes of you.'

'Hm.' Arkannis didn't sound convinced. 'Still – it was an audacious plan. Hiding amongst the enemy. It must have turned your stomach.'

'The Emperor's devotion breeds a strong constitution. I happily tolerate the association with deviants if it leads to their destruction.'

'So you planned to expose the Underchurch. When? As it rose up against the city?'

'Exactly. Merely infiltrating and destroying the Council isn't enough – one must force every hybrid, every infected abomination, every last Emperor-damned freak into the light. Only then will the purge be complete. This church is – and has always been – a poor excuse for an insurgence. It would have failed with or without my intervention.'

The inquisitor was gloating now, enjoying his own cleverness. G'hait, still reeling in misery at his master's treachery, realised that Arkannis was keeping him talking. Trikara, meanwhile, was inching forwards. He wondered if she could move faster than a finger tightening on a trigger, and decided that she probably could. His heart raced.

'Ha,' said Ariale, staring directly at him, eyes flashing with psychic incision. 'My thanks, G'hait. Your thoughts always have had a habit of getting you into trouble, haven't they?'

G'hait groaned inwardly.

Ariale aimed his gun directly at the Cardinal's head, taking careful aim. 'Call off your freak, Arkannis. She might be able to dodge bullets, but I sincerely doubt that you can.'

Without a word exchanged, the giggling hybrid slunk away behind Arkannis. The Cardinal curled a lip.

'Better,' Ariale grinned. 'You know, until you arrived, this was shaping up to be a rather humdrum project. I can't tell you how delighted I was at your acceptance of my invitation. We've been investigating the Elucidium for decades, did you know that?'

'I did.'

'Ha, yes. Yes, you would. Quite the bright spark, aren't you? Things have been much more, heh… challenging, since you showed up. Still, it's all over now. The vigilators know the Underchurch is here and I have a truly fascinating prize. I shall enjoy interviewing you in my workshops, Arkannis. I'm very interested in your organisation. Very interested indeed.'

'You think I'd tell you anything?'

'They all do, sooner or later. I think that's enough talk for now. I want you to walk very slowly to the door. I want you to keep your hands – and your acolytes, at that – where I can see them. No sudden moves, no sharp sounds. No mind-tricks. We are leaving.'

'You're quite wrong. About it being over, I mean.'

'Spare me, Arkannis. I've won.'

'I'm afraid not. You say you sent a communiqué to the Vigilators. That would be Marshall Delacroix, then?'

'I told you. Enough talk.'

'That would be the same Marshall Delacroix that I just watched being cut into thirteen pieces. I could have his head fetched, if you'd like.'

Beads of sweat sparkled on Ariale's head. He flicked the gun angrily, like some semaphore signal. 'Enough lies!'

'It's no lie, inquisitor. I had every military officer in this city torn to shreds. It's over. The armies are beheaded. You warning didn't get through.'

'It's not over, warpshit!' Ariale's eyes narrowed, sinister. 'Even if you're telling the truth, you think I can't command the grunts myself?'

'Indubitably. You might even be able to prevent the uprising, if you reach a comms-post fast enough. But you aren't going to.'

'What?'

Now slick with sweat, the inquisitor brandished his gun with the insectile jerks of a desperate man. G'hait regarded him with contempt, silently praying that Arkannis's icy cool wasn't a bluff.

'Inquisitor Ariale,' Arkannis said, utterly unconcerned with the weapon fixated upon his head. 'The Elucidium have known your name for some time. We learned of your presence in this sector years ago.'

'Shut up! I'll shoot you, Emperor's oath! I'll shoot you where you stand!'

'I want to thank you, inquisitor, for making my search so much easier. I had despaired of ever unearthing you when you did me the courtesy of inviting me to your side. It was an… entertaining moment.'

'That's enough.' Ariale was beginning to recover his composure, resolve hardening. 'That's enough, you freak. Y-you xeno-spawn bastard. That's enough!' Only his eyes remained wild; full of the uncertainty of his own success. His knuckle, drawing on G'hait's attention with morbid fascination, turned white upon the trigger.

'Since the beginning of their supposed evolution,' Arkannis intoned, lip curled with distaste, 'humans have had a weakness. A ridiculous thing. A flaw, I say. An oversight in their minds. It turns the most acute intelligence into a thing of dumbstruck naivety. Don't you want to know what it is?'

'Shut u–'

'I'll tell you. Here. Listen. It's a fascination, like the magpie, for anything that glitters.'

Slowly, like planets rolling out of their orbits, like icebergs overbalancing and tilting, base-over-tip, into an arctic sea, the inquisitor's eyes swivelled downwards. Pinned to his own lapel, a work of exquisite beauty, the brooch gifted to him by Arkannis shimmered in the gloom.

'Goodbye.' Arkannis said, and tapped the tiny trigger stud of the remote detonator he'd cradled in his hand since entering the chamber.

Inquisitor Ariale fragmented like an overripe fruit.

Excerpt Seven:
Interior passage, Volume V ('Matriarch Ascendant'), '*Primacii*: Claviculus Matri'

Let it thus *be known:*

I am a prisoner here. I am stolen from my world, my congregation, my church. They are dead, I expect. They are victims of the Carrion God, crushed utterly by his unhappy attentions. I am a prisoner of his demagogue son, his secret disciple. I am the captive of his Inquisition, and – behold – I have not denied the Mother's love.

She is within me. She resides. She endures, yes.

They call for my confession. They strip me and gag me and strike me, they beat me with barbed rods and cut at my flesh with hooked knives. They say that I shall be redeemed, if only I recant. If only I renounce my patroness. If only I betray Her glory, Her honour, Her mercy.

They are fools.

Behold, inquisitor and soldier and peasant. Behold, disciple of the withered messiah. Behold, you frail thing, you ugly thing, you loveless thing, you empty thing:

The Great Sky Mother is coming! Blessed be!

I die.

THE LATCHCRAFT SWAYED horizontally, its grip upon the tether-cable sustaining its upward motion despite gyrating freely along its central axis. G'hait resisted the urge to vomit.

Sitting opposite him, head buried in a sheaf of yellowing papers, nodding or 'ah'ing to whatever material interested him, Cardinal Ebrehem Arkannis paid no attention whatsoever to his travelling companions. At his side Trikara licked a thick syrup of blood from her claws, long tongue coiling and slurping at razor edges with snakelike prehensility.

There had been a minor battle at the launchsite when the crowds saw that one final craft was due to travel. Trikara had been obliged to cut her master a pathway.

G'hait sat in silence, sullen and confused and angry all at once, and remembered:

HIS MASTER'S DEATH barely even registered. Even as his shattered body, pulverised and violated by the force of the brooch-charge, slid to the ground, G'hait's mind felt nothing but rage at his betrayal.

There was nothing beyond his master. He'd as much as admitted it to Arkannis: his loyalty was owed to Kreista first and the Church second. A chasm had opened in his mind.

Before even the echoes of the detonation had faded, before the Council had recovered their decorum and wiped themselves clean of the blood-drizzle that covered them, a scurrying Contagii arrived with the news:

The patriarch was ascending from its lair.

'About time.' Arkannis said, turning to face the Council. 'Spread the word. It's started.'

A HEAVY LURCH rocked the craft, dislodging G'hait from his seat. He righted himself silently, neurotically imagining Trikara laughing at him from the shadows of her robe. Arkannis had barely moved.

'We've left the ionosphere, I imagine.' he said, not taking his eyes from the paperwork.

G'hait fidgeted, uncomfortable with the decision he'd taken. He wondered how it would be for his maelignaci brothers and sisters when She arrived. He wondered if their absorption would be as wondrous as he'd been taught to expect. He wondered if they would truly ascend to sit at Her side.

He wondered whether he'd ever find out.

The memories of his last hours on Garial-Fall became a cavalcade of impressions, speeding to a single point, and G'hait lost himself in their fractured kaleidoscope.

WHEN THE REMAINS of the traitor-magus had been dragged away and hurled into the purii pits, to be fought over and split amongst the hungry predators, the Council sang. A choir of psychic instruction that effervesced through air and stone, embedding the commands that Arkannis provided in each distant Contagii, in each hissing maelignaci, in each slouching purii brood.

They sang their call to arms, and in every district of every quarter, in every neighbourhood and ghetto-tier, in every slum and archeotech skyrise: the Mother's faithful responded.

THE PDF REGIMENTS did not last long. Those few companies whose remaining petty officers had been able to affect some degree of command quickly schismed as the contagii hidden in their midst revealed themselves; stalking with blank expressions through dormitories and mess halls, serenely fingering autogun triggers or slashing out with jagged combat knives. If they enjoyed or regretted their betrayal of men who had once been counted amongst comrades, if indeed they were even conscious of it, they gave no sign.

Other groups were less fortunate still. Lacking their commanders they fragmented across the city; separating into twos and threes to combat the growing anarchy or to feed it, as whim dictated. The riots exploded to cover every district, and at every street corner uniformed men were set upon by mobs, dragged screaming through the streets with regs tearing and bare flesh shredding upon the icy rockcrete.

To an outsider it might seem as though the insurgents were already amongst the crowds, but no: at this early stage any violence was the product of fear and anger – natural and indiscreet. There was no xenogen agenda here, no whispering psionic voice to direct the carnage.

IT WAS MIDNIGHT when the cultists emerged. Singing joyful hymns to their approaching godhead, draped in white and red robes with the embroidered mark of the New Dawn, they spilled from secret meetings and impromptu prayer session across the city.

Only the Vigilators, leaderless and run-ragged from its perpetual clashes with the angry crowds, were left to face them.

The Church of the Celestial Womb broke upon their synthiplex shields like the first breakers of an onrushing tsunami, and by the time the first heavy stubbers were in place, the first long-hoarded Leman Russ had crawled from its secret depot, the first scripture-daubed flamers had reached the front of the crowd; the armoured judges were backing away and dropping their power mauls, scrambling for cover.

It was carnage.

* * *

AND ARKANNIS HAD asked G'hait. 'Will you come with me?'

And G'hait had looked at the blood-slick-smear that was all that remained of his master, and had nodded without thought.

AN HOUR AFTER the congregation first unfurled its banners and began to chant in anticipation of the Mother's arrival, the civilian militia (now swamped with amateurs and hotheads that had seen the vigilators' massacre), together with the few scattered morsels of the PDF that remained, regrouped in the vast plaza beneath the Foildom's mezzanine-tier. They were a horde of ants, parading and drilling at the heart of a mighty nest, and when their petty officers and sergeants gave their awkward, stilted speeches they were received with all the rage and venom of the mightiest orations by the greatest of heroes.

These people had been deceived. They'd been attacked from within by a cancer that had gone undiagnosed and untreated. They were angry, above all, and as they marched upon the holding zones that the Church had captured it seemed briefly that they might turn the tide and spare the city.

Then the patriarch led his blood-relatives to battle.

TO THE CITIZENS, it must have seemed as though nightmares had risen from the ground.

From bolt-holes and sewage conduits, from steaming ventilators and ruptured charnel pipes. Scuttling with crustacean dryness, drawing back ossified segments of chitin to leer with gumless canines bared. Clacking and clattering, claws scissoring together. Formicating. Swarming.

The purii were at their head – snaking forwards, long limbs propelling them onwards, talon-claws curled inwards. Spider-like, they came. Across walls and ceilings with as much grace and speed as across the body-strewn floor, grappling claw-over-claw, barbed shoulders roiling with each effortless motion.

The maelignaci were a misfit army: a gallery of variety. Here the ogre-like broods of the first generation battered aside an Arbites tank, there the slinking raptor-packs of second generation hunter-killers snapped at their squealing prey through the collapsed remains of a PDF encampment.

And towering above, bloated, shrieking and roaring and crackling with psionic spoor, the patriarch rode on a surf of blood and bone, hot breath curling with red mist, ice settling then steaming from his gore-streaked flanks.

G'HAIT AND TRIKARA and Arkannis rode the last latchcraft to the orbit-platform.

G'hait had boarded without a single backwards glance.

IN COMPARISON TO the insanity, spreading like some infectious pox throughout the city below, the orbit-platform was a silent mausoleum. Slipping through automated docking doors, each new clash of metal-on-metal threatening in vain the totality of the quiet, the three found themselves invaders within a frozen grave.

Bodies lay casually discarded, crooked limbs cut and broken by imprecise blades. Thick chords of blood, congealing in viscous swirls where the uneven deck dipped or rucked, were smeared broadly, as though some deranged redecoration had been attempted.

Cross-legged in the reception chamber they found the contagii – eight men and women, singing hymns, splattered with meat and blood. Their mission complete, they ignored Arkannis's small group as if it didn't exist, and briefly G'hait found himself again considering the nature of vapidity. Not for them the pain of doubt, the recognition of betrayal. They might as well be machines – and G'hait envied them.

The Cardinal's shuttle, the *Mawgetair*, was a small affair: a long-tubed craft, dwarfed by its bulging generarium and

warp engines, ribbed around its central portion with a filigree of struts and pylons, minor ventricles comprising
domestic chambers – austere cabins, perfunctory mess
hall and sickbay – to either side. To G'hait, to whom the
notion of ever seeing beyond the perpetual clouds of his
home, let alone stepping foot upon a spacecraft, was
unthinkable, it was a peculiar space, filled with inexplicable components and obtuse machinery. Lights flickered
like burning constellations, auspexes chattered and
glowed, brass gauges ticked with heartbeat regularity, or
else oscillated in time to the weird fluctuations of the
engines.

There seemed to be nobody else aboard.

'How do you… How do you travel in the warp?' G'hait
asked, surfacing briefly from the melancholia that had
struck him mute since his master's death.

Arkannis regarded him with a shrewd smile.

'How do you mean, acolyte?'

'I… I've read documents, my lord. My master, he…'

'Your master taught you rather more than most primaciis ever know, let alone maelignacis.'

G'hait relapsed into silence. Even the memories were
painful now.

'In answer to your question, G'hait, I carry aboard a
Navigator of the noble house Predantir, to negotiate the
eddies of the warp. He lies entombed above the bridge,
sustained by servitors and logic machines, where he has
remained inert during my absence.'

'And he serves you freely?'

'Of course. His loyalty is commendable.'

'Then… he is contagii?'

The Cardinal's gaze bored into G'hait. He imagined his
skin flaying, peeling back in protest at the razor glare.

'No, G'hait. He is not contagii.'

'Then how d–'

'Rest. You've been through a great deal. All will become
clear.'

* * *

THE MAWGETAIR PEELED from the orbit-platform with solemn magnificence, jointed holding-limbs retracting, folding away like the spines of some void-birthed urchin. It pitched sideways across the silent satellite that had anchored it, dipping a flank in unthinking salute before moving glacially away, engines flaring in the void.

G'hait pressed his face against a small porthole, the bony ridges of his brow clicking lightly against the cold synthiplex. The vast pearl that was Garial-Fall, clouded surface a mass of white and grey whorls, tumbled slowly below him. For a second his mind lurched with the scale of the world before the corkscrew-whirl of the vessel carried its horizon-terminator from view, filling his window with nothing but endless inky black.

G'HAIT SAT MOROSELY, glaring into the middle distance, when Arkannis returned to the round gallery where he had left his two companions.

He smiled broadly at G'hait.

'We're underway.' he proclaimed needlessly. 'I suggest we take the opportunity to rest before entering the warp. It can be… difficult to sleep whilst crossing the Empyrean.'

He dropped the sheaf of papers he'd been inspecting into a chair and crooked a finger at Trikara, who regarded him with her head cocked.

'Come, my little fiend,' he trilled. 'Back into your cage.'

G'hait frowned, introspection interrupted. 'Cage?'

'Heh. Oh yes. You didn't think I'd allow her the run of the ship whilst I slept?'

'But… You said she's loyal to y–'

'I did no such thing. I said that she does what she's told. And I can't control her when I'm asleep.'

Trikara hissed, pearly fangs glinting from the shadows of her cowl. For a second her deranged giggling faltered; leaving in its stead just a whipcord monster, filled with rage and hate. She glared at Arkannis as if confused, working her jaw.

'She'd slice me limb from limb, given the chance. I told you: her mind is a broken jewel. She's a puppet, G'hait. An insane, beautiful, terrible puppet. And I've been pulling her strings so very, very long.'

'H-how?'

'A simple little illusion. I poke around in her skull and reclothe myself in her eyes. To her, I'm a magus-farseer, a primacii of her long dead brood. Her mind tends to wander somewhat, but I assure you it doesn't take her long to remember my true identity when the illusion slips.' His eyes flashed, that same amused grin painting his lips, and without appearing to change at all Trikara's venomous rasp petered away.

A question surged in G'hait's mind, heavy with portent. 'Have… have you ever…?'

'Have I played with your mind?' The cold eyes filled his world. 'No. And for a very simple reason.'

'What reason?'

'I haven't needed to.'

Without another word Arkannis led Trikara away, leaving G'hait profoundly disturbed. Again what he had regarded as certainty crumbled around him, and at the centre of the deception was Arkannis. Something wasn't right. Something didn't add up. He felt it in his blood.

His eyes fell upon the paperwork that the Cardinal had been reading. Frowning, feeling exposed and lost and childlike, he reached out and focused on the first page.

It was a letter. It began:

WE ARE THE *unclean*.

We are reviled (so they say). We are despicable and pestilent and abominable. We are known as 'thing', as 'freak', as 'heretic'. The derision is as tedious as it is endless.

G'HAIT CHEWED HIS lip, confused. And then, with his heart sinking, he read the rest.

* * *

ARKANNIS RETURNED TO him as he reached the final page.
The Cardinal sat silently, not interrupting, and watched.
G'hait's literacy was far from perfect, and at times he
would pause to squint at the characters, lips moving
soundlessly as he wrestled with a difficult word. Arkannis
regarded every movement of his eye, every crease in his
ossified brows, every tremor of his lips.

And then G'hait was finished, and he stacked the
papers carefully, placing them on the seat beside him.

'What do you think?' Arkannis asked.

G'hait worked his jaw. 'I think… I don't know. I'm not
sure. Where are these excerpts from?'

'They come from a book. A volume titled *"Primacii:
Claviculus Matri"*. It's the testimony of a magus, G'hait.
His life, in his words.'

'And he wrote it of his own free will?'

Arkannis chuckled. 'No. He was a prisoner. He was captured by a man named Agmar. An inquisitor.'

'He was forced to write this?'

'My research suggests he was… given a choice. Write an
honest testimony or return to the interrogation suite.
Agmar was notoriously… skilled, in the art of pain.'

'What happened to him? The magus, I mean.'

Arkannis peered at G'hait through shrewd eyes.
Appearing to make some form of decision, he dug a hand
into his robes and withdrew a single sheet of paper,
folded with bladelike precision. He opened it out and
handed it G'hait.

'The epilogue of the volume.' he explained. 'Agmar's
chance to pass judgement on what his little pet had written.'

G'hait frowned as he took the sheet, then craned his
neck and read.

Epilogue, *'Primacii*: Claviculus Matri'

LET IT BE *recorded that on this day, 02.05.750.M41, the prisoner that has composed this volume was discovered at first light*

dead in his cell. I am told by the sisters of the Order Panacear, whose efforts have sustained him throughout his interrogation, that his expiry is attributable to a devastating brain haemorrhage, caused (they suggest) by exposure to intolerable excesses of physical pain. I remain unconvinced.

Regardless of how the heretic succumbed, he went to his doom unabsolved; and if it should please the reader to know, I am confident his soul remains ungathered to that Brightest of lights; the Golden Throne. Long may he dwell in damnation in payment for his sin.

His final testimony, this testimony which you now read, is all that remains of him. I shall not hide it. I shall not seek to deny his eulogy from the light of scrutiny for, heretic though he be, it is in our interests to know his mind.

The Imperium, reader, is a vast thing. One might almost be forgiven for confusing its scale with its strength; for is it not simple to believe that something so massive, so mighty, so sprawling, must also be impenetrable; unbreakable; stalwart?

Would that it were so. The Imperium, great as it is, is a flickering light in a sea of darkness. It is a thing so fragile that to look upon its facets, like some brittle jewel, brings even me – I, an inquisitor of the Emperor's divine law – to the verge of tears and terror.

The race of man must acknowledge its fears. It must face the darkness that creeps at its edges. Only in acceptance are we strong. Only in conflict may we prevail.

Seek not to ignore or hide the heresy that abounds on every side. Expose it! Bolster it! Feed it with false strength, so that in its purgation the Emperor's heart is swollen with mighty victory!

Herein lies the testimony of a heretic. I urge that it be absorbed, for only in knowing their ways can we hope to crush our enemies.

Inquisitor Agmar, 750.M41

G'HAIT LOOKED UP from the text, more confused than ever. A question nagged at his mind.

'How did you come to possess this?' he said. 'All of these excerpts… They can't be just… just freely available.'

Arkannis brushed aside the question with a wave of his hand. 'That's not important. What do you think of it all?'

'I… I don't know. I can't see why these things matter. Not here and now.' A thought occurred. 'Is Agmar still alive?'

'No, no. He died long ago. But his legacy lives on. He was a great man, in many respects.'

'He was human! He served the Withered God!'

'Mm. Yes. Yes, he was.'

A fear gripped G'hait's chest abruptly. Something formless but cold, a certainty that evaded him but that grew in specificity with every moment, that sat in his guts and began to rise.

'Agmar,' Arkannis said, cradling his fingers like the spars of a ribcage, 'was renowned for his pragmatism. He believed in knowledge. He believed in revealing the enemy. He believed in strength through conflict.'

The fear slipped into G'hait's throat. He felt as though he was falling.

'Agmar's philosophies were passed, through the years, to his novices. Most notable amongst them was a man named Istvaar. He took Agmar's ideas, his theories, his disparate records of muse and whimsy, and structured around them a modus. A way of working.'

'H-how do you know all of this…?' The fear gripped G'hait's tongue and he wondered briefly whether he might choke.

'Today the Istvaanian inquisitors are a secret society, G'hait. Their ways are considered extreme – and they would be the first to agree. Extremism is sanctioned, they would say. Extremism is required. Are the enemies of the Imperium concerned with moderation? With liberalism? Of course not!'

The fear struck G'hait's mind like a mallet, and the truth that had crept into his blood and limbs and bones invaded his consciousness as a cancer, digging claws of ice into his brain.

'You aren't a magus.' he said, voice dead. 'You... you're a....'

Arkannis smiled, and his teeth twinkled like supernovae in the half gloom of the vessel.

'The Instvaanians gave a name to their secret society, so that they could organise their movements away from the spying eyes of other, less enlightened members of the Emperor's faith...'

'This is.... you can't.... Oh, Mother...'

'We called ourselves the Elucidium.'

Something exploded behind G'hait's mind. One final betrayal, one final act of confusion and treachery. He'd been played for a fool – and (he could see it now) he was. Oh, Mother, he was! Such a fool! Such an idiot to believe the lies of the Emperor's agents!

His legs lifted him from his seat, unbidden. He would set things right, he told himself. He would finish this. His claws snapped open.

'You die!' he hissed, feeling the world turn red around him.

A gun barrel pushed itself into his forehead and Arkannis stared down upon him from beyond its dark circle.

The thought hit him: It doesn't matter! Better to die than submit!

His heart didn't agree.

'I know you, G'hait.' Arkannis said, a world away. 'Any other maelignaci wouldn't stop. They'd be lashing out right now, not caring about dying. They're born for it. Born to kill or be killed, at the Mother's whim. Not you. You're a mistake. A freak. You're too human.'

G'hait sobbed, telling himself not to listen, wrestling with the fear, with the self-preservation, with the self-disgust.

'You don't want to die, G'hait.' Arkannis said. 'That's your weakness.'

'...kill you...' the words didn't work, lost behind snot and tears.

'No you won't, child. We both know you won't. I want you to do something for me, G'hait.'

And though he mumbled and trembled and spat, G'hait knew that he'd do whatever the inquisitor asked.

'I want you to look through the window.' The voice was a cold knife, slicing through his defences, cutting at his control. Unable to disobey, G'hait pressed his face for the second time against the cold plate, a delicate fresco of ice scuttling across its exterior surface. 'Tell me what you see.'

Aching blackness, without form or end or distinction. It swallowed his eyes, it sucked at his mind, it made a lie of perspective.

And then something moved. Impossibly, something shifted, and had form. As it clarified against the blackness something beside it arose from the murk, and another. And another. The void blossomed with faint ghostlight, reflected from the planet surface now lost from G'hait's view, playing across uneven surfaces of a dozen, a score, a hundred vast shapes...

Here the wan luminescence played across a fronded gill, there a vast tentacle coiled with colossal precision. Scattered across the blackness without end, the shapes drew near. A fierce triumph gripped G'hait, like a fire rising in his chest.

'It's the Mother!' he crowed, all thoughts of Arkannis's betrayal scattering. 'She comes! She approaches! Blessed be!'

The Cardinal's expression didn't change. 'Perhaps,' he said, 'you should look again.'

The shapes in the void were closer now; easier to discern.

The fronded gill, at this distance, seemed less fluted, less organic in its sweeping rills. One might be forgiven for instead imagining the chromic spars of a sensor array, or the brandished muzzles of atmospheric cannons. The tentacle, unravelling across the vacuum, a million tiny clavicules dotting its surface, now seemed more regular; segmented in slabs of connected metal. A fuel umbilicus.

Great leathern wings became lance arrays and bridgeheads, gaping spoor-mouths at this distance were rendered as flight hangars and torpedo tubes. Scales became buttresses, spines were the steeples and turrets of human construction, gaudy skin-colourations became the blocky designs of heraldry and symbol.

'Battlefleet Ultima Secundus,' Arkannis intoned over G'hait's shoulder, 'incorporating the fifteenth, seventieth and ninety-third regiments of the Karadmium Guard, plus the principal attack vessels of the Tarantulas Chapter of the Adeptus Astartes. I requested their presence in this system one week ago.'

G'hait sagged to his knees.

'The Mother is not coming, G'hait. Not today.'

The world fell from his eyes. Bile rose in his throat, bitter and hot against his teeth.

'Why...?' he choked, strangled by the duplicity.

Arkannis patted him on the shoulder, almost fatherly. 'Because Garial-Fall was a weak world. A weak world with a weak Governor, ruled by weak laws and weak politicians. Its Vigilators were second rate, its PDF regiments lacklustre. And to top it all it harboured a weak inquisitor – an enemy of the Istvaanian school – whose execution I have pursued for some time. Call it... call it personal, if you will. That the city also hid your Underchurch was a happy bonus.'

'Y-you... you used us..'

'Of course. I told you, G'hait: one doesn't cure the cancer of indolence through repair, or supplementation. One must destroy before rebuilding can begin. I lit the spark, G'hait. I swept away everything that the hivedome thought was stable and secure. Imagine their surprise!'

'You're mad....'

Arkannis stared, eyes bulging, cloak billowing. 'Wrong. Wrong, G'hait. There's a distinction between madness and pugnacity. I have done exactly what was required. That world, down there, that useless ball of rock and snow. It will be purged! The ferocity of its cleansing will be a sight to behold. Your petty little church won't stand a chance.

'There will be fire and blood and death. Oh yes, it will be carnage, to both sides. But from the ashes a new

Garial-Fall will arise. Tighter, more secure. And those that have survived will be stronger for it!'

G'hait was a husk. He felt it: a profound emptiness that gnawed at his skin from inside. All that was left was betrayal – and it swirled in his mind like a storm.

'Why me?' he croaked, 'why spare me? Why involve me!'

Arkannis smiled his lazy, reptile smile, and blinked.

'Because you're special, G'hait. A maelignaci whose loyalty can be bought by an inquisitor – even one as ineffectual as Ariale – is a worthy prize indeed.'

'Y-you… you expect me to be loyal to you?' the notion sickened him, squeezed at his consciousness, lifted the bile into his mouth again.

Arkannis shook his head, slowly, lips pursed. 'No. No, I think you're beyond trusting me.'

'Then what?' Great tears snaked across his human nose and lips.

Arkannis lifted the sheaf of papers from where G'hait had left them, flicking across the crisp sheets with a wry smile.

'I should like to add my own research to that of Inquisitor Agmar. Knowledge is power, G'hait.'

'R-research…?'

'Yes. It shall be titled "*Maelignaci: Abnormalities and Weaknesses*".'

He dipped his spare hand into his robes and withdrew a long, bone-handled stylus.

'Here,' he said, eyes flashing, gun barrel yawning menacingly. 'You'll be needing this.'

CALCULUS LOGI

Darius Hinks

HEAT RISES FROM the sands like a living thing. It shimmers and rolls over the dunes with a silent menace, bringing tears to my eyes. I blink, and an array of filmy geometric shapes shifts slowly across my retina, the minute mathematical symbols blurring in the salty water. Then I close my eyes for a moment to rest them from the harsh light.

Not that there's much to look at anyway.

Belisarius IV is barren beyond anything I have ever experienced. Not a single river breaks the monotony of the view; not so much as a sapling lifts its leaves above the sweeping dunes. If it weren't for the distant wreck of the *Sardanapalus*, it would seem a lifeless wasteland; but I know otherwise.

In three and a half seconds the planet's fierce sun will reach its zenith. The heat will become sixty degrees celsius: a heat so great that the planet's scarce fauna will be forced to burrow and hide to escape the seething furnace. For a short while peace will descend, and only then can our daily race begin.

As my chronograph reaches the end of its countdown,
I flex the pistons in my augmented legs, tensing the muscles and stretching the artificial fibres in preparation.
'Envisage a circle of which the centre is nowhere, and the
circumference is everywhere,' I murmur, taking comfort
from the old catechism as I lower myself into a crouch,
'for that is the Emperor.'

The ticking of my device is audible in the otherwise
silent cave, and I sense the anticipation of the others as
they ready themselves. Their fear is almost palpable, and
I can't help but smile as I consider their pitifully
unadorned limbs. Every day they make the attempt, and
every day another one dies.

A bead of sweat rolls slowly down the bridge of my
nose, and I feel the immense heat beginning to rise
through the soles of my boots.

'Now!' I cry, and launch myself into the light.

One by one we spring from the darkness of the cave,
blinking like new borns as our eyes struggle to adjust to
the harsh glare. I race ahead: sprinting lightly over the
dunes with the sun sparkling along my dials and cogs,
and the pistons in my legs wheezing musically as they
power me across the desert.

Behind me trail the other survivors, those faithless flot-
sam and jetsam who are now my only companions:
Amaryllis, Hasan, Rabanus and Valens. Humans of
course, but as alien to me as everything else on Belisarius.

I can hear their pained gasps as they struggle to breathe
the stifling air and without even turning to look, I can
envisage the desperation on their sweating faces as they
attempt to find purchase on the shifting sand. The sun
will be at its hottest for only seven minutes and forty-two
seconds, and they each know that a moment's hesitation
could be fatal. Seven forty-two: the numbers are embedded in their thoughts like a prayer.

I sprint like never before, as though I have daemons
bearing down on me. The desert becomes an incandes-
cent blur, and the sound of my heart fills my ears. Speed

is everything, speed and faith, and as a pleasing pain begins to tighten around my muscles, I wonder absently who will survive the day.

Soon, our goal is in sight: a small fraction of the ruined colossus that was once the *Sardanapalus*. It straddles the horizon like the carcass of a slaughtered beast, slowly collapsing in on itself under the heat of the midday sun. During the crash, this tiny section, containing the detention cells, split from the rest of the ship and landed close to the rocky outcrop we now call home.

I am the first to arrive at the wreckage, ducking under a blackened support strut and staggering into the relative cool of the shade. Then, four point eight seconds later, the convicts arrive – groaning with relief as they escape from the smouldering sun.

There is a frantic clattering and banging as we begin to scour the debris-strewn rooms.

'Here, servitor,' gasps Valens. 'Quick!'

Servitor. He knows what I really am, and the word grates on me, but I feign indifference and hurry to his side nonetheless.

A cracked pipe is spitting dark viscous liquid onto the sand. 'Is it safe?' he asks, clutching my arm, his tattooed face full of hope.

I stoop down beside the pipe, take a small piece of faded vellum from within my dusty robes and hold it briefly under the trickle of liquid. 'As a rock I shall be, with Him by my side,' I whisper, and press the damp parchment gently to my cracked lips.

For a few seconds I remain silent, my eyes closed as I relish the sensation of the moisture soaking into my dusty mouth.

'Well?' hisses Valens eventually, a note of desperation creeping into his voice.

I open my eyes and calmly meet his fierce gaze. 'Its composition is only seven parts water,' I tell him with a shrug. 'There are three quite noisome contaminants present.'

Valens massages his shaven head, trembling with barely-restrained anger. With a rush of adrenaline I realise that he might strike me. He leans forward until his blistered sweating face is almost touching mine. 'But is it safe?'

'Oh, yes,' I reply with a polite smile, and take a deep gulp.

THE RETURN JOURNEY is always more difficult. Every second wasted during the search for water now hangs heavily around our necks – almost as heavily as the ten litre flasks tied to our heaving chests. My footing remains true, however, and soon the rocks are in sight, along with the safety of the cave.

'Thirty point three eight seconds!' I call over my shoulder, holding up the chronograph. I am ahead of the others by eighteen metres and will soon reach safety. Neither heat nor fear has any hold over me: while the convicts run hunched and clumsy with weakness, I spring smoothly over the sand with my head held high, remaining utterly calm even as the hairs on my face begin to shrivel and burn.

One by one we reach the cave, tumbling desperately down the final dune and flinging ourselves onto the hard rock. I am of course the first, closely followed by Amaryllis – all one and a half metres of her small, wiry form collapsing to the ground with a staccato laugh of relief. Then comes Valens, his eyes rolling wildly as he runs past me into the shadows, and a few seconds later Hasan, his massive silhouette briefly blocking out the light as he careers through the cave's narrow entrance, and then... and then no one.

'Where is Rabanus?' Hasan's deep voice echoes ominously around the cave. Amaryllis looks up from where she lies, her face suddenly taut with fear. 'How... how long, logi?' she gasps, struggling for breath. I take the chronograph from within my robes, and examine its delicate glyphs. I prolong the moment for two point seven seconds, aware that in the device's radium glow my face must look strange and menacing, then I shake my head nonchalantly.

'Time's up.'

They rush to the mouth of the cave and squint out into the blinding light. At first there is nothing to be seen, but then Rabanus appears, sprinting wildly towards us. Even at this distance I can see the animal terror on his face, the pitiful lack of self-control. Somehow he must have fallen behind, and he is still two minutes and three seconds from the safety of the rocks.

'Look there,' says Amaryllis, pointing a trembling finger at the sand near the cave's entrance, but her words are unnecessary – we can all see the dunes beginning to roll and shift.

With inexplicable relish I realise Rabanus is already dead, and all we can do now is watch.

Amaryllis leans heavily against Hasan. 'Oh, Rabanus,' she groans. 'Poor Rabanus.'

The dunes begin to churn and boil more violently, and from beneath the ground comes a horrendous noise: a tearing, rumbling grinding that fills each of their faces with dread. Hasan turns away, unable to watch, knowing all too well what will happen next.

Then the movement ceases.

We strain forward to watch. Rabanus is now only thirty-two seconds from the cave, and in the deathly quiet I can hear the hoarse barking of his breath as he races towards us.

'Maybe some days the heat lasts longer,' Valens wonders aloud, turning to me, his voice suddenly full of hope. 'Maybe he can still make it?'

Receiving no reply, he looks once more out at the desert to see that Rabanus is now twenty seconds away – his legs pounding the sand like pistons and a relieved grin beginning to spread across his sunburnt face. 'He is going to make it!' cries Valens eagerly.

The desert explodes.

A blinding eruption of sand and air throws me to the ground, and in the din and confusion someone screams horribly. When the air clears, only Hasan is still standing, but from the floor of the cave we all see the same terrible, surreal scene that he does.

Rabanus is hanging twenty-two metres up in the air, his eyes wide with incomprehension as he looks down at us from his strange perch. He's obviously dazed with shock, and his head thrashes violently from side to side as he tries to grasp the terrible reality of what's happening to him.

Then I notice his legs, lying on the desert floor, far below, spraying a powerful torrent of blood across the sun-bleached sand. Rabanus gives a hoarse cry of denial, and strains to free himself, but the blood loss overcomes him and he collapses into a lifeless slump.

The creature holding him in one of its monstrous claws raises him higher, seeming to savour the moment, then it rams the man's ruined torso greedily into one of its many gaping mouths and crashes heavily back down onto the sand. The impact sends out such a huge seismic tremor that fifteen pieces of the cave's roof fall down around me.

The behemoth has returned.

'HE WHO JUDGES me is the Emperor,' I whisper, as I sit alone in the moonlight, 'I shall not judge myself.' The words bring me little comfort however. Emotions do not sit easily with a calculus logi, and the guilt that has recently settled over me stings like an open wound. I nervously finger the nest of wires that snake from under my scalp – twisting and plaiting them as though they are strands of hair. Logarithms and ciphers, interpolation and statistics – these are the emotions of a calculus logi. The dogma of logic and obedience. Certainty is all, certainty and blind faith. So this terrible seed of self-doubt gives me a sense of foreboding I cannot seem to quell.

The sources of my confusion are asleep at my feet, huddled together for warmth and snoring contentedly. As I look down at them, my certainty returns. Of course, I know where my duty lies, and I must be strong. I must protect these criminals, however unworthy they might seem. If the Emperor wishes me to die here, on this barren world then so be it, I will die with pride. Although – my thoughts cloud over once more – would the Emperor really wish to lose one faithful servant in the name of three faithless ones? I shake my head in confusion and look out into the desert to distract myself from such shameful thoughts.

Even in the inky blackness, I can see the monstrous shape of the creature: ever patient, ever hungry, waiting silently on the horizon. Its huge eyes are blind and sealed, but I know that it senses my every move, every subtle odour of my flesh. Should I be foolish enough to step out from the safety of the cave, even for a second, it would pounce. Tearing me limb from limb, as it did those poor souls who never made it to the safety of the cave.

Still, it will not have long to wait. Days, weeks at most before it will have us all. Dehydration, hunger and the constant heat will finally take their toll, and even I will be too slow to survive the daily scavenging runs back to the detention cells. Unless…

I turn to look once more at my companions and notice with a guilty start that Amaryllis has awoken, and is watching me intently. 'You should rest,' I say, with what I hope is a reassuring smile.

She says nothing in reply, but continues to stare up at me from the shadows. The whites of her eyes are just visible in the moonlight, and I have the uncomfortable feeling that she has somehow read my thoughts. 'And what about you, logi? Do you ever sleep? Or did the tech-priests take even that pleasure away from you?'

I frown, despite myself. 'Do you find sleep pleasurable? How can oblivion be a pleasure?'

Amaryllis laughs softly to herself. 'Oh, you'd be surprised at the things I find pleasurable.' She crawls over to sit next to me and arches her eyebrows enigmatically. 'I'm not the nice girl you might think I am.'

My tongue cleaves to the roof of my mouth, so I simply smile awkwardly and nod. Amaryllis fills me with a nameless fear that I cannot explain. The others scare me too, but for reasons I can at least identify: Valens is clearly insane – a novice Helio Cultist whose sun-worship has frazzled his brain to such an extent that the Ecclesiarchy were forced to lock him up. For all his fierce facial tattoos and piercings he is too much a prisoner of his own mind to be a threat. And Hasan is simply a thug. Although he claims to have once been an Imperial crewman, I somehow doubt it. His brutal slab-like face and colossal frame mark him for what he really is: a belligerent simpleton. But Amaryllis... she is altogether more mysterious. Her faithlessness seems somehow wanton.

Annoyed by the strange power she seems to have over me I attempt to embarrass her. 'I hope you don't mind me asking, but I was wondering–'

'This sounds interesting,' she says with a smirk.

I hesitate, and clear my throat self consciously. 'Well, you may not wish to talk about it... of course...' I wait for her to interrupt again, but she just continues to smile coyly at me. 'Well, it's just... at the time of the crash you must have been in the vicinity of the detention cells... in fact you must have been in one of the detention cells, and I just wondered – please don't think me impertinent – but what crime had you committed?'

She looks blankly at me and says nothing in reply. Her face assumes an expressionless mask that seems, in the half-light, horribly sinister and I have the disturbing feeling I am sitting with an automaton. I suddenly regret my question, and begin to shuffle awkwardly on the cold floor. Then, after a painfully long time, she finally moves. She takes a slender piece of rock from within her coat and begins to drag it along the cave floor – so that its edge sparks slightly in the dark, and an unpleasant scraping sound cuts through the silence.

I cough nervously again. I have noticed her toying with the stone on two previous occasions – it's one of the many things I find inexplicably disturbing about her. As she continues to hone the edge of the rock, I feel suddenly afraid, and look out once more at the behemoth.

She follows my gaze, but only after twelve seconds of awkward silence does she finally speak. 'Strange, isn't it? We can't escape – we may as well have died with all the others during the crash – and yet every day we put so much effort into postponing the inevitable. Silly really. It would be easier just to end it all now.' She flicks a pebble out onto the sand, and watches as the creature shifts its monstrous head in our direction. 'It could all be over so quickly.'

'Don't say such things,' I reply. 'Your substance is not your own, to be cast aside like an empty shell, it is a vessel for the Emperor's grace.' I tap my chest to reinforce the point, and quote from memory: 'The greatest and most precious form He has given us, that we may partake in His divine light!'

Infuriatingly, Amaryllis simply rolls her eyes. 'Oh, yes – the Emperor… how could I forget him?' She shakes her head, and I feel my muscles tensing with anger.

'You should not speak lightly of such things.'

'Calm down, logi, suicide isn't really my style.' Then she smiles coyly. 'Besides, death may not be the only option.'

I narrow my eyes, but say nothing.

'You know what I mean, friend, you've seen it too.'

I shake my head vigorously. Maybe she has read my thoughts. 'It could not be done,' I say, all too aware of what she is referring to. Further out in the desert, beyond the remains of the detention cells, lies the main wreckage of the *Sardanapalus*. If anyone could reach it, within the allotted time, they would surely find refuge within its huge labyrinthine shell.

Amaryllis leans forward, her small elfin face full of excitement. 'It could be done,' she says, with the moonlight flashing in her eyes. 'We could make it, you and me. We're still fast enough, not like the others, and we wouldn't need to allow time for a return journey – we'd be safe within the

ship. The creature could never break through the hull.' She
gently touches my hand, and I withdraw it with a start.
'There would be enough water to last for months, and
food! Think,' – she pauses to catch her breath – 'the ship
must have a signalling device of some kind, some kind of
distress beacon. It needn't just be our mausoleum, we
could be rescued. Think, logi!'

I shake my head again. These are the very thoughts that
have been haunting me. With my implants, and the
coolants running through my veins, I have no doubt that
I could make it, but it would be I alone who reached the
ship: none of the others would survive the attempt, I'm
sure of that. If I were to try and reach the main part of the
ship it would mean deserting Amaryllis and the others to
their fate. Seven forty-two: the numbers are their death
sentence, but somehow she refuses to see it. As I watch
her, fidgeting with excitement, I feel a sudden rush of pity,
and my mind is finally made up: I can't leave these people
to die. I must remain until the end, keep them alive as
long as possible, and if necessary, perish with them. The
decision gives me a warm glow of righteousness.

'No,' I say, raising my chin proudly, 'there is not enough
time.' I gesture to the numerous ciphers and clockwork
devices that litter my battered copper outfit. 'I have examined every possibility, every differential, every possible
equation, and we would not have enough time to reach
the *Sardanapalus* before the sun began to cool.'

I feel sure that my authoritative tone will finally silence
the girl, but she simply smiles enigmatically and toys
with the sharpened stone. Then, without taking her eyes
off me she begins spinning it on the ground. 'Can you
only think like an adding machine, Regulus? Can you
only see the world as arithmetic?' I say nothing, and she
shakes her head, her smile becoming a grimace. 'They
threw me in those stinking cells simply because I can see
things as they really are. I can see the world from another
point of view!' She tosses the rock into the air, and to my
amazement it vanishes. An inexplicable feeling of nausea

rushes up from my stomach. Then she leans forward until I can feel her warm breath on my face. Fear grips me, and I try to back away, but the cave wall is behind me.

'You cannot account for every variable' she whispers, and rests her hand gently on my neck. I would be more comfortable with a snake at my throat than this strange woman, and as she slides her hand across my skin, I squirm uncomfortably. I feel suddenly powerless, and unable to move. She reaches under my leather skullcap and I feel her fingers shifting delicately back and forth across my skin. Then, to my dismay, she pulls something from beneath the matted cerebral wires. 'Life is more than an equation,' she says showing me the stone. 'You must learn to trust to chance.'

'Cheap tricks will not save you from that,' I say, gesturing out of the cave and trying to still the tremor in my voice. 'You're nothing but a faithless conjuror!'

'I need no cheap tricks, logi! Trust me,' she hisses, 'you cannot account for every variable, you cannot see every eventuality. If you would just– '

A rustling noise comes from behind us.

We turn to see that Valens has awoken and is watching us in silence.

Even in the dark of the cave I see the blood rush into Amaryllis's cheeks, and I wonder how much the Helio Cultist has heard.

For a few seconds he remains silent, obviously confused by his surroundings, then he sits up with a yawn. 'What are you two gossiping about, ' he says, stretching his arms with an audible crack. 'Not me, I hope?'

We both laugh awkwardly.

'Well, no point trying to sleep now, I suppose,' he says, rising to his feet, 'it will soon be light, and my master will rise from his slumber.' I look out through the cave entrance, and sure enough, on the distant horizon, beyond the great mass of the beast, the black of the sky is already changing to a deep, vivid blue. 'Another hour and it will be dawn.'

'Seventy-two minutes and forty-three seconds,' I say.

Amaryllis laughs dryly, but Valens seems suddenly annoyed. He glares at me. 'What would we do without you logi?'

I smile innocently in reply, and Valens moves to the back of the cave, where he lies down on the ground again and begins to moan strangely.

'What is he doing?' Amaryllis whispers, arching her eyebrows.

'It could be some kind of religious rite – maybe he's praying?'

Amaryllis peers through the darkness at the man, obviously amused. She watches as he spreads his limbs into a star shape and grins inanely at the cave's ceiling while continuing to chant. 'He is,' she murmurs, 'utterly insane.'

'You TRIPPED ME!' screams Valens, scrambling to his feet and squaring up to Hasan. 'You retarded ape!'

'I did not, ' replies Hasan in his deep slow voice.

Amaryllis and I sprint past them both without pausing.

As I run, I turn to see Hasan drawing himself up to his full height of two metres, so that he towers above the priest. 'You fell.'

With an enraged scream, Valens flies at him, and the pair fall – punching and kicking – down the side of a steep dune.

I turn away again, and concentrate on running. With Amaryllis straining to match my speed of twenty-five kilometres an hour, I fly over the dunes. Each day, rather than growing weaker, I seem to be becoming faster, more powerful than before. Adrenaline has replaced blood as my vital fluid, and I wait impatiently each day for noon – and the race – to arrive.

I reach the cave with two point three minutes to spare, and trot calmly onto the safety of the rocks. Amaryllis soon follows, her face flushed with exertion, and her limbs trembling uncontrollably. As she falls to the floor, coughing violently, I look back out across the desert. 'No,' I say, stifling a laugh, 'surely not!'

Out across the dunes, Valens and Hasan are still rolling and tumbling over the sand – laying blow after blow on each other. The sand around the convicts is now red with their blood, and they seem, with only seconds until the creature rises once more, utterly oblivious to their danger, intent only on killing each other. 'Animals,' I mutter under my breath, and shake my head.

Amaryllis rushes to my side. 'Oh, no,' she gasps, 'what have they done?'

We watch in silence as the distant figures wrestle and kick, lost in their rage. Then, with almost comic surprise, they freeze, mid-punch, and remember where they are.

'Too late,' breathes Amaryllis next to me, shaking her head with disbelief. 'They don't have enough time.' She looks at me with her mouth hanging open like a simpleton. 'Do they?'

The ground is already beginning to shift and roll, and I shake my head slowly. The men finally continue their sprint in the direction of the cave, but they have wasted far too much time, and I can see the fear on their faces. Animals, I think, is this worth dying for? They are not utterly without guile though, I notice. In an attempt to confuse the stirring behemoth they take separate paths towards the cave – presumably thinking that this way at least one of them might survive.

Valens is thirty-three seconds from the cave when the creature takes him. At first it seems as though he has fallen into an unseen pit. The ground suddenly disappears from beneath his feet and he simply vanishes from view. Then the pit rises from the ground around him and is revealed as a great gaping maw of impossible size.

'Save us,' breathes Amaryllis as the creature rises up into the sky, lifting its huge mass up from beneath the ground.

'It's incredible,' I murmur, shaking my head in awe.

'Look,' says Amaryllis in a small voice, 'Hasan.'

The usually brutal looking man seems suddenly child-like as the creature slams its massive body back into the ground and speeds in his direction. He staggers to a halt, seeing that the creature is now between him and the cave.

'What is he doing?' hisses Amaryllis, as the man drops dejectedly to the floor.

'Dying,' I reply.

'WE COULD MAKE it,' says Amaryllis, pacing around the cave. 'You've got to trust me, logi. I see things you can't – you can't see every eventuality! You must see beyond the numbers. The universe revolves on an axis of luck and circumstance... not science!'

I look up at her from where I sit. It has been two days, eight hours, fifteen minutes and sixteen seconds since the deaths of Valens and Hasan, and Amaryllis's mouth has not closed once. Her exhortations are becoming more and more hysterical. 'I've told you,' I say, 'I've looked at every possible variable.'

'But you don't know every possible variable!' she cries, with tears of frustration appearing in her eyes. 'Are you a god, that you can foresee the outcome of all things?'

'There is only the God-Emperor.'

'Pah! And what is He? A corpse... at best!'

'He is not this or that, but He is all things, for He is the cause of all.'

Amaryllis clutches her shaven head in her hands, and howls. 'Oh, what did I do to deserve this? Marooned with a... with a sanctimonious abacus!' She sits heavily down on the floor opposite me, and begins to scrape her stone angrily across the ground.

Once again I feel alien emotions stirring within me. As the days wear on, the woman's endless bullying entreaties are fuelling a growing rage in me. Why should I, a loyal servant of the God-Emperor, end my days on this lifeless world, in this pointless vigil – so that a faithless criminal need not die alone? In a few more days, even I will be too weak to make the longer journey – to the main wreck of the *Sardanapalus*.

Is this what the Emperor would really want? How can I be sure? It can only be days now before I will no longer have any option, but to stay... and die. I vigorously shake my head as though trying to dislodge my shameful thoughts. No, I assure myself, I must not question my duty. I must be true to my training. The forge world of Zopyrus VI seems a distant memory – it has in fact been two centuries, eight months and three and a half days since I knelt before the tech-priests and memorised the sacred tracts of my order – but nevertheless, even here I must remain true to my faith. My role is to protect my fellow humans, and if I deserted this woman now, I would be no better than a heretic.

'It cannot be done,' I say softly.

'Fool!' says Amaryllis through gritted teeth. 'You make me sick.' She slams the stone on the ground angrily. 'It's drones like you who make me ashamed to be human! Not you that you are much of a human anyway!'

Anger rises unbidden in my mind, and I feel my pulse quicken unpleasantly. The woman seems to be capable of stirring utterly useless and unproductive emotions in me.

'How much of you is actually a man? Half, if that? The tech-priests have made a freak of you, Regulus.' She rises to her feet and levels a trembling finger at me. 'You talk of the Emperor, but what are you to Him? Nuts and bolts! A walking box of cogs!'

'My faith is sufficient to ensure His protection, where as you are nothing but a...' – I hesitate before uttering such a potent word – 'heretic!'

'Maybe, but at least I'm a human! What are you? A servitor? A machine? How could the Emperor love that?'

I feel my pulse throbbing angrily in my forehead. Her words cut through me like knives, and my head is beginning to spin with anger. Where have these emotions come from? I have never before lost my temper – has the sun corrupted my thought patterns?

'But worst of all,' she shouts, 'you are a coward!' Then she whirls around and strides to the back of the cave, where she sits down with her back to me.

I find I am sat bolt upright, my fists clenched with anger. She is a worthless traitor. It cannot be right that I should die for such a wretch. It cannot! I could easily reach the *Sardanapalus*. What do I care that she could not? Like the final part of an equation I feel something in my mind slotting into irreversibly place. Almost without volition, I find I have made a decision.

'Very well,' I say, trying not to let my voice betray my emotions, 'tomorrow we will make the attempt.'

Amaryllis turns to look at me with a shocked expression. Then she grins. 'I knew you had it in you.'

As I PATIENTLY watch the glyphs on my chronograph, I feel a growing sense of joy. 'Ten seconds,' I say, turning to Amaryllis, who is crouched beside me at the mouth of the cave. She nods, her sun-lit face full of eagerness for the race ahead. 'We take the same route as before, pause for twenty seconds at the remains of the detention cells to catch our breath … then just keep running until we reach the *Sardanapalus*.'

I flex the pistons in my legs, watching the hydraulic cables as they slide smoothly back and forth. Strange, that such insignificant things should make all the difference between survival – I turn to look at Amaryllis – and death.

'Now,' I cry, and throw myself out into the desert.

I run as before, with a loping easy stride. Dashing comfortably over the shifting sands at twenty kilometres an hour, and hurdling the dunes as though they aren't there, I have no need to push myself. I know to the exact millisecond how long it will take me to reach the *Sardanapalus*, and even allowing for errors, seven minutes and forty-two seconds will give me plenty of time.

At the sound of Amaryllis's gasping breath, I find it difficult not to laugh. 'Machine' she called me. What a fool. The Emperor's gifts of augmentation are bestowed on only the most faithful of His servants; but that's something a worthless apostate like her couldn't hope to understand.

I look over my shoulder, and see that for the moment she is keeping up with me, although a combination of the heat and exertion have already coloured her face an unhealthy purple. She grins eagerly back at me, and once more I have to stifle a laugh. I can barely wait to see the expression on her face when she realises that I have been right all along. I hope that before the creature devours her, she will have time to consider the superiority of my 'freak' brain.

When I reach the detention cells I am barely short of breath, but I nevertheless lean against the twisted metal frame and attempt to lower my heart rate a little. Amaryllis is still four point six seconds away and I look out in the direction of the *Sardanapalus*. My heart swells as I see that large sections of the hull are still intact – it will be a perfect refuge from the creature. It is even possible that I will find other survivors, hopefully of a more pious sort than my recent companions. I check the chronograph. Twelve point eight seconds and I will need to start the next section of the run.

A hoarse gasping alerts me to the arrival of Amaryllis. She slumps next to me against the cell wall with whimper, and then crouches down on the ground as she tries to catch her breath. Sweat is rushing over her face in torrents. 'How... how are we... doing?'

I smile, relishing the moment. 'No time for a rest, I'm afraid,' I say, tapping the chronograph. 'In three minutes and thirty-two seconds it will be cool enough for the creature to rise. We need to go now.'

I bend down beside her and whisper in her ear: 'In fact, as it would take you three minutes and fifty-eight seconds to reach the wreck, you may as well start preparing yourself for the afterlife now. This will be your last trip.'

Amaryllis looks up at me in alarm, and I feel a thrill of power. I see now how right I was to lead her to her death. I am more than she could ever be – I am more than human... I am calculus logi. As the sun beats down on me, I feel the Emperor's grace flooding through me – mingled in with the blinding light.

Then, strangely, I notice that Amaryllis is smiling.

'I have other plans,' she says, and with surprising speed shoves something towards me. Before I can react, there is an explosion of escaping air and my legs give way. As I crash heavily to the ground I see that her sharpened stone is embedded deeply in my femoral hydraulics.

Amaryllis steps calmly away from me as I thrash around awkwardly on the ground, cursing and spitting. 'Do you see now, friend,' she says, dusting herself down demurely, 'that you cannot account for every variable?' She stoops so that her face is just out of my reach. 'But maybe you would have to be a little more human to truly understand that, Regulus.'

With an inarticulate roar I try to pull myself to my feet, but my shattered limbs won't hold me and one point two seconds later I hit the floor again with a crash. I land heavily on my side, and watch as Amaryllis sprints lightly away across the desert – towards the *Sardanapalus.*

My mind is blank with animal rage, and at first I fail to grasp what she has done. Then, as my thoughts clear, I realise. Of course: by the time the creature has finished with me, Amaryllis will be safe. She has bought her escape with my life. She has planned this all along. All those days spent sharpening the stone...

My wrath consumes me. I turn my head and glare furiously into the sun – letting the light burn through my eyes, as though the heat can somehow scorch away my fury. As pain blossoms from behind my retina I hear the tech-priests' mournful litany, coming back to haunt me from across the centuries: 'Deception is the corruption of science.'

'No!' I scream as the ground beneath me begins to roll and shift. 'No! No! No!'

CRIMSON NIGHT

James Swallow

THE SEWER'S AWFUL stench would have crippled a normal man with stomach-knotting nausea. It was a heady, foul cocktail of repellent, putrid matter, stagnant water and base stinks that signalled ripe decay.

Tarikus rose from his hands and knees where he had slipped into the sluggish embrace of the liquid effluent, and spat out the matter that had choked his mouth. The gobbet impacted the hard-packed bricks of the sewer tunnel wall with a wet slap; something small and chitinous, an insect scavenger he had almost swallowed, skittered away. He glanced backward, in the dimness catching the merest glint of metal from his armour, the paldrons and plates piled perhaps a quarter-league behind him, at the mouth of the access channel.

Tarikus shook off the oily remnants of the muck and came up as far as the tunnel confines would let him. His bulk filled the conduit, the edges of his shoulders clipping the bricks, his head forced down into a cocked angle. Even bent at the knees, it was all the Space Marine

177

could do to fit his mass into the narrow passageway. Had
he still been clad in his ceramite armour, he would have
been wedged like a bolt shell jammed in a cannon breech
after just a handful of paces. In his service to the Golden
Throne, Tarikus had lost count of the number of Light-
forsaken worlds he had fallen upon in the name of the
Emperor, carrying the savagery and the cold fury of the
Doom Eagles with him; and if his captain wished it, he
would venture on and fight naked, with tooth and nail if
that were to be the order of the day.

He spat and took a measured breath, concentrating for
a moment, casting his hearing forward. Beyond the drips
and spatters of falling water, past the slow slopping current of effluent, there were voices: faint sounds that
someone without the enhanced senses of the Adeptus
Astartes might had missed, murmurs borne to him on
breaths of reeking air. The voices were indistinct,
ephemeral, but laced with the touch of terror. Tarikus
nodded to himself. He was close now.

His knuckles whitened around the grip of his bolt pistol, the solid shape of the gun and the weight of it in his
fist familiar and comforting. Bringing it up to sight along
the stubby barrel, he pushed forward, the rhythm of his
footfalls sending ripples out before him, rings of liquid
catching the faint glow of organic biolumes set into the
tunnel roof. As Tarikus walked, he strained to catch a
sound from his quarry, some random noise that might
give away its position and alert him, but he heard nothing, only the pitiable crying of its victims. No matter, the
Marine told himself, there can be no other way out of this
stinking warren. He's in there.

After a hundred more steps, the tunnel suddenly bal-
looned out into a circular atrium, an open flood chamber
fed by a dozen more channels, each of them – unlike this
one – blocked by a heavy iron grate. Tarikus scanned
them in an eye-blink: not one had been forced open. As
he had planned, the foe had been caught in his lair and
trapped there. Tarikus hesitated a moment, licking at the

sickly air. In the near-absolute darkness down here even his abhuman eyes strained to make out anything more than gross shapes, and his scent senses were fogged with the sewer's fetor. With a hiss of effort, Tarikus leapt from the mouth of the channel and dropped the seven metres to the chamber floor, the wet crash of his landing sending a surge of liquid roiling away. The moans he could hear jumped an octave. He could see people arranged like some grotesque exhibition in the chamber's centre, each in a box-like cage, piled randomly atop one another. A tiny flicker of child-memory blinked through Tarikus's mind: a nest of building blocks, a tottering tower built by small hands towards the sky.

In that second, the foe exploded from beneath the knee-deep fluid, a massive man-form spitting a reeking rain out behind it. Tarikus reacted with impossible speed, the bolt pistol turning to target, barrel winking like a blinded eye. The Marine's finger tightened and rounds screamed from the gun, finding purchase in the creature's chest – impossibly, ineffectually, bursting through it to spark away into the walls.

Tarikus ducked as the heavy head of a massive hammer hummed through the air. A split-second too late, he realised the blow had not been aimed at his skull; the arcing trajectory of the hammer dipped down and caught him squarely on the forearm. The impact knocked the gun from his hand and it vanished into the dark, claimed by the murk with a hollow splash. The foe pressed the attack, emboldened by disarming the Space Marine, looping the hammer around for a crushing stroke. As it strode towards him, the Doom Eagle caught the glitter of a lengthy silver probe emerging from his assailant's other palm. Tarikus let him come on, let himself be pushed back toward the wall. As he retreated, he used his free hand to shrug a metallic tube from a strap on his wrist. Consciously willing his optic nerves to contract, he thumbed a stud at one end of the tube. With the brilliant fury of a supernova, a sputtering blaze of light erupted from the flare rod, filling the chamber with shuddering, actinic colour. The caged ones screamed, their faces caught in a frieze of cold white. Tarikus's eyes were fixed on the enemy before him, the foe revealed at last before the flare's illumination.

It stood a metre or so higher than he, clad in shrouds of rust-pocked armour, the broad feet anchored in the churning pool of effluent, the great mailed fists thrown up to protect its head, and the head itself concealed behind a helmet with dark eyes and the fierce grin of a breath grille. Except for its crimson hue, it was the virtual double of the armour Tarikus had discarded at the tunnel entrance, and staring back at him from its breastplate was the twin-headed eagle of the Imperium of Man.

BROTHER-SERGEANT TARIKUS first cast eyes on the planet Merron as the Thunderhawk made a sharp roll to port. The craft turned inbound toward the starport – the barren desert world's only link to the greater galaxy beyond – and Merron's rumpled orange geography presented itself to the Space Marine. He gave it a practiced survey: there was just one large conurbation, toward which they were flying, and the rest of the land as far as Tarikus's eyes could see appeared to be nothing more than a great web-work of ruddy-coloured scars.

'Open-cast mines,' said a voice beside him. 'Merron is rich in iridium.'

'Indeed?' Tarikus said mildly. 'Thank you for telling me, Brother Korica. Having ignored Captain Consultus's briefing this morning, I of course knew nothing of that.' He turned to give Korica a level stare.

The younger Marine blinked. 'Ah, forgive me, sergeant. I had not meant to imply you were ill-informed about our new garrison posting–'

Tarikus waved a dismissive hand. 'You need not prove your eagerness by reciting the captain's words, lad. Sufficient enough that you have committed them to memory.'

'Lord,' Korica said carefully.

The sergeant allowed himself a small smile. 'You are ready for a new world's challenge and that speaks well of you, Korica. That is why you were promoted from novitiate rank to the status of battle-brother with such rapidity... but this is not a place where we will find combat awaiting us. Merron is a way-station garrison, somewhere to re-arm and lick our wounds while we watch the Emperor's mines for him.'

'But if that were so, why not use the Imperial Guard to protect it? Are not we more valuable elsewhere?' There was a hint of wounded pride in the youth's voice.

'Mere men? Ha! Iridium attracts the greed of weaker souls like a candle does moths. We could not expect mere men to stand sentinel over it, nor expect them to repel any of the warp-cursed traitors who prey on the Imperium's riches.'

The Thunderhawk rumbled through a pocket of turbulence and Tarikus gave a curt shake of his head. 'No, only the Adeptus Astartes can truly place duty before base desire.' The disappointment on Korica's face was clear as day, and Tarikus waved him away. 'Fear not, lad. If the Corrupted return to this world as they have in the past, we'll be in the fray soon enough.'

The younger Marine looked downcast and Tarikus watched him for a moment. So raw, so untried, he thought, was I ever the same as he? He had not exaggerated when he praised Korica for his swift rise to full status as a Doom Eagle, but still Tarikus regretted that such a promotion had been necessary. On the ice planetoid Kript his company had met an overwhelming force of rot-souled Traitor Marines and lost fully a quarter of their number. Although the enemy had been routed, the blood cost they exacted was paid back with new men, new brothers advanced from the scout squads. Under Tarikus's direct command, Korica, and with him Brother Mykilus and Brother Petius, were among many newly fledged Doom Eagles. Tarikus gave himself a moment to remember his fallen comrades; they had met death at last on Kript's airless plains, and gone to Him willingly with the blood of the impure on their hands. The sergeant had personally recovered a relic from the field of battle, the shattered blade of a chainsword that was now a memorial to one of his brothers. When his time came, Tarikus hoped that the Emperor would grant him so perfect an ending.

THEY RODE OUT across the blasted ferrocrete plain of the port in a line of Rhinos, bikes and speeders, carrying at the head the metallic banner of their standard. From his vantage point at the hatch of his squad's transport, at the rear of the procession, Tarikus nodded at the clean dispersal and formation of the vehicles. Before him, the full might of the entire third company was spread, a glittering steel parade of tactical, assault and terminator squads – a suitable first impression for the Doom Eagles to make on their inaugural posting to Merron.

His gaze wandered to a force of vessels clustered at the southern quadrant of the airfield. They too were Thunderhawk transports, but wine-dark in colour where Doom Eagle craft were gunmetal silver. Their brooding livery looked like old, dried blood beneath the light of Merron's red sun. On their tail-planes they sported a disc-shaped sigil, a serrated circular blade kissed with a single crimson tear. The ships belonged to the Flesh Tearers, one of the smallest but most savage Chapters in the Adeptus Astartes.

Tarikus let his helmet optics bring them closer. Dozens of Marines were trooping aboard the Flesh Tearer craft while helots and workers, probably Merron locals, were busily loading cargo pods. As he watched, one of them slipped and dropped a case, the labourer's face a sudden mask of fear. A Marine walked to him and gestured roughly, the worker nodding frantically, thankful his mistake had not cost him his life. Tarikus looked away and dropped back into the Rhino.

'...nothing but carrion eaters,' Korica was saying to Mykilus. The other young Marine glanced up at the sergeant with a questioning gaze.

'Have you ever served with them, sir?' He jerked a thumb in the direction of the ships. 'There are rumours–'

'You're not a child, Brother Mykilus. Your time to give credence to fantasy tales is long gone,' Tarikus snapped.

'You deny the reports that they eat the flesh of the dead?' Korica pressed. 'Like the Blood Angels that spawned them, the Flesh Tearers feast on corpses–'

Tarikus took a heavy step forward and the rest of Korica's words died in his throat. 'What tales you may have heard are of little consequence, lad. Soon the Flesh Tearers will be gone and we will assume their garrison here. In the meantime, I expect you to contain your half-truths and speculations – clear?'

'Clear,' Korica repeated. 'I meant no disrespect.'

Tarikus was about to add something more, but without warning the Rhino suddenly lurched to the right, the forward quarter of the vehicle dipping sharply. Loose items flew across the cabin and only the sergeant's quick reflexes kept him upright. The Rhino skidded to a shuddering halt with a heavy iron clang.

An attack? Tarikus's first thoughts were of battle and he snapped out orders. The squad did as he commanded and boiled out of the vehicle in a swarm, bolters to the ready, scanning for an enemy. As Tarikus rounded the Rhino, Captain Consultus's voice crackled in his earbead, demanding a report.

Tarikus expected to see a smoking impact hole or the burnt traces of a lascannon hit, but the vehicle was undamaged. Instead, the very road the Rhino had been passing over had given way, a massive disc of ferrocrete cracked and distended into a shallow valley. 'The road, brother-captain, it seems to have collapsed...' Tarikus banged his mailed fist on the Rhino's hull and signalled the driver to put the vehicle in reverse, and the slab-sided machine began to edge backward. The sergeant frowned.

The ground opening up beneath them was hardly an auspicious omen.

As the Rhino pulled back, a contingent of locals approached, cautious and fearful around the Space Marines, giving them a wide berth. They carried iron sheets and makeshift blocking to repair the collapse, and they went to work without speaking. Tarikus studied them for a moment to determine which one was the leader, then strode over to him. The man recoiled, his hands fluttering over his chest like birds.

'You,' Tarikus said. 'How did this happen?'

The man blinked fear-sweat from his eyes. 'B-by your leave, Lord Muh-Marine,' he stuttered. 'The airfield here, it was built over the old quarter. The cesspools are still beneath our, uh, feet. Sometimes, subsidence...' He trailed off, his frayed nerves robbing him of any more speech.

Tarikus looked past him. Some of the workers were covering the centre of the new crater with a rough cloth, trying to conceal something and making a poor try at it. 'You there, hold!'

The man reached out to touch Tarikus's armour and thought better of it, drawing back his hand as if it had been burnt. The Doom Eagle ignored him and stepped forward; the Merrons scattered like frightened dogs. Tarikus ripped up the cloth with one hand and peered into the crater. Where the road surface had sunk into a dark chasm, a small void had been cut into the old sewers below. From the hole a dozen scents assaulted the Marine, but one came to him with the cold familiarity borne from a thousand battlefields. In the cesspool beneath the road were the naked forms of two corpses, pale and drawn, bleached by months of discorporation. 'What depravity is this?' Tarikus boomed, turning to face the Merrons. 'Answer me!'

'Don't concern yourself, Doom Eagle.' The words buzzed over the general channel of his helmet communicator, and Tarikus looked up to see who had spoken. Six

Flesh Tearers had arrived, the black and red of their armour shining darkly.

'Concern?' Advancing on the Marine who had addressed him, Tarikus's voice was almost a snarl. 'Who are you to decide what should concern me?'

The Flesh Tearer removed his helmet and placed it under the crook of his arm, a casual gesture but one calculated to show Tarikus the skull painted on his shoulder plate and the rank insignia he bore. 'I am Gorn, Brother-Captain of the Flesh Tearers 4th company. I command the Marine garrison on Merron,' and here he hesitated, showing a little flash of teeth in a feral smile. 'At least until the end of this day.'

'My apologies, brother-captain. I did not recognise you.' Inwardly, Tarikus fumed at his own indiscretion.

Gorn made a dismissive gesture. 'No matter, sergeant. We will handle this.' The captain directed his men into the crater.

'If I may ask, what transpired here?' Tarikus pressed. 'I will have to make a report to my commander.'

'A report, of course,' said Gorn, lacing the comment with barely concealed disdain. 'There have been minor incidents of unrest in the city, which we recently suppressed. This–' he pointed at the crater, '–is no more than a sad reminder of the same, most likely a few misguided fools who took their own lives in a death-pact. Nothing more.' Gorn laid a level gaze on Tarikus. Clearly, the conversation had come to an end, as far as the company commander was concerned.

Tarikus glanced back at the Rhino. Korica had arranged the squad to remount the transport and stood waiting for him to return. 'By your leave, then, brother-captain.'

Gorn nodded. 'Of course, brother-sergeant…?'

'Tarikus, lord.'

'Tarikus. Tell Consultus I will receive him in the garrison tower within the hour.'

'As you wish, lord.'

Am I a mere messenger now, Tarikus wondered as he walked away? Korica seemed about to speak as he boarded the Rhino, but Tarikus silenced him with a glare. 'Get us out of here. Make haste to rejoin the column or else I'll see you carry this heap of pig-iron into town.' The sergeant regretted the sharp words almost as soon as he had said them; his anger was at the arrogant Gorn, not his own men.

CAPTAIN CONSULTUS SAID nothing as Tarikus relayed the details of the incident, the two of them standing in the stone annex before the Space Marine garrison. The sergeant kept his eyes straight ahead as he spoke, but even in his peripheral vision he noted a stiffening of Consultus's jaw as Gorn's name was mentioned. Tarikus had served under the captain for over a century, and knew that this subtle sign indicated an irritation that in other men would have manifested as a shouting rage.

'Strange that he and I should cross paths after so long,' the officer mused. 'I had not thought I'd see Gorn again in this life. I'd thought the Flesh Tearers would have torn themselves apart by now.'

'This Gorn, brother-captain – you fought with him?'

Consultus nodded. 'Our Chapters met briefly on Kallern. You know of it?'

'The Kallern Massacres.' Tarikus recalled the records of the conflict from the indoctrination sessions of his training. 'Millions dead. Terror weapons unleashed in untold numbers.'

'And the Flesh Tearers in the middle of it all. What they did there earned them the attention of the Inquisition, from that day to this. They embrace the tactics of the berserker, rending and destroying all that stand in their way – enemy and ally alike. If I could command it, I would never place Doom Eagles alongside them, even in the darkest of days.'

Tarikus shifted uncomfortably. 'The brothers... tell stories about them.' The sergeant was almost ashamed to give voice to the thought.

'There are always stories,' Consultus said simply. 'The trick is to know if they are just stories.'

The door before the two Doom Eagles opened to reveal the chamber beyond, silencing any more conversation. A group of Flesh Tearers stepped past, among them a blunt-faced codicier. 'Captain Gorn will see you now,' he said, his grey eyes flicking over Tarikus's face. The sergeant said nothing, wondering if the psyker had heard every word they had uttered; as if in reply, the codicier gave Tarikus the smallest hint of a scowl.

Consultus entered the chamber, beckoning Tarikus with him. The exchange of commands was a formal ritual, and it required witnesses. Inside, Gorn was overseeing another Flesh Tearer as the Marine removed the company standard from the wall. This was a solemn duty, the banner a sacred artefact that no helot would dare lay hands upon. As the blood-red pennant was taken down, Tarikus heard the Flesh Tearers murmur a prayer to their Chapter's progenitor, Lord Sanguinius.

The two commanders met each other's gaze. 'Consultus.'

'Gorn.'

'My men are ready to take our leave of this sandpit. I can think of no better a company to take our place here than yours.'

If Consultus noticed the derisive tone in Gorn's voice, he gave no sign. 'The Doom Eagles will strive to be worthy of the honour of this posting.'

'Indeed.' Gorn removed a long ivory rod from a small altar before him. 'This token was granted by Merron's governor, as a symbol of our command here. Accept it from me and you will be this world's new defender.' He held out the rod to Consultus like an unwanted gift.

'A moment,' said Consultus coolly. 'First, I would address the report Brother Tarikus brought to me. These "uprisings" of which you spoke.'

Gorn grimaced. 'The report, yes. It is, as I told the sergeant, of no matter. A circumstance we dealt with. It will not trouble you.'

'All the same, I would have a full accounting of it before you leave.'

The Flesh Tearer commander gave a sideways glance at the other Marine, in shared, unspoken scorn at the Doom Eagle's expense. 'As you wish. Sergeant Noxx will see to it.'

'Lord.' Noxx spoke for the first time.

'Now,' Gorn continued, still proffering the ivory wand, 'For the Glory of Terra, I transfer command of the Merron garrison to Captain Consultus of the Doom Eagles. Do you accept?'

Consultus took the rod. 'In the Emperor's name, I accept command of the Merron garrison from Captain Gorn of the Flesh Tearers.'

'So witnessed,' Tarikus and Noxx spoke together.

Gorn's mouth twisted in self-amusement as he took the banner from Noxx. 'You'll find this an agreeable assignment, Consultus.' He patted the chamber's only other item of furniture, a simple carved chair. 'This seat is most comfortable.'

Tarikus frowned; from any other man, such a thinly veiled insult would have had him knocked to the stone floor. Gorn and Noxx left, the heavy ironwood door slamming shut behind them.

'He mocks us,' Tarikus grated. 'Forgive me sir, but by what right–'

'Keep yourself in check, Tarikus,' Consultus said mildly, the words instantly stopping the sergeant in his tracks. 'You're not a novitiate any more. Quell your enmity and save it for the foe. Let Gorn and his men play at their games of arrogance. They have little else.'

Tarikus stiffened. 'As you wish, brother-captain. Your orders?'

Consultus weighed the ivory token in his fist, then handed it to the sergeant. 'Place this somewhere out of sight. We have no need to validate our command here with the display of vulgar trinkets. All of Merron will understand, the dedication of the Doom Eagles is symbol enough of our devotion to the Emperor.'

'So witnessed,' Tarikus repeated.

THE GARRISON TOWER stood ten storeys tall, dwarfing the largest of the other buildings in Merron's capital, and beneath the surface were a dozen basements and sanctums carved from the sandstone. It was cool and damp down here, a comparative comfort to the uncompromising heat above. Tarikus made a circuit of the lower levels. Squads of Flesh Tearers were everywhere, completing their final preparations for departure, securing weapons for transit and storage. He checked here and there on the numerous Doom Eagles mingling among them, setting up storage dumps for ammunition and equipment. The groups of Marines moved around each other in a controlled dance of parade-ground efficiency, with little interaction.

Tarikus secured the rod in a weapons locker, and turned to discover he was being watched. A Merron male, half-hidden in the shadows, gave a start as he realised he had been discovered.

'Are you lost?' Tarikus asked.

The Merron's head darted back and forth, clearly weighing his chances at running away.

'Speak,' the sergeant said carefully.

The man flinched at the word and dropped to his knees, hands coming up to protect his face. 'Lord Marine, please do not kill me! I have a wife and child!'

Irritation flared in Tarikus. 'Get up, and answer my question.' He did so, and Tarikus felt a flash of recognition. 'Wait, you led the work crew at the starport.'

'I am Dassar, if it pleases you, sir.' The man was trembling, terror-struck in the Doom Eagle's presence. 'I beg you, I was just curious... about your kind.'

Tarikus had often seen common men cower before him. It was the manner of a Space Marine to expect this, as the

greater populace of the Imperium – especially on backwater medieval worlds such as this – saw the Adeptus
Astartes as the living instruments of the Emperor's divine
will; but something sat wrongly with Dassar's behaviour.
The Merron's fear was borne not from awe and veneration, but from outright terror. 'I am Sergeant Tarikus of the
Doom Eagles. You have nothing to fear from me.'

'Y-yes, honoured sergeant.' Dassar licked his lips. 'But,
p-please, sir, may I leave?'

'What are you afraid of, little man?'

At these words, the Merron began to weep. 'Oh, Great
Terra protect me! Lord Tarikus, spare me! My family will
have nothing if I am taken, their lives will be forfeit–'

Tarikus felt a mixture of confusion and disgust at Dassar's craven display. 'You are a helot in the service of the
Emperor! What cause would I have to take your life?'

Dassar's sobbing paused. 'You… you are of The Red…'
he said hesitantly, as if the statement would answer all
questions. 'You are predators and we are prey…'

'You talk in riddles.' Tarikus bent down and placed his
face by Dassar's. 'What is this "Red" you speak of?'

'The children sing the rhymes,' Dassar hissed, 'Here
come The Red, they stalk while you sleep. Here come The
Red, your blood do they seek. Here come The Red, to
your soul they lay claim, and you'll never be seen in sunlight again.' He gingerly laid a finger on Tarikus's armour.
'Only the colour is different. We prayed we would be free
of them, but now you have come as well, in numbers five-
fold.'

Stone crunched underfoot behind him and Tarikus
came up on his heel, whirling about. Framed in shadow,
Sergeant Noxx pointed past him at the cringing servant.

'You, vassal! Where is that case of grenades I ordered
you to find? Your lassitude will not be permitted!'

Dassar bolted away into the dark, calling over his shoulder. 'Of course, Lord Marine, I shall do as you order!'

Noxx gave Tarikus a hard look. 'These locals. They are a
superstitious lot, brother-sergeant.'

'Indeed?'

Noxx nodded. 'They're full of naïve fables. I would pay them no mind.'

Tarikus cast a glance in the direction that Dassar had gone and then pushed past Noxx, back up toward the surface. 'I'll try to remember that,' he said.

NIGHTFALL ON MERRON was a slow, languid process. Out on a long orbit around its huge red star, the planet had lengthy days far beyond those of Terran standard, and nights that were longer still. Tarikus watched the sky's gradual drift toward red-orange twilight through the window behind Captain Consultus, the colour shimmering off the shapes of a dozen armoured Space Marines outside as they drilled in tight-knit groups.

'You were right to bring this to me,' he said carefully, 'but Noxx is correct. I have examined the Adeptus Ministorum records of this world and its natives, and their culture is disposed toward myths and idolatry. The Ecclesiarchy allowed it to continue with guidance toward veneration of the Golden Throne, but some anomalies of doctrine might still exist.'

Tarikus shifted slightly. 'Captain, that may be so, but this helot, I saw nothing but absolute dread in his eyes. Reverence breeds a different kind of fear.' When Consultus gave no reply, he continued. 'A commissar once spoke to me of the Flesh Tearers' legacy of Sanguinius, of' – and here Tarikus had to force the words from his mouth – 'the curse of the Black Rage.'

'What you are insinuating borders on heresy, sergeant,' the captain stated coldly. 'You understand that?'

Tarikus found himself repeating Korica's words aboard the Rhino. 'I meant no disrespect.'

'I have seen the Flesh Tearers in their unbounded fury,' Consultus said quietly. 'They would take prisoners for interrogation, and we would never see them again. Once, I found a mass grave on the edge of my patrol zone, filled to the brim with enemy dead. I thought to check the bodies for any whom still lived, but there were none. Instead, I found men with hearts torn out by human teeth, bloodless and bone-white.'

An image of the corpses in the crater returned to Tarikus's mind. 'If the Merron people are being preyed upon by...' He paused for a moment. 'By someone, and the Imperium does not protect them from it, their faith in the Emperor's divinity may falter.'

Consultus nodded. 'There are always dark forces that seek uncertainties such as this. If they were to gain a foothold on Merron, the consequences could be disastrous. That shall not come to pass while we stand sentinel here.'

'Will the inquisitors hear of this?'

The captain shook his head. 'This is a matter for the Adeptus Astartes. You, Tarikus, will take a few men and investigate these circumstances. I will have you put down this fable for all of Merron to see.'

'It will be my honour, captain.' The sergeant met his commander's gaze. 'I will follow this malfeasance to its source.'

'I know you will, Tarikus. Wherever it takes you.'

THEY FOUND THE body after only an hour of searching. Dassar's thin screech cut through the blood-warm air and brought Tarikus and Korica running, to where he stood flanked by Mykilus and Petius. Between the hulking forms of the two armoured Space Marines, Dassar looked waif-like by comparison, a child's crude sketch of a man against the brutal shapes in silver-grey ceramite. The servant had panicked when Tarikus had ordered him to accompany them, but it was the Merron's reluctant direction that had brought them here, to a landscape of wreckage and broken stone on the city's outskirts. Brother Petius raised his faceplate to the sergeant and flicked a glance at the ground.

'Elderly male, no clothing or identifying marks. I'd estimate he's been dead for two standard days.'

Tarikus accepted Petius's report with a nod. The young Marine's skills with matters of the dead were trustworthy; he would one day become a fine Apothecary for the Chapter. 'Show me.' Tarikus stepped around the shuddering form of Dassar and peered at what they had discovered.

'We found him concealed beneath some rubble,' began Mykilus. 'Not too well hidden, either. I suspect he was meant to be found, sir.'

The sergeant dropped to one armoured knee to get a closer look at the corpse. Like the bodies he had seen in the sinkhole, the frail old man's papery skin was fish-belly white and anemic. 'Drained of his vital fluids,' Tarikus murmured. 'Exsanguinated...'

'It is as he said,' Korica indicated Dassar, 'these ruins around the airstrip are a warren of tunnels. The ideal place to dispose of a body.'

'The others were found like this?' Tarikus asked.

Dassar nodded slowly. 'Y-yes, Lord Marine. Sometimes weeks, even months after they go missing from their homes.'

Mykilus's brow furrowed. 'Are all you Merrons sheep? You did nothing about these abductions, you did not speak of them to the garrison commander?'

After a long moment, Dassar spoke again, his voice thick with fatigue. 'We were told to keep our petty problems to ourselves.'

Tarikus stood up and gestured to Korica. 'Wrap the body in Dassar's sandcloak and take it back to the Rhino. We will treat the dead with the respect they are due. How was he killed, Petius?'

'Look here, sir.' The Marine pointed at a circular wound on the body's chest. 'A puncture point, just beneath the heart. This poor fool was sucked dry through some kind of instrument, perhaps a metallic proboscis or tube. I believe he was alive and conscious at the time.' Petius removed a thin scalpel blade from a pack on his belt and picked at something on the dead man's flesh.

Dassar turned away and retched into the scrub. 'Oh, Emperor, deliver us from this evil, save our brother Lumen–'

'You knew this man?' Korica asked.

'The metalsmith's father-in-law,' Dassar choked. 'Taken last month during the two-moon festival.'

'Whatever kills these people does not murder before it is ready,' said Tarikus. 'How many others are still missing?'

'A-a dozen, perhaps more...'

'Then, where are they if they are not already dead?' asked Mykilus.

Tarikus nudged a loose stone with his broad, metalshod foot. 'Beneath us...'

'No one ventures into the tunnels!' said Dassar sharply, 'A foetid place running with pestilence. Any man who enters would surely sicken and die!'

'Any man,' echoed Tarikus. 'But we are not mere men.'

'Brother-sergeant,' said Petius, a warning in his voice, 'I have something.' He held up a tiny sliver of metallic material that glistened in the fading daylight. Tarikus examined it closely; such an artefact would surely be imbued with the despair of so terrible and tragic a death – a relic well suited to be taken to the Chapter's Reclusium on Gathis when this mission was at an end.

Mykilus intoned a prayer to the Machine God and gently waved his auspex over the fragment. 'A piece of ceramite,' he pronounced, 'old and corroded. It seems crimson in colour.'

'The Red!' Dassar husked, but the Marines did not answer him. Their enhanced senses caught the sound of tracks long before the servant's human ears registered the approach of a vehicle.

A Razorback tank in Flesh Tearer livery rolled into view between piles of rubble, which had once been brick-and-mortar buildings in the old quarter. The vehicle halted and for a moment there was silence. With a squeak of poorly maintained hinges, the tank's upper hatch opened and a trio of Marines exited. Dassar shrank back, shifting to hide himself behind Petius.

'Ho, Brother-Sergeant Tarikus.' Tarikus recognised Noxx's voice.

'Noxx,' he replied with a nod. 'What brings you here?'

The Flesh Tearer sergeant looked around. 'I could ask you the same.'

Tarikus was suddenly very conscious that Noxx and his men were carrying their bolters in battle-ready stances. The same awareness seemed to flicker out to Korica, Mykilus and Petius, and from the corner of his vision, Tarikus saw them shift their hands close to the triggers of their own guns. 'We are conducting an investigation.'

'For another of your reports?' Noxx said archly. 'The Doom Eagles must be a well-documented Chapter indeed.' When Tarikus did not rise to his barb, the Flesh Tearer indicated the nearby airstrip. 'In answer to your question, I am supervising the transfer of this vehicle to one of our Thunderhawks.'

'Through a debris zone?' said Mykilus.

Noxx's words became a snarl. 'Not that it is any concern of yours, whelp, but this route is quicker than the paved road. After all, we are doing our best to remove ourselves from Merron as fast as we can.'

A sideways glance from Tarikus kept Mykilus from answering with an angry riposte. 'We need no assistance,' he said in a neutral voice.

One of the other Flesh Tearers spoke. 'What have you there?' He gestured toward the cloak-wrapped body. 'Another deader?'

'Nothing of consequence–' Tarikus began, but Dassar spat loudly behind him.

'Fiends! Eaters of men!' the bondman hissed, emboldened by the Doom Eagles' protection. 'Your time is at an end! Merron will fear you no more!'

Noxx gave a chug of harsh laughter. 'Careful, vassal. The Adeptus Astartes does not take kindly to insults from lesser men…'

Dassar began to speak again, but Petius cuffed him with the flat of his gauntlet and he fell to the ground. The Marine had saved his life; had the servant vented his hostility any further, Noxx's men would have been within their rights to discipline him as harshly as they saw fit.

'You should keep him quiet.' said the other Marine. 'They never spoke out of turn when we were in charge here.'

Tarikus took a menacing step forward. 'But you are not in charge here any more. The Doom Eagles are Merron's protectors now, and the Emperor has duties for you elsewhere, Flesh Tearer.'

The sergeant's words brought the tension in the air to a knifepoint. But after long moments, Noxx broke it with a nod to Tarikus. He ordered his men back aboard their tank, and the vehicle lumbered off, kicking up spurts of dust.

CONSULTUS'S RIGID EXPRESSION did not alter as Tarikus relayed the discovery of the body to his commander. Only when he handed over the metal fragment did the sergeant see anything more than cold contemplation on his face. Finally, Consultus put the ceramite shard aside.

'Meaningless, Tarikus. If this is the best you can do, the chief librarian will laugh you out of the chambers.'

'I suspect Noxx and his men knew about the corpse before we did.'

'Conjecture. I cannot even begin to countenance the idea of placing doubt on a brother company without hard, irrefutable evidence.'

'They were goading us,' Tarikus said. 'I won't stand by and have my Chapter derided by carrion eaters–'

Consultus came to his feet with a snap of boots on stone. 'You forget your place, sergeant, for the second time today. Do you plan to make a habit of it?'

Tarikus felt his colour rise. 'No, brother-captain.'

'Good, because the last thing I want is for one of my most trusted squad leaders to begin behaving like the novitiates I put him in charge of, clear?'

'Clear, lord.'

The captain turned away. 'Night has fallen. You have until dawn to find something substantial, otherwise the Flesh Tearers will leave and this matter will be closed.'

TARIKUS STEPPED OUT into the Merron evening. The crimson glow of the sunset still lingered at the horizon, and above, the largest of the planet's moons was full and gibbous, hanging in mute judgement over the city. The sergeant walked the perimeter of the garrison block, along cloisters thick with shadow. Other Doom Eagles passed him by, leaving Tarikus alone with his thoughts. It was the nature of a Space Marine to be instilled with supreme self-belief, and like any other member of the Adeptus Astartes, Tarikus knew with all his heart that they were the strongest, the most dedicated, the most fearless warriors in the Emperor's arsenal.

Despite their arrogance and savagery, Tarikus had a grudging respect for the Flesh Tearers. They had weathered more than their share of misfortune and hardship; from the jungle hell of their homeworld, they numbered merely four full companies, and their only starship was an ancient hulk crowded with ill cared-for equipment, like the patchwork Razorback he'd seen earlier. They were Brother Marines, and Tarikus found the idea that members of the Legion Astartes would stoop to such pointless barbarity as preying on innocent civilians disgusting. It was his duty, he decided, not just to his Chapter and to the Merrons, but to the Flesh Tearers and to the Emperor, to end the circle of suspicion without delay.

'Tarikus.' The voice cut through his musings. He became aware of three figures standing around him in the darkness, their blood- and black-coloured armour blending into the night.

'Captain Gorn: I thought you were at the airstrip.'

'I have other matters to attend to.'

The sense of threat from the ruins rushed back to him. 'What of them?'

'It has come to my attention that certain… rumours are being circulated. This displeases me.'

Tarikus said nothing; although he could not see their faces, he could taste the familiar scent-trace of Noxx and one of his men from the Razorback.

Gorn continued: his voice coloured with annoyance. 'We have had our fill of this worthless sand pile, sergeant, and we wish to leave it behind. It would not go well for our departure to be delayed by needless hearsay. Do you understand?'

'I believe so, brother-captain.'

'Then I hope for your sake I will hear no more of this unworthy prattle.'

Without another word, they left him there, turning over Gorn's cryptic half-threat in his mind; but then another voice called his name, and this one was screaming it, crying and shrieking into the moonlit night.

TARIKUS FOUND DASSAR in a shuddering heap at the feet of Brother Mykilus, the Marine's face split with confusion over how he should deal with the wailing servant. Tarikus pulled him upright.

'What is wrong?'

Dassar's face was streaked with tears. 'My Lord Tarikus, I am undone! I came to you with the truth and now I have paid the price – they took them! They took my wife and my son!'

'He claims the Red abducted his family and dragged them into the sewers,' said Mykilus.

Tarikus's eyes narrowed. 'Summon Korica and Petius,' he told the Marine. 'Tell them to bring weapons for close-quarter combat.' As Mykilus did as he was ordered, Tarikus questioned Dassar. 'These tunnels, what do you know of them?'

'A web of sewers,' the man said between sobs, 'feeding to a central chasm. It was once an underground reservoir, but now it is barren.'

A lair, thought Tarikus. Like a trapdoor spider, the Red was hiding concealed in the stone tunnels – just as the sergeant had begun to suspect.

'Mira and my boy Seni, they'll be killed! Please, I beseech you, save their lives!'

Tarikus looked up as Mykilus returned with the others. 'I have heard enough. This ends tonight.'

Korica handed him a loaded bolt pistol, and the four Space Marines advanced into the gloom.

Mykilus used a shaped charge to blow open a rusted manhole cover in the plaza near the garrison, and with Korica on point, the quartet dropped down into the foetid runnels beneath.

'The stench – I have never encountered the like before!' Petius gasped.

'Like a breath from a slaughterhouse,' said Korica with a grunt.

'Hold your chatter!' Tarikus barked. 'Look sharp! We can only guess at what we are facing.' He glanced up and down the tunnel they stood in: it was a wide pipe, a main tributary or flood channel.

After a few hundred strides, Korica pointed toward a small branch tunnel. 'Sergeant, see here. I believe this is one of the vents that joins the main chamber.'

'Too narrow for us,' noted Petius.

From behind him, Tarikus heard Mykilus give a growl of frustration. 'The auspex senses something, but I cannot interpret the runes…'

The squad halted, the echoes of their footfalls dying away. Over the licking of the effluent around them, Tarikus strained to listen. Dimly, he was aware of an organic rustling sound, like matted fur on cobbles.

'Above–' began Korica, leaning back to look at the tunnel ceiling. Without warning, a dozen bulky black shadows detached themselves from the crumbling bricks and fell across Korica's upper torso. The sewer was suddenly filled with high-pitched squeals as dozens of rat-like vermin bit into the Marine's armour, acidic saliva

melting through the ceramite. Blinded, Korica squeezed
the trigger on his bolter and the gun crashed into life, a
fusillade of shells arcing from the muzzle as he twisted in
place. The bolts sparked off the walls in brilliant red ric-
ochets.

Tarikus leapt forward, shoving Petius aside as a round
whined off the tip of his shoulder plate; the Marine was
unhurt, but his Battle-Brother Mykilus reacted seconds
slower than the veteran Tarikus, taking hits in his chest
and thigh. Mykilus sagged, slipping down the curved
wall.

Brother Korica gave a bubbling scream; some of the rat-
things that swarmed over his chest plate had bored into
his armour and were scratching and tearing at him from
the inside. One of the rodents leapt at Tarikus, spitting
venom, and he caught it in mid-jump, crushing the animal in his fist. For a moment, it hissed and snapped at
him, and Tarikus saw the tell-tales signs of mutation and
corruption across its form. The tiny body bulged and
popped beneath his fingers like an overripe fruit.

Korica's bolter clicked empty and still the injured, mad-
dened Doom Eagle swatted at himself with the inert
weapon, desperately trying to pick off the darting, biting
shapes. Dark arterial blood ran in thick streams from the
joints in his armour.

Tarikus grabbed at Petius's weapon – a narrow-bore
hand flamer – where it had fallen and trained it on his
brother Marine; the rat-beast's eyes had glowed with the
same infernal hate that the sergeant had seen in the Traitors at Kript, and suddenly he had no doubt as to what
quarry they were tracking. Korica seemed to sense his
intentions and nodded his consent. Tarikus whispered a
litany under his breath and pressed down the trigger stud,
engulfing Korica and his myriad attackers in wreaths of
glowing orange flame. The verminous creatures hissed
and spat, catching ablaze and falling away from the
Marine's armour. Korica shrugged off the licking fires,
beating them out with his gloves, his breath coming in

harsh wheezes. The Marine's skin was bloodied, burnt
and cracked, but he lived.

'Thank you, brother-sergeant,' he coughed. 'Only the
flamer's kiss can dislodge these warp-spawned abber-
ants…'

'What were those creatures?' asked Petius.

'Mutants,' said Tarikus, handing back the flamer. 'The
twisted lackeys of Chaos.'

Behind them, Mykilus gave a hollow groan. Petius went
to his side. 'He's alive, but the bolter shells hit a primary
artery. The bleeding must be staunched or he will perish.'

'Do it,' Tarikus snarled, removing his helmet. With the
ease of hundreds of years of practice, the sergeant began
to divest himself of his armour.

'Sir, what are you doing?' Petius asked. 'You cannot
think to–'

'You said yourself, the channel is too small for one of
us. I must leave my armour here and venture on without
it.'

'Let me come with you,' grated Korica, ignoring his
injuries.

Tarikus shook his head. 'You are blinded and Mykilus
will be lost without aid. You must carry him to the surface. I will see this through to its ending.' The Marine
shrugged off his torso plates and stood, unadorned and
ready. 'Get Mykilus to safety and inform Captain Consultus of the situation.'

Petius nodded. 'As you command, sergeant. Terra protect you.'

Gripping the bolt pistol in his hand, Tarikus pushed on
into the narrow channel alone.

STARING BACK AT him from its breastplate was the twin-
headed eagle of the Imperium of Man.

The shock of recognition sent a thrill of adrenaline
through Tarikus; bare-chested and unarmed, he was
face-to-face with a fully armoured, crimson-clad Space
Marine, the unmistakable broad shoulders and the

fearsome mask of the helmet pressing down on him. The light from the flare tube began to gutter out in pops and splutters of greenish-white chemical fire, and as it did the foe let out an echoing cry that was half-pain, half-rage.

TARIKUS STABBED THE dying flare forward like a knife and connected with the red Marine's torso – but instead of blunting itself on the toughened ceramite exterior, the tube pierced the chest plate, flakes of metallic armour crumbling away under the impact. Like the fragment Brother Petius found, he realised. His surprise robbed him of the initiative, and the foe's hammer whistled through the foul air, catching Tarikus in the shoulder. The impact spun him about, and he stumbled, splashing through the muck in gouts of oily liquid. The sergeant's right arm went loose; the dislocated joint sang with pain, the edges of bone grinding together. Tarikus gave a bellow of anger as he dragged the limb back into place with a sickening crack. The hammer came out of the dimness at him once more, but this time Tarikus was ready and blocked it with a cross-handed parry. The slow, heavy weapon's path could not be quickly halted and it struck the wall, the head burying itself in the rotted bricks. The vague shape of the red Marine pulled impotently at the handle, spitting out wordless, hollow noises of frustration.

'Woe betide!' Brother Tarikus answered with a battle-roar and leapt at his enemy with a powerful kick that shattered the red Marine's greaves. The foe fell back, letting go of the hammer, and raised its hands in a poor approximation of a fighting stance. As he circled it, on some higher, analytical level, Tarikus's mind was marvelling at what he saw. What madness is this, he wondered? No Adeptus Astartes, not even the foul cohorts of the Traitor Legions would dare show such ineptness!

Tarikus saw an opening and took it, his fist striking his attacker's chest with such ferocity that the torso plate broke apart, crumbling like rotten pastry. The Imperial eagle sigil snapped under his knuckles, revealing itself as nothing more than painted glass. Tarikus reached inside the rent he'd made in the crimson armour and dug his sturdy fingers into the folds of flesh and clothing within. He felt thick blood ooze out around his wrist, heard a gasp of pain. The sergeant balled his free hand into a fist and struck the red Marine across the helmet; the blow landed with a hollow ringing collision. His muscles bunching, Tarikus hit out again with all his might and his backhand took the helm off his foe's head, arcing away to clatter against the walls.

Revealed within the armour was a pasty-skinned parody of a man, his face riven with blotches and his eyes sepulchral with hate. Across his brow was a livid brand: a grinning skull surrounded by an eight-pointed star. Exposed, he seemed pathetically small and weak, a faint shadow of Tarikus's rugged, broad form.

'Who are you?' Tarikus demanded, shaking him. 'Answer, you wretch!'

Above, the sergeant heard the cough of impact charges as the chamber roof gave way; stones crashed to the floor around him, but he did not spare them a glance.

'Talk, or I'll tear the truth from you!' His grip tightened, and the little man spat up thin, greenish-tinted blood.

When he finally spoke, it was in a fluid, gurgling murmur: 'Here come The Red, they stalk while you sleep. Here come The Red, your blood do they seek. Here come The Red, to your soul they lay claim, and you'll never be seen in sunlight again…'

The sergeant hesitated for a moment, then tore his hand from the little man's chest, ripping bone, lung and flesh out along with it. The ruined figure dropped away and sank into the torpid black water.

PETIUS FINISHED APPLYING the salve to a small wound on Tarikus's face and pronounced him healthy. His Space Marine physiology was already flushing the toxins from the sewer out of his system, and the salve would help it in the process. He watched as the Merrons brought up the caged ones from the chamber, as men and women greeted their families with tears; some joyful at finding those they loved still alive, some weeping as bloated, pallid corpses were hoisted to the surface. He noted with some small satisfaction that Dassar had been reunited with his wife and son; at least for the helot, the Emperor had moved through Tarikus this day to deliver him from his pain.

He rose to his feet as Captain Consultus approached, with Gorn and Noxx a step behind.

'Tarikus, you performed well. A citation may be in order.'

Gorn gave a reluctant nod of agreement. 'Perhaps so, brother-captain.'

'This is at an end, then?' he asked.

'It is,' said Consultus. 'When Petius returned to the garrison with news of what transpired, I asked Captain Gorn to lend us the arms of his Flesh Tearers.'

'It seemed a logical course of action,' noted Gorn.

Petius jerked a thumb at several impact craters nearby. 'We are storming the tunnels, flushing them out with flamers and plasma-fire. It is a nest of foulness and corruption down there.'

'The man,' Tarikus began. 'He wore our armour…'

'Not quite,' said Gorn, 'it was a well-crafted copy, but made from a poor ceramic compound. Not even strong enough to deflect a punch.'

'But it was similar enough to convince the Merrons.'

Consultus nodded his assent. 'He preyed on their fears to discredit the Flesh Tearers and the Adeptus Astartes.'

'To what purpose?' said Petius.

In reply, Noxx tossed a spherical white object at the youth, but Tarikus snatched it from the air before it reached him. It was a human skull, and etched into its bone were whorls and patterns of lines. The matrix of thin bands seemed to shimmer in the half-light, forming the shape of a many-angled star. 'Ask him,' said Noxx.

Gorn cocked his head and subvocalised a message into the comm-net. 'Our transports are approaching orbit. By your leave, brother-captain, if you have no further use for us, the Flesh Tearers would quit this troublesome world.'

'Thank you for your assistance, Brother Gorn,' said Consultus, offering his hand. 'Perhaps we will meet again under better circumstances?'

'Perhaps,' Gorn replied, returning the gesture. He gave Tarikus a wary nod and walked away. Noxx followed and did not look back.

The Doom Eagle sergeant watched them go in silence.

TARIKUS FOUND HIMSELF in the company of his captain once again a few days later, as he completed his prayers after early morning firing rites.

'Brother-captain,' he began, 'have the tunnels been cleansed?'

'The taint of evil has been purged,' Consultus replied.

'Were all the missing civilians accounted for?' Tarikus said after a moment.

Consultus gave him a neutral look. 'We only found live victims in the cavern where you killed the cultist, the Red. There were several caches of bodies scattered around the sewer complex.'

'They were all killed in the same manner?' he pressed.

'Not all,' said the captain. 'A handful were found with different wounds.'

'In what way?'

'It is of little consequence now, Tarikus, but if you must know, there were some that sported torn, ragged wounds from claws and teeth. From human teeth.'

Despite himself, the sergeant felt a shudder of cold run along his spine. 'The Red killed only by draining blood. If he was not responsible, then who was?'

'Who indeed?' said the Captain as he walked away.

Tarikus looked up into the sky, where the crimson night was fading into dawn; if he had an answer to that question, he kept it to himself.

HUNTER/PREY

Andy Hoare

GASPING FOR BREATH in the darkness, Neme Fortuna stifled a scream.

She felt the beast lunge towards her scant moments before its tremendous weight barrelled into her chest, its claws gripping her wrists and slicing into the flesh as she was slammed into the flagstone paving.

The beast's snarling face was right in her own, its animal breath huffing against her skin, saliva specking her cheek. It wore dull, grey armour, and a glint of light reflected in huge canine teeth as it opened its mouth to roar. She screamed in denial, the beast bellowed in fury, and for an instant her eyes locked with the two dark pits mere centimetres from her face, tiny, malevolent sparks of animal rage glowing crimson in the darkness before her.

She thrashed and wrestled and screamed, but the beast's claws sank into the raw flesh of her wrists, blood seeping through her sleeves and turning the stones beneath slick.

The beast reared, and Neme Fortuna knew with a stark clarity that the events of the previous twenty-four hours would lead to her death, here in the dark, on a cold stone floor on an Emperor-forsaken wasteland at the edge of hell.

INCENSE DRIFTED UPWARDS in a lazy spiral from the ornate censer set on the floor, its cloying scent permeating the room and turning the light from the dim glow-globe a cold blue.

Neme sat cross-legged and still before the censer, her shaven head lowered as she breathed the ritual incantations that would allow her to enter a state of meditation in which she could send her consciousness beyond the confines of her physical body. She breathed deeply, feeling the hot smoke fill her lungs. After a moment of warm light-headedness she began to perceive the room around her, to sense its dimensions and textures despite the fact that her eyes were closed in deep concentration.

Reaching beyond the boundaries of her chamber, the psyker allowed her spirit-self to drift on the zephyrs of consciousness gusting around the station. Down cramped, darkened corridors, hooded tech-priests of the Adeptus Mechanicus and shuffling acolytes of the Adeptus Astra Telepathica passed. She could sense their unease, for she felt it too, a tangible miasma permeating the very air, circulated by the millennia-old atmosphere conditioners. On instinct, she allowed her spirit-self to coast on the emotional slipstream of a trooper as he marched purposely towards the control centre of the Ormantep Listening Station.

The trooper, a member of the elite Kasrkin company that had been dispatched from Cadia to garrison the post, swung open the heavy blast door of the control centre and stepped into a scene of barely controlled mayhem. Tech-priests and acolytes crowded around cogitators and pict slates, some issuing orders, others hurrying to carry them out. Some debated with fellows while others raised voices in denial. Still more knelt in prayer to the God-Emperor of Mankind, while others sat with head in hands.

Into this scene Neme followed the trooper, who strode calmly amidst the turmoil to stand at attention before a man who was clearly his superior. The trooper saluted, handed the officer a data-slate, and was dismissed.

The officer surveyed the room, his rugged, noble features showing barely contained disdain at the lack of discipline surrounding him. He lifted the slate, his piercing eyes speed-reading the information displayed on its glowing pict screen. He turned, issuing an order to an acolyte, though Neme's spirit-self could make out no more than a ghostly echo as he spoke.

The acolyte hurried to a cogitator bank, his hands speeding over the dials and levers. A massive display at the centre of the chamber came to life, grainy static splashed across its surface. The image resolved into a view of the barren oxide wastes of Ormantep: low, jagged hills serrated the horizon.

The officer barked an order, and the acolyte adjusted the controls. A crosshair appeared in the centre of the screen, and the scene zoomed in on a patch of sky, a numeric counter set in the corner of the target icon counting up the magnification.

Even at maximum zoom the picture was barely discernable, yet Neme could make out a trio of white contrails streaking across the night sky towards the distant mountains.

She concentrated, allowing her spirit to lift. Up through the vaulted ceiling of the control chamber, through dark access ways and service ducts, through plates of armaplas sheathing and out into the night. The domed form of the control centre squatted on the barren surface below, secondary structures adjoining it at seemingly random points. She drifted higher, imagining herself buffeted by high altitude winds that her spirit-self had no way of perceiving. Turning her sight on the distant horizon, she sped in the direction she had been shown by the pict.

Several kilometres out into the oxide wastes, Neme caught sight of the streaks of fire slashing across the dark sky. The three lights passed across the livid purple stain that was the distant, though still too-close edge of the Ocularis Terribus, the Eye of Terror, the cosmic-scale rent in the fabric of reality through which the most dreaded of humanity's foes had fled ten thousand years before, and through which no sane man should pass. Steeling herself, Neme sped on, until she saw a distant cloud billow up from the base of an ancient crater.

In her chamber, Neme Fortuna gasped as her spirit-self returned to her body. She bent double, dry retching as a wave of nausea hit. She had seen them. Massively armoured warriors in black and gold, disembarking from dread engines of daemon-spawned technology.

Intruders had made planetfall on Ormantep.

'IS THERE ANY danger of you actually finishing today, deacon?'

'Just gimme a sec, will ya? I'm almost done.'

'Shift ended ten minutes ago. Get a move on or we're off without ya.'

Guido Sol hefted the power pack of his drill rig as he exited the mine-shaft. His bulky pressure suit was encrusted with the dust and grime of another fruitless, ten-hour shift at the face. Deacon, his partner in this fool's errand of a contract, emerged a moment later, gloved hand raised to shield his visored face from the glare of the warp-spawned energies of the Ocularis raging in the night sky above.

While Deacon struggled with his power packs and feed-lines, Sol strode over to the ledge of the cliff into which the mine was sunk. The desolate plains stretched for kilometres below him, the rust-coloured deposits of eons tinged a sickly violet by the glow of the Eye of Terror. A low wind swept across the barrens, stirring eddies of dust that skimmed off towards the distant horizon.

'I hate this place.'

Sol and his crew were indentured workers, miners shipped in from off-world to work the mines of

Ormantep for what had seemed, at the time they had signed up, a tidy profit. But on their arrival they had found themselves indebted to their Adeptus Mechanicus employers for the cost of the interstellar journey, and that cost had amounted to the equivalent of a lifetime in service to the Adeptus overseers.

Finally, Deacon was ready, and Sol set off towards their crawler where the rest of the miners waited. But the other man had stopped again, and was staring up into the sky, his squinting eyes visible through the plastic shield of his pressure hood.

'For the Emperor's mercy, what now?'

Deacon pointed, and Sol turned. As he did so a super-heated mass of screaming metal thundered overhead, throwing both men to the ground with the force of its backwash. Sol felt the rubber of his pressure suit melting into his back and he fought to remain conscious as the mountainside was churned with dust and flying rock.

Sol raised his head, his ears ringing with the force of the object's passage. As the tumult of its passing settled, he could make out the form of his companion rising from the ground and dusting himself off. Standing up, he was afforded a view of a blossoming mushroom cloud at the base of an unnamed crater, not half a kilometre distant.

'Ya reckon we should check it out?' Deacon asked, uncertain.

'Might be a claim in it, Deac. Split two ways we might be able pay off the techs and ship outta here, I guess.'

'Split two ways, Sol?' said Deacon, a wry grin touching his lips as realisation dawned.

'Aye, vox down to the crew. Tell 'em to head back without us.'

THE ADEPTUS ASTRA Telepathica acolyte led Captain Vrorst into the vaulted chamber of the astropathic choir. Neme hurried to keep up with the Kasrkin officer. He halted abruptly in the centre, causing the psyker to stumble as she barely avoided colliding into his back.

The acolyte approached a shadowed niche at the head of the dimly lit chamber, and bowed before his master, Astropath Primus Grenski, who reclined amidst a mass of purity sealed pipes and cables on a spartan couch within. Grenski did not acknowledge the younger adept, as he was deep within the trance that would allow him to transmit his thoughts light years across the gulf of interstellar space, to commune with his peers on a thousand other worlds.

Captain Vrorst surveyed the chamber, obviously impatient with such matters. He preferred to leave this sort of thing to Fortuna, the sanctioned psyker attached to his command. Neme could sense he was ill at ease in the company of those who did not serve the Emperor as he did, with cold logic and cold steel.

'What's the problem, adept? Why have you interrupted my sweep?' Vrorst had been busy overseeing the station's security in the aftermath of the sighting of the intrusion, and Fortuna's subsequent report of her viewing trance.

'My master has been within the auto-séance for three hours now, captain. He should have established contact with another terminus long ago. His life signs indicate he has not, and that he is locked within his trance. Those signs have started to fluctuate wildly.'

'So?' asked Vrorst, his ignorance at the adept's words plain.

'He means,' interrupted Neme, as the acolyte stumbled over an explanation, 'that something out there is blocking him, stopping him from getting the message out that the intruders are here.'

'Well, there's no way to be sure of that.' The acolyte glanced at her lapel. 'Lieutenant.'

Neme scanned the chamber, wrapping her arms around herself against the cold. Another seven niches were arrayed around the room, an astropath reclining within each one. Her breath fogged as she spoke.

'No? Well something isn't right, and we all know that an intrusion this close to the Gate is bad news.'

'I can assure you, lieutenant, that everything is…'

An alarm blared from a brass horn above Adept Grenski's niche, and every astropath in the choir suddenly sat bolt upright before collapsing back down within their couches. A look of horrified disgust crossed the captain's face, but Neme was looking at the reader mounted next to Grenski's niche. A series of green lines crossed the display, each zigzagging wildly.

The adept was clearly on the verge of panic, and Vrorst was barking an order to the Kasrkin in the lobby without. Neme's eyes left the reader and settled on the face of the astropath. She shivered, and realized abruptly that it was not nerves turning her skin to goose flesh, but the temperature. It was falling rapidly.

A drop of blood appeared at Grenski's nostril. Something stabbed into Neme's mind, a spike of indescribable agony at the centre of her brain that withdrew as suddenly as it had appeared, sending her crashing to her knees, clutching her head in her hands.

The acolyte was praying, and Neme opened her watering eyes to see that the astropath's face was covered in a thin skein of ice. She turned her head, seeing the occupants of the other niches were similarly affected. She tried to stand, but her knees were stuck fast to the frost glazing the paved floor.

Two Kasrkin rushed into the room and grabbed Neme under her armpits, dragging her back towards the chamber door.

The acolyte collapsed at his master's feet and let out a piteous wail, the sound Neme imagined a lost soul might voice as it writhed in the flames of purgatory. The last thing she saw as she was pulled from the choir chamber was steady streams of blood from every astropath's nose, freezing, even as they poured, to shatter into a thousand ruby shards as they hit the cold stone floor.

* * *

SOL RAISED HIS head over the rock to get a clear view of the base of the crater. Glimpsing movement below, he ducked back down as Deacon reached the top of the path and collapsed, out of breath, beside him.

'Whadya see, Sol?'

The miner raised his hand to silence him, and edged around the base of the rock. Less than fifty metres below he could make out three towering metal forms, mechanical claws sunk into the hard ground, with strange symbols etched on every surface. Large figures moved around them. Sol had never seen suits the like of which they were wearing. The machines were moving, and Sol's eyes widened in disbelief as he realized their claws were digging down into the earth with an insect-like scurrying motion that he had never seen a machine do before.

'Now that's some rig,' whispered Sol, anger passing over his features at the prospect of another crew working his claim.

'That ain't no rig, Sol. I don't for the life of me know what it is, but I'm tellin' ya, that ain't no rig I ever seen.' Deacon was leaning out over the rock face, and the pair saw the three machines sink entirely beneath the dusty ground as the figures below dispersed.

'Ok, ok. We gotta think this through,' said Sol. The thought that perhaps the intruders were not merely competing prospectors, but something far worse, caused him to reconsider the wisdom of his decision to send the crawler home without them.

'Right, I got a plan...'

A single shot rang out from scant metres behind them. Sol spun, only to be confronted by a giant in black and gold armour standing over him. Edging back against the rock, he glanced to his side at Deacon. The other miner was spread-eagled, the back of his hood a ragged mess and a fan of blood and bone spattered across the boulder.

The black-armoured warrior swung his aim across, and Sol found himself staring down the barrel of the pistol.

'Damn,' cursed Sol. The harsh report of the bolt pistol echoed off the sides of the cliff face and rolled out over the barren wastes as the Black Legionnaire pulled the trigger.

CAPTAIN VRORST STOOD at the centre of the control chamber, hands clasped behind his back. Before him, a bank of pict-screens lined the wall, each manned by a Cadian staff officer. Each viewer relayed the scene from a surveyor; some set atop the armoured towers of the listening station, others mounted on remote pylons several kilometres out into the wastes.

Seven of the viewers had gone off-line in the last twenty-nine minutes.

An ensign, turned and beckoned to his captain. 'Sir, squad three reports Sector Epsilon clear. The surveyor shows no sign of interference.'

Vrorst grunted and the officer returned to his vigil, relaying the order to the squad to move on to Sector Gamma. Picking out surveyor Epsilon Seven from the bank of screens, Vrorst could make out the men of squad three as they prepared to depart. They were deployed in textbook fashion: the perimeter secured and a two-man detail investigating the survey unit. The squad leader was Sergeant Heska, a man who had served under Vrorst for the best part of two years. If they got through whatever was headed their way, thought Vrorst, he was due a promotion.

'Tell Heska to move his men on,' Vrorst ordered, turning as Lieutenant Fortuna appeared at his side.

'Wait,' Neme called, and the staffer turned, looking to his superior for confirmation.

Irritation crossed Vrorst's face as he turned to look down at the psyker. 'Lieutenant Fortuna, either leave my command centre, or hold your tongue!' Silence descended and none dared turn to watch.

Fortuna raised her flushed face to meet the captain's steely glare. She was much shorter than the veteran officer, and her voice trembled as she replied.

'Captain, please listen to me. I'm schooled in these matters. Something's wrong out there, I know it.'

Vrorst turned and gestured at the viewers. 'Of course something's wrong, Fortuna.'

'Surveyor Gamma Twelve has just gone off-line, sir,' the ensign said, confirming Vrorst's statement.

'I can see, ensign. Put me through to Sergeant Heska, right now.'

The ensign's hands moved over a series of dials and switches, and he spoke quietly into his vox set. 'On the vox, sir,' he eventually replied.

Addressing Sergeant Heska, Vrorst spoke clearly, the tone of an experienced leader of men ringing clear in his voice. 'Heska? Listen to me and follow my orders to the letter. Squad nine is holding station at Gamma Three. I want you to fall back and regroup with Klorin's squad. It's only half a kilometre due west of your position. Confirm.'

Static burbled from the vox horn for a moment, before Heska's voice cut through amidst a storm of interference. 'Confirmed, captain, moving out now.'

'Tell him to hurry. Something's close.' Neme stood beside Vrorst, her expression betraying uncertainty warring with the determination to make him appreciate the danger she sensed was near. Vrorst bit back a caustic reply, instead ordering a staffer to call up the view from surveyor Gamma Three.

The picture appeared on the large screen in the centre of a wall. The scene was one of controlled, drill ground efficiency as squad nine took position in what little cover was afforded by the scattered boulders and low defiles out in the wastes. The minutes stretched out, punctuated by a staffer confirming Heska's position and status. Each time a curt, 'no contact,' was the reply.

After thirty-three minutes, the staff officer drew Vrorst's attention to the main screen. A dust blizzard was closing in on squad nine's position, reducing visibility to less than twenty metres. Another five minutes passed, and a silhouette emerged from the storm. The men of squad nine raised their hellguns at the figure, and the challenge came loud over the main vox.

'Identify. Arcadia.'

'Arcadia est,' came the swift and correct reply.

Sergeant Klorin stepped out from cover to shake the hand of his comrade, Sergeant Heska, while the next man followed in. Neme's indrawn gasp caused every head in the chamber to turn towards her.

'Tell him...'

Sergeant Heska tumbled forward against Klorin as his chest exploded. Klorin must have assumed his friend had stumbled, and bent down to lend a hand. The movement saved his life, as a fusillade of bolter fire erupted from the storm, pinning the Kasrkin of squad nine behind cover. Klorin, reading the situation, dragged Heska's limp form into the cover of a low rock, bellowing orders to his men.

Vrorst stepped forward, addressing a tech-priest hovering near the cogitator banks. 'Adept, I need that surveyor set to read the body heat of whoever's assaulting my men. Can you do it?' The tech-priest nodded and began a recitation of the Canticle Machina over the surveyor bank.

Turning to a staff officer, the captain barked his next order. 'Ensign, I want a Valkyrie out there right now. Those men must be evacuated immediately.'

'But, sir,' the staffer began to protest, 'the storm will make–'

'Don't give me excuses, damn it. Just do it!'

The scene on the main screen switched to a kaleido-scopic riot of colour as the tech-priest petitioned the machine's spirit to relay an image based on thermo graphic readings. The colours resolved into solid masses, the cold air of the dust storm visible as swirling, deep blue vortices and the forms of the Kasrkin as distinct, red shapes. The surveyor altered its focus, seeking to penetrate the veil of howling dust that obscured the attackers.

A score of orange forms emerged from the blue, the heat issued from them so intense the surveyor could not resolve their exact shapes beyond this formless mass. Twin stars of bright white sat at the shoulder of each figure, and further strobes of glaring light indicated muzzle flashes as bolters spat high velocity explosive rounds into the Kasrkin position. A clutch of fading red smears indicated that the men of Heska's squad had fallen, cut down from behind before they could reach the dubious safety of squad nine's position.

Vrorst addressed the remaining squad leader with an authoritative calm. 'Klorin. I have a Valkyrie closing on your position, ETA...' He glanced at the tactical reader, 'ETA three minutes thirty. Until then you have some soldiering to do.'

Sergeant Klorin's voice came across the vox, barely audible above the chatter of bolter shells, the crack of hellguns and the howl of the dust storm. 'Confirmed, sir. We'll hold them, pending extraction.'

'You'll do as I say, sergeant, or there will be no extraction. Now listen to me...'

Captain Vrorst relayed a series of instructions to the squad leader, specifying targets that the Kasrkin could not acquire through the dust, but that he could read clearly on the thermographic surveyor. Over the next minute, three of Klorin's men fell to bolter fire, before Vrorst ordered the men to fall back to a small ravine they could defend should the position be attacked frontally. Thirty-eight seconds later one of the attackers fell to the disciplined fire of the remaining defenders, and a brief cheer filled the control chamber before a stern look from Vrorst silenced the staff. Another ten seconds, and the attackers had moved around to outflank the Kasrkin. Vrorst redirected Klorin's squad to fire on the new threat, and another attacker fell.

Another twenty seconds, and only three of the squad remained. Massive forms emerged from the dust, and the Kasrkin were firing at will.

Vrorst turned to a staffer, grim resolution etched across his features. 'Recall the Valkyrie.'

Neme turned on him. 'You can't! You've got to get them out of there. You can't just let them die without…'

Vrorst met her gaze and indicated the screen. The last of the Kasrkin had fallen, and the attackers had taken the position.

Dejected, the psyker made to leave the chamber, but turned once more to speak.

'You knew they didn't have a hope, didn't you?'

'Of course I knew, lieutenant. But those men were Cadians, they were Kasrkin. They deserved nothing less than a warrior's death. And that's what I gave them.'

OVER THE COURSE of the next six hours, Captain Vrorst supervised the preparations for the attack he was now certain would come. Though the base was well defended, he made certain every conceivable eventuality was covered, above and beyond that which the layered defence hardware and the elite of the Cadian military were trained for. Every entrance to the listening post was welded shut, booby trapped with frag grenades and guarded by a squad of Kasrkin. Flak board barricades were erected across every corridor, and heavy weapon positions placed at each intersection. Every last man of the company knew his role in the defence, and manned his post with the determination the Cadians, and in particular, the elite Kasrkin, were famous across the Imperium for.

Plans were laid, fire solutions calculated and rally points identified. If a position should collapse, the defenders would fall back to the next, under covering fire from the men occupying it. The final stand would be made at the central keep, the chamber of the astropathic choir. If that should fall, then there would be no further point in a fighting withdrawal, for all would be lost.

Throughout this period, Neme meditated. She had prayed to the Emperor, so many light years away on distant Terra, that she would not fail in her duty to Him. She had prayed that Astropath Primus Grenski, the sole survivor of the events in the astropathic chamber, would awake from his deathbed and somehow summon the strength to get a warning to Cadia, to anybody, to warn of the attack. She prayed that, should the attack come and Vrorst's defences fall, the Emperor would lend her strength to face her death in the manner the teachings of the Cadian progeniums proscribed: on her feet and with her wounds to the fore.

In the apothacarium, Astropath Primus Grenski awoke from feverish dreams of worlds in flames and the diabolic hordes of the Arch Enemy vomiting from the hellmouth of the Cadian Gate. He was too weak to call out. Sensing his death was near, he attempted once more to broadcast an astrotelepathic plea for aid. But another mind sensed his own, and unleashed the full extent of its powers against his frail, battered psyche. As life ebbed from his ancient frame, Grenski consoled himself that he had tried, though whether he had succeeded, he would never know.

THE FIRST WARNING of the attack came when the power cut out across the complex. The bank of surveyor screens went black in a second, and the consoles died. The omnipresent background vox-chatter fell silent. Standing in the centre of the command chamber, Neme found her world plunged into disorientating darkness.

There was a moment of preternatural still and then a harsh white beam cut through the gloom, dazzling her. An instant later more beams illuminated the chamber. With a sigh of relief, Neme realized that the Kasrkin guards had activated the torches slung under the barrels of their hellguns.

A beam swung across the chamber, to pick out Captain Vrorst. 'Get that light out of my face, trooper!' he ordered testily. 'Adept, where are the back-ups?'

A hooded adept of the Machine God, visible only as a bent form in a shadowed corner of the chamber, began a low chant as he prised open a purity-sealed access panel. He paused in his work long enough to issue a sibilant hiss of annoyance, before striking an illuminated rune he had uncovered amidst the innards of the machinery.

A bass thrum, felt deep in the gut rather than heard with the ear, filled the room. The drone soared painfully up the scale until it was an ultrasonic squeal, beyond the range of human hearing. An instant later, a heavy jolt shook the chamber and a deep red illumination grew in brightness from emergency glow-globes, casting a hellish radiance across the occupants as the reassuring hum of the back-up generator settled into the background.

The surveyor screens spluttered back to life, and the staff officers manning their posts began the rituals necessary to bring their consoles back on-line. Vrorst knew from experience that he would be tactically blind until his command centre was fully operational again, but that was one of the reasons the Cadians, along with other Imperial Guard regiments, employed sanctioned psykers.

'Lieutenant Fortuna, if you'd be so kind?'

Neme started, realizing the captain had addressed her. 'Sir?'

'Lieutenant, you may have noticed that we've just lost all command and control capability short of the squad-level vox. I have no idea what has caused the power shut down, and I have no way of finding out until the security net is back up. If you wouldn't mind, and if you're not too busy, perhaps you could find the time to use those vaunted powers of yours to find out what the hell is going on?'

Neme resolved to rise above Vrorst's sarcasm. Though he was her commanding officer by dint of rank, she answered to the officio psykana back on Cadia, and would no longer be cowed by his bearing. She stood firm, lifted her head in defiance, and faced the captain.

'I'll need absolute silence,' she said.

Vrorst merely nodded and stalked off to the surveyor stations to hurry up their restarting. Neme watched him for a moment, reading the emotions radiating from him in palpable waves. She was a psyker, and well accustomed to the distaste, or outright hostility, most people felt towards her kind. It was often only in the service of the Guard that a sanctioned psyker could earn respite from the distrust of others and find a productive outlet for their powers. Ironically, a life of isolation or persecution was often violently curtailed upon the battlefields of the Cadian Gate, as many a psyker would lay down their lives in defence of those who hated them.

Neme closed her eyes and, taking a deep breath, allowed her extrasensory powers to absorb the emotions of those around her. She filtered out the tension in the command chamber, and cast her psychic net further afield. One sector at a time, she scanned the perimeter of the complex, seeking out thoughts that did not belong to the defenders. At the edge of her inner-hearing, she caught an echoing whisper, like the sound of malicious plotting in the nave of an empty cathedral. Bracing herself, she homed in, a feeling of utter menace welling up inside her. Suddenly she realised the nature of the threat and severed the psychic link.

She broke the contact a moment too late. An explosion of pain erupted behind her eyes, the psychic backlash throwing her several metres across the chamber. She caught a railing and braced herself as a second wave hit, fighting with all her resolve against the white-hot lance of another's psyche. She drew strength from years of conditioning, calling upon deep reserves of her own power. With a tremendous effort of will, she forced the probing claws of agony from her mind, exorcising the other's intrusion with a primal scream of denial.

Gasping for breath, she shouted at Vrorst, 'Sector twelve!' before slumping to the floor in exhaustion.

A THUNDEROUS EXPLOSION rocked the station, shaking the command chamber and setting off wailing alarms.

The squad level vox burst into life and a staff officer called to Vrorst over the din, 'Sir, sector twelve is under fire, reporting unidentified contacts assaulting their position.'

'Command group, with me. That means you too, Fortuna. On your feet. Squads seven and twelve form up, one and two, get this chamber secure and stay alert.'

The Kasrkin moved into position without hesitation, and Vrorst's command squad was at his side in an instant. A sergeant ushered Neme foward, along with a vox-operator, a medic and two troopers carrying flamers.

The guards stationed at the entrance to the command chamber hauled open the massive blast doors, and Vrorst led his men out into the emergency-lit passage. Jogging down the corridor, the troopers of squad seven took the point, hellguns levelled and covering every angle from which an attacker might appear. The point man reached a bulkhead door that led to the loading bays, and the group covered the trooper as he turned the locking wheel.

The door ground aside, revealing a scene of desperate combat. A squad of Kasrkin poured a fusillade of hellgun fire the length of the loading bay from behind a flakboard barricade. At the far end, a score of two and a half metre tall giants were advancing, halting periodically to fire off explosive bolter rounds that tore great chunks from the defenders' cover.

Vrorst took position at the barricade, his men following his example. 'On my mark… fire!'

As the attackers advanced, thirty hellguns opened fire as one. Though not individually as powerful as a bolter, massed hellgun fire is capable of overwhelming most foes, no matter how well armoured they may be. The nearest attacker faltered, great chunks of his breast plate disintegrating as the volley hammered home. The armour fused and bubbled, a single bright las-round exploited the weakness opened up, and speared through the figure's torso to erupt from its back in a shower of sparks. The giant fell. It did not bleed, for its wounds were instantly cauterised.

Vrorst ordered a second volley, and this time three more of the armoured behemoths fell. The advance slowed, and one of the attackers sought cover in a side corridor rather than risk another fusillade. The defenders took a collective breath, but kept up their surveillance of the bay.

Vrorst was proud of every one of his men, knowing that a less well-disciplined unit than the Kasrkin would erupt in cheers at this stage, creating a moment of vulnerability an experienced enemy could exploit.

'Sir?' Vrorst's vox-operator crawled to his side, a portable scanner held before him. 'They're moving down corridor delta seven, sir, I think they've overridden the lock-out. They'll be on us in thirty seconds.'

'Fall back by squads, to rally point secondus delta seven. Go!' Vrorst yelled as he ushered the first of the Kasrkin past.

With drilled proficiency, each squad withdrew from the barricade, covering one another as they stepped down. Vrorst was the last to quit the loading bay, and the clang as he slammed the blast door shut rang down the corridor as he jogged after his men.

An explosion tore into the head of the file, ripping apart the point men. The corridor was instantly choked with reeking smoke and the screams of the wounded. A trooper tumbled out of the turmoil, one arm hanging limp and blasted at his side, while the other fired his hellgun into the darkness behind. The medic ran to his side to usher him to safety as more Kasrkin knelt and poured suppressive fire into the roiling smoke. The vox-operator was at Vrorst's side, trying all he could to get a fix on the situation.

'My set's wasted, sir. I can't get a clear reading.'

Vrorst cast his gaze around, and located Neme. 'Can you tell what's going on up there, lieutenant?' Though visibly shaken, the psyker nodded, and after a moment of stillness shook her head.

'I can't, sir, someone's–'

A hail of explosive bolts scythed from the smoke, followed a moment later by the silhouette of a massive, bulky form. The figure was revealed as its passing caused the smoke to part: a giant of a man in baroque power armour, the evil of millennia writ large across his helmeted visage. He stooped and with one hand choked the life from a nearby Kasrkin, whilst putting a bolt round into the throat of another, a fountain of arterial blood, that looked like black tar in the red emergency lighting, sprayed across the wall.

In Vrorst's long career he had never seen such a foe, but there was no doubt in his mind now as to the identity of the attackers: Traitor Marines of the Black Legion, the praetorians of Warmaster Horus himself, the Arch Traitor. Seeing his men being slaughtered where they stood, and judging that they were on the verge of being overwhelmed, he bellowed the order to retreat to the command chamber.

'No, wait,' stammered Neme. 'Not the command centre, there's something... someone... the Star Chamber! We've got to get the astropathic choir.'

Rounding on Neme, the captain was silenced by the certainty in her expression. His command was falling apart and he was expected to trust psyker witchery? Cursing the vagaries of fate, he rescinded his order, instructing the squad leaders to head for the Star Chamber instead.

The Kasrkin fought a fighting withdrawal down the length of corridor and past a bulkhead door that was blown open by a thundering blast almost as soon as it was sealed behind them.

The Black Legion pursued relentlessly, the Kasrkin unable to bring their own weapons to bear in any meaningful way in the confines of the passageways. Men fell screaming, and Vrorst took a bloody wound to the shoulder from a ricocheting bolt as they made for the final junction before the Star Chamber. Rounding a corner, they found themselves running towards a hastily erected barricade across the chamber entrance, and threw themselves over it as reaching arms dragged stragglers to safety.

Vrorst took in his command. Less than a score of men had survived, and his vox-operator and medic were missing. Taking position with the barricade's defenders, the remaining Kasrkin prepared to sell their lives dearly at this, the last rally point.

The Black Legion gave chase, emerging into the junction before the Star Chamber and a dozen, towering men spreading out as they raised their bolters. At their head was a figure from a nightmare, his armour wreathed in arcane sigils, black robes billowing behind him. Cold blue electrical discharges wreathed his hand as he gestured towards the defenders.

None behind the barricade knew the tongue in which the sorcerer spoke, but all felt the meaning behind his dark words deep within themselves. Here was a follower of the Ruinous Powers, and he intended to offer every soul in the complex to his corrupt masters.

NEME FORCED THE sorcerer's incantation from her mind, attempting to gather her strength for one last stand against the impossible odds facing them. But her thoughts were interrupted by a new presence, a shift in the ebb and flow of the powers raging around her. She tilted her head as if straining to discern a single whisper above a thunderous chorus. What was it she could hear?

THE BLACK LEGIONNAIRES opened fire, a storm of bolts punching through the flakboard barricade and cutting men down in bloody swathes. The Kasrkin returned fire, though for every las-blast they unleashed ten bolt rounds were returned.

The Black Legionnaires were almost on the barricade when a piercing sound cut through the din of battle and the haze of gun smoke. A mournful howl, low and feral echoed down the corridors.

The roaring of the Black Legionnaires' bolters fell silent, and the sorcerer's blasphemous utterances caught in his throat. Another howl split the air mere metres behind the Traitor Marines. They paused, casting uncertain glances into the shadows.

Neme raised her head above the barricade in time to see a Black Legionnaire snatched from behind and dragged into the dark. A bestial snarl grew to a savage outburst of rage and the sound of splitting ceramite armour rang from the walls.

The Traitor Marines began firing into the shadows around them, emptying entire magazines at targets none of the defenders could see. Taking advantage of the distraction, Vrorst led his men back into the Star Chamber, and the massive, embossed doors slammed together as the last man stumbled through.

The sounds of battle increased to fever pitch on the other side of the portal, screams of rage and pain muffled by the barrier. Then silence for a moment, broken an instant later by the doors exploding inward.

The Black Legion sorcerer stood framed in the doorway, arcs of blue lightning creeping from his hands and along the bulkhead. He scanned the chamber, his visored gaze sweeping the survivors until it came to rest upon the form of Neme Fortuna. She sensed his recognition, for he knew she was a pysker, the last person with any hope of calling for outside aid. As he strode towards her, Captain Vrorst drew his chainsword and threw himself at the Traitor, only to be batted aside with contemptuous ease with a single back handed stroke. Vrorst flew across the chamber, slamming into the stone wall with a sickening crunch of splintering bone.

The sorcerer advanced on the defenceless psyker, more Black Legionnaires flanking him. The last of the Kasrkin made to intercept them, but were cut down by bolt rounds or hacked apart by screeching chainswords. The reek of gun smoke and freshly spilled blood assaulted Neme's senses, as she pulled herself upright, determined at least to face her death on her feet.

As she straightened, back to the cold wall, a Black Legionnaire screamed in pain and rage, his back arching and his arms spread wide. His bolter clattered to the floor, as a white hot light speared from his eyes and mouth. The point of a sword, afire with pristine energy burst through his chest plate, transfixing him for an instant before it was withdrawn, sending the Traitor's blasted body crashing to the ground.

Another man stepped through the entrance, fully a match for the Black Legionnaires in bulk and height. But in stature the similarity ended, for this mighty warrior wore dark grey armour, adorned with a panoply of pelts, totems and fetishes. Mounted over his bald head was a hood of intricate crystalline nodes that formed a halo of psychic bale-fire around him. Neme was overwhelmed by the power emanating from him, and knew that here was a master of the pysker's craft, infinitely more accomplished than she could possibly aspire to become.

The Black Legion sorcerer turned, a low hiss sounding from the mouthpiece of his helmet. Issuing a guttural incantation, he pointed at the chamber entrance, and a violet-hued barrier of warp-spawned power sealed it so that none could interfere. He took a step back, clearly making room for the clash he knew would ensue. As dulled sounds of battle emanated from beyond the barrier, the warrior stepped forward, the glow from his crackling hood becoming more intense. He raised his sword, the sorcerer raised his staff, and the two lunged at precisely the same instant.

The warrior-mystic was faster, deflecting the Traitor's weapon with a back-handed parry. Stepping inside his opponent's guard, he brought his knee up hard, slamming it into the sorcerer's stomach. The Legionnaire doubled over, but cart-wheeled his staff up behind him as he did so, driving it into the warrior's chest armour. The newcomer staggered as arcane fire flickered across his body, a mighty crack in the ceramite of his breastplate evidence of the sorcerer's strength.

Indistinct shadows appeared at the entrance, mighty claws raking at the mystical barrier.

Putting space between them, both combatants stepped back. Neme could sense the build up of arcane energies.

Pure white light danced across the warrior's blade, while a black nimbus appeared before the Traitor. Both men stood immobile as the energies built, accompanied by a roar of psychic feedback that caused Neme to drop to her knees, her hands clamped over her ears.

As one, both combatants unleashed their pent up energies, which jumped the centre of the chamber in a heart beat and thundered into the other caster. Both were thrown sprawling to the floor, and through the play of sorcerous powers Neme saw that the warrior-mystic was grievously wounded, a terrible gash running along one side of his head and blood seeping from the crack in his chest.

The warp-barrier was assailed by frenzied shapes throwing themselves against it, accompanied by a savage roar of anger and pain.

The Traitor gained his feet and stood, unsteadily at first, but then with an arrogant swagger as he crossed to the fallen warrior. The energies playing around his hood spat and sputtered, the pure light of his force sword fading, to be replaced with the gleam of ordinary steel. The sorcerer raised his staff high above his head with both hands.

Neme saw with absolute clarity that she could not allow this to happen. In the infinite chasm between one moment in time and the next she drew every last shred of energy she possessed, drawing so deep on reserves of psychic power that she could feel the creatures of the warp scratching at her soul as she channelled the very stuff of their realm through her flesh.

She screamed as her body became a vessel for a tidal wave of arcing energies, unleashing it in a mighty, uncontrollable burst at the Black Legion sorcerer. The force of her attack sent him reeling, an upraised hand attempting to repel the lightning that enveloped him. Caught up in the blizzard, the sorcerer never saw the sweeping blow of the warrior-mystic's sword that clove him in two from the crest of his helm to his groin in one mighty downward slash.

* * *

NEME FOUGHT TO hang on to the last shreds of conscious-ness. Through eyes that refused to focus she saw the warp-barrier blink out of existence, and a creature from nightmare leap through the Star Chamber entrance. It lunged at her, pinning her to the ground, animal jaws snapping in her face as its claws raked the flesh of her forearms.

A SINGLE WORD in an unfamiliar tongue cut through the snarling, and the beast was gone. Neme opened her eyes to see the back of the warrior as he stalked from the chamber, a loping creature with wolf-like features wear-ing the mangled remains of tarnished dark grey armour, at his side.

'Wait...' she said. He paused, silhouetted in the fires raging in the passage beyond. 'Who are...'

The warrior held up a hand and uttered words Neme could not understand, before reforming the sentence in a tongue he had clearly not used in many years.

'Who I am is immaterial, girl. That I was here is all that matters. We leave now to continue the hunt, for the Great Betrayer is abroad once more.'

A massed, doleful howling echoed down the corpse-strewn passages of the Ormantep Listening Station.

'Wait!' she called again.

But the stranger was gone.

THE BEGUILING

Sandy Mitchell

NIGHT AND THE rain had both been falling for some time and I'd been getting steadily colder, wetter and more hacked off since the middle of the afternoon before we saw the light, glimmering faintly through the trees which bordered the road. The two gunners in the back of the Salamander with me hadn't helped my darkening mood either; they were fresh out from Valhalla, had never seen rain before, and found the 'liquid snow' a fascinating novelty which they discussed at inordinate length and with increasingly inanity.

To add insult to injury they had an ice-worlder's indifference to low temperatures, chattering about how warm it was, while I huddled into my greatcoat and shivered. The only upside to their presence was their transparent awe at being in the company of the famous Commissar Cain, whose heroism and concern for his men was fast becoming legendary.

Legendary, that is, in the literal sense of being both widely believed and completely without foundation.

Since my attempt to save my own miserable skin by deserting in the face of a tyranid horde on Desolatia had backfired spectacularly, leaving me the inadvertant hero of the hour, my undeserved reputation had continued to grow like tanglevine. A couple of narrow scrapes during the subsequent campaign to cleanse Keffia of genestealers, which aren't strictly relevant to this anecdote but were unpleasant enough at the time, had added to it; mostly I'd run for cover, kept my head down, and emerged to take the credit when the noise stopped.

So I should have had the sense to sit back and enjoy the relative peace the post I'd gone to some trouble to arrange for myself ought to have guaranteed; a rear-echelon artillery battery, a long way from the front line, with no disciplinary problems to speak of. But, true to form, I just couldn't leave well enough alone.

We'd been campaigning on Slawkenberg for about eight months standard, or about half the local year, putting down in the southern hemisphere of the main eastern continent just as the snows of winter began to give way to a clement, sweet-scented spring. Tough luck on the Valhallans, who bore the disappointment with the stoicism I'd come to expect, but just gravy so far as I was concerned. True to form we spent the spring, and the sort of balmy summer that vacation worlds build their entire economies on, flinging shells into the distance, secure in the knowledge that we were doing the Emperor's work without any of the unpleasantness you get when the enemy can shoot back at you.

I wasn't even sure who the enemy was, to be honest. As usual I'd given the briefing slates only the most perfunctory of glances before turning my attention to matters of more immediate concern, like grabbing the best billets for myself and a few favoured cronies. Since my instincts in this regard remained as finely honed as ever, I managed to install myself in a high class hotel in a nearby village along with the senior command staff, most of whom still cordially detested me but who weren't about to turn down a soft bed and a cellar full of cask-matured amasec. I had equally little time for them, but liked to be able to keep an eye on them without too much effort.

I made sure Colonel Mostrue got the best suite, of course, selecting a more modest one for myself which better fitted my undeserved reputation, and which had the added advantage of a pair of bay windows which afforded easy and unobserved access to the street through a small garden which was only overlooked by the apartment belonging to the hotel's owner. He wasn't about to challenge anything an Imperial commissar might do, and with the indispensible Jurgen, my faithful and malodorous aide, camped out in the anteroom, there was no chance of anyone wandering in to discover that I was entertaining company or had wandered off to amuse myself in the many houses of discreet entertainment the locality had to offer.

In short, I had it made. So, as the summer wore on, it was only a matter of time before I found myself getting bored.

'That's the trouble with you, Cai.' Toren Divas, the young lieutenant who was the closest thing I had to a friend among the battery, and was certainly the only member of it who would even dream of using the familiar form of my given name, tilted his glass and let the amber liquid slide down his throat, sighing with satisfaction. 'You're not suited to this rear-echelon soldiering. A man like you needs more of a challenge.' He fumbled for the bottle, found it was empty, and looked around hopefully for another.

'Right now I've got enough of a challenge with that winning streak of yours,' I said, hoping to bluff him into doubling his bet again. The best he could be holding was a pair of inquisitors, and I only needed one more Emperor to scoop the pot. But he wasn't biting.

'You're going stir crazy here,' he went on. 'You need a bit of excitement.'

Well, that was true, but not in the way he meant. He'd been there on Desolatia and seen me take on a swarm of tyranids with just a chainsword, hacking my way through to save Jurgen's miserable hide completely by accident, and bought the Cain the Hero legend wholesale. His idea of excitement was being in a place where people or aliens or warp-spawned monstrosities wanted to kill you as horribly as possible and doing it to them first. Mine was finding a gambling den without a house limit, or a well-endowed young lady with a thing for men in uniforms and access to her father's credit slip. And in the last few months I'd pretty much run out of both locally, not to mention other recreational facilities of a less salubrious nature. So I nodded, mindful of the need to play up to my public persona.

'Well, the enemy's leagues away,' I said, trying to sound rueful. 'What can you do?'

'Go out and look for them,' he said. Maybe it was the amasec, maybe it was the stage of the evening when you start to talk frak just for the hell of it, but for whatever reason I found myself pursuing the topic.

'I wish it was that easy,' I said insincerely. 'But then I'd have to shoot myself for desertion.' Divas laughed at the feeble joke.

'Not if you made it official,' he said. There was something about his voice which sounded quite serious, despite the amasec-induced preternatural care with which he formed the words. If I'd just laughed it off at that point, it would all have turned out differently: a couple of eager young troopers wouldn't have died, Slawkenberg might have fallen to the forces of Chaos, and I definitely wouldn't have ended up fleeing in terror from yet another bunch of psychopaths determined to kill me. But, as usual, my curiosity got the better of me.

'How do you mean?' I asked.

'LET ME GET this straight.' Colonel Mostrue looked at me narrowly, distrust clearly evident in his ice-blue eyes.

He'd never fully bought my story on Desolatia, and although he generally gave me the benefit of the doubt he was never quite able to ignore the instinctive antipathy most Guard officers harboured towards members of the Commissariat. 'You want to lead a recon mission out towards the enemy lines.'

'Not lead, exactly,' I said. 'More like tag along. See how the forward observers are doing.'

'They seem to be doing fine,' Mostrue riposted, his breath puffing to vapour as he spoke. As usual he had the air conditioning in his office turned up high enough to preserve grox.

'As I'd expect,' I said smoothly. 'But I'm sure you've seen the latest intelligence reports.' Which was more than I had, until my conversation with Divas had drawn my attention to them. 'Something peculiar seems to be happening among the enemy forces.'

'Of course it does.' His voice held a faint tinge of asperity. 'They're Chaos worshippers.' I almost expected him to spit. 'Nothing they do makes sense.'

'Of course not,' I said. 'But I feel I'd be shirking my duties if I didn't take a look for myself.' Although I didn't have the slightest intention of going anywhere near the battlefront, I really was mildly intrigued by the reports I'd skimmed. The traitors seemed to be fighting each other in several places, even ignoring nearby Imperial forces altogether unless they intervened. I didn't know or care why, any more than Mostrue did; the more damage they inflicted on each other the better I liked it. But it did give me the perfect excuse to comandeer some transport and check out the recreational possibilites of some of the nearby towns. Mostrue shrugged.

'Well, please yourself,' he said. 'It's your funeral.'

So I FOUND myself later that morning in the vehicle park, watching a couple of young gunners called Grear and Mulenz stowing their kit in the back of a Salamander. Jurgen, who I'd co-opted as my driver, glanced up at the almost cloudless sky, his shirt sleeves rolled up as usual, a faint sheen of sweat trickling across his interesting collection of skin diseases. Even though we were in the open air, and he wasn't perspiring nearly as much as he had when we first met in the baking deserts of Desolatia, I kept upwind of him through long habit.

Jurgen's body odour was quite spectacular, and even though our time together had more or less immured me to it there was no point in taking any chances. Physically he was much less prepossessing than he smelled, looking as though someone had started to mould a human figure out of clay but became bored before they finished.

Though I strongly suspected Mostrue had assigned him as my aide more as a practical joke than anything else, Jurgen had turned out to be ideally suited to the role. He wasn't the biggest bang in the armoury by any means, but made up for his lack of intellect with a literally minded approach to following orders and an unquestioning acceptance of even the mutually contradictory parts of Imperial doctrine which would have done credit to the most devout ecclesiarch. Now he looked at a faint wisp of cloud on the horizon, and shook his head.

'Weather'll be changing soon.'

'It seems fine to me,' I said. I suppose I should have listened, but I grew up in a hive and had never quite got the hang of living in an environment you couldn't adjust. And besides, it had been warm and dry for weeks now. Jurgen shrugged.

'As the Emperor wills,' he said, and started the engine.

WHAT THE EMPEROR willed on this particular morning was a steady increase in the cloud, which gradually began to attenuate the sunshine, and a slowly freshening breeze which stole the remaining warmth from it. The sky darkened by almost imperceptable degrees as we rattled along, making good time towards the nearest town, and I wasn't too surprised to feel the first drops of moisture on my skin while we were still some way short of our destination.

'How much further?' I asked Jurgen, wishing I'd comandeered a Chimera instead. The noise in the enclosed crew bay would have been deafening, but at least it would have kept the rain off.

'Ten or twelve leagues,' he said, apparently unperturbed by the change in the weather. 'Fifteen to the OP.'

I had no intention of accompanying Grear and Mulenz all the way to the forward observation post, but we were close enough to civilisation to make the quarter hour or so of mild discomfort I still had to look forward to seem bearable. 'Good,' I said, then turned to the gunners with an encouraging smile. 'You'll be there in no time.'

'What about you, sir?' Mulenz asked, looking up from his ranging scope. It was the first time I'd let them know I wasn't planning on checking in on the observation post; every artillery battery needs its forward observers, but it's a hard, thankless job, and a fire magnet for every enemy trooper in the area once they realise you're there. I smiled again, the warm, confident smile of the hero they expected me to be.

'I'll just be poking around to see what the enemy's up to,' I said. 'I'm sure you don't need me getting in the way.' That was always my style, making the troops feel as though they had my full confidence. A pat on the back generally works better than a gun to the head, in my experience; and if it doesn't you can just as easily shoot them later. Grear nodded, his chest swelling visibly.

'You can count on us, sir,' he said, positively radiating enthusiasm.

'I'm sure I can,' I said, then lifted myself up to look over the rim of the driver's compartment again. 'Jurgen. Why are we stopping?'

'Roadblock,' he said. The palms of my hands began to tingle, as they often do when something I can't quite put my finger on doesn't seem right. 'Catachans, by the look of it.'

'They can't be,' I said. I glanced ahead of us: a squad of troopers was fanning out across the road, lasguns at the

ready. Jurgen was right, from this distance they did seem
to have the heavily-muscled build which distinguishes
the inhabitants of that greenhouse hell. But there was
something about the way they moved which rang alarm
bells in my mind. And besides... 'They're all assigned to
the equatorial region.'

'Then who are they?' Jurgen asked.

'Good question. Let's not wait to find out.' No other
instructions were necessary: he killed the drive to the left-
hand tracks, and the Salamander slewed round to face the
way we'd come. Grear and Mulenz sprawled across the
floor of the crew compartment, taken by surprise by the
violent manoeuvre; more used to Jurgen's robust driving
style I'd grabbed the pintel mount to steady myself.

A few las-bolts shot past our heads as the ambushers
realised we were getting away, followed by barely coher-
ent curses.

'Emperor's blood!' I swung the heavy bolter around
and loosed off a fusilade of badly-aimed shots at our pursuers. Grear and Mulenz gaped at me, obviously stunned
at seeing the heroic legend come to life, until I grabbed
Grear and got him to replace me at the weapon.

'Keep firing,' I snapped, pleased to see that I'd got a couple at least, and dropped back behind the safety of the
armour plate. That required an excuse, so I seized the voxcaster. 'Cain to Command. We have hostiles on the forest
road, co-ordinates...' I scrabbled for the map slate, which
Mulenz helpfully thrust at me, and rattled them off. 'Estimate at no more than platoon strength...'

'There's more of them up ahead,' Jurgen cut in helpfully.

'Command. Wait one.' I peered cautiously over the rim
of the crew compartment. Another squad had emerged
from the trees lining the road, then another, and
another... I could estimate at least fifty men, maybe more,
straggling across the highway towards concealment on
the other side. 'Make that company strength. Possibly a
full advance.'

'Confirming that, commissar.' Mostrue's voice, calm and collected as usual. 'Targeting now. Firing in two.'

'What?' But the link had gone dead. We only had one chance. 'Jurgen! Get us off the road!'

'Yes, sir.' The Salamander swung violently again, las-bolts spanging from the armour on all sides now, throwing us around like peas in a bucket. The ride became a succession of sickening lurches, as the smooth rockcrete of the highway gave way to a rutted forest track. The flurry of bolts began to dwindle as we opened the distance from our pursuers. All except a few, which continued to pepper the front armour to little effect.

I risked another peek over the armour to see a small knot of men scattering in front of us: a couple of them weren't quite fast enough, and the Salamander lurched again with a sickening crack and a smell of putrescence which made Jurgen's odour seem like a flower garden.

'Who are these guys?' Mulenz asked, grabbing a lasgun and sending a few rounds after them for good measure.

'Care to guess?' I suggested, drawing my chainsword as one of the enemy troopers began clawing his way aboard. Despite everything I'd seen in my career up to that point, it was still a shock. The face was distended with infection, pus seeping from open sores, and his limbs were swollen and arthritic. But inhumanly strong, for all that. Even an ork would probably have thought twice about trying to board a vehicle moving at our pace...

With an incoherent scream, which the two gunners fortunately took for a heroic battle cry, I swung the humming weapon in a short arc that separated the head from his body. A fountain of filth jetted from it as it fell, fortunately away from the Salamander, making us gag and retch at the smell. By the time I was able to blink my eyes clear I could hear the first shrieks of the incoming shells.

The roar of the barrage detonating behind us was almost deafening, splinters of wood from shattered trees spattering the armour plate, and stinging my cheek as I ducked for cover. Jurgen kept us moving at a brisk pace, deeper into the cover of the woods, and the noise gradually receded. Grear and Mulenz were looking back at the flashes and smoke like juvies at a firework display, but I guess being forward observers they were used to being at the sharp end of one of our barrages. For me it was a novel experience, and one I wasn't keen to repeat.

'What do we do now, commissar?' Jurgen asked, slowing to a less life-threatening speed as the noise grew fainter behind us. I shrugged, considering our options.

'Well, we can't go back,' I said. 'The road will be impassable after that.' A quick conversation on the vox was enough to vindicate my guess; things had been chewed up so badly regimental headquarters was having to send patrols in on foot to confirm that the enemy had been neutralised.

I looked at the map slate again. The forest seemed awfully big now that we were inside it, and the rain was starting to fall in earnest, gathering on the over-hanging branches to drip in large, cold drops onto my exposed skin. I shivered.

'What I don't understand is what they were doing out here,' Grear said. 'There's nothing of any strategic importance in this area.'

'There's nothing in this area at all,' I said, mesmerised by the map. 'Except trees.' A faint line was probably the forest track we were on. I leaned forwards to show it to Jurgen. 'I reckon we're about here,' I concluded. He nodded.

'Looks about right, sir.' He switched on the headlights; the twisting track became a lot clearer, but the trees surrounding us suddenly loomed more dark and threatening. I traced the thin line with my thumbnail.

'If it is,' I said, 'it comes out on the north road. Eventually.' It was going to be a long, arduous trip, though. For a moment I even considered going back the way we'd come, and taking our chances on the shattered highway, but that was never really going to be an option; the Salamander's suspension would be wrecked in moments, and there were bound to be enemy survivors lurking in the woods. Pushing on was the only sensible choice.

FOUR HOURS LATER, cold, tired, hungry, and seriously hacked off, I was beginning to think fighting our way out through a bunch of walking pusbags wouldn't have been so bad after all. We'd probably have linked up with the first of our recon patrols by now, and be on our way back to the battery in a nice cosy Chimera...

'What's that?' Grear pointed off to the left, through the trees.

'What's what?' I brushed the fringe of raindrops from the peak of my cap, and followed the direction of his finger with my eyes.

'I thought I saw something.' Shadows and trees continued to crawl past the Salamander.

'What, exactly?' I asked, trying not to snap at him.

'I don't know.' A fine observer he was turning out to be. 'There!' He pointed again, and this time I saw it for myself. A glimmer of light flickering through the trees.

'Civilisation!' I said. 'Emperor be praised!' There could be no doubt that the light was artificial, a strong, warm glow.

'There's nothing on the map,' Jurgen said. He killed the headlights, and brought us to a stop. I glanced at the softly-glowing slate screen.

'We're almost at the highway,' I concluded. 'Maybe it's a farmhouse or something.'

'Not exactly agricultural land around here though, is it, sir?' Mulenz asked. I shrugged.

'Forestry workers, then.' I didn't really care. The light promised warmth, food, and a chance to get out of the rain. That was good enough for me. Except for the little voice of caution which scratched at the back of my mind...

'We'll go in on foot,' I decided. 'If they're hostile they can't have heard our engine yet. We'll reconnoitre before we proceed. Any questions?'

No one had, so we disembarked; the three gunners carrying lasguns, while I loosened my trusty chainsword in its scabbard.

The ground was ankle-deep in mud and mulch as we squelched our way forward. I ordered us into the trees to make for the light directly, cutting the corner off the curve of the track. The going was easier here, a carpet of rich loam and fallen leaves cushioning our footfalls, and the thick tracery of branches overhead keeping most of the rain off as we slipped between the shadowy trunks.

A line of thicker darkness began to resolve itself through the trees, backlit by the increasing glow behind it.

'It's a wall,' Mulenz said. No wonder they made him an observer, I thought, nothing gets past this one. I raised a cautious hand to it: old stonework, slick with moss, about twice my own height. I was about to mutter something sarcastic about his ability to state the obvious when we heard the scream. It was a woman's voice, harsh and shrill, cutting through the shrouding gloom around us.

'This way!' Mulenz took off like a startled sump rat, and the rest of us followed. I drew my laspistol, and tried to look as though I was heroically leading the charge while keeping the rest of the group between me and potential danger.

Something was crashing towards us through the undergrowth, and I drew a bead on it, finger tightening reflexively on the trigger.

'Frak!' I held my fire as the looming shape resolved itself into a young woman, her clothing torn and muddy, who I suddenly found clamped around my neck.

'Help me!' she cried, like the heroine of a cheesy holo-drama. Easier said than done with a good fifty kilos of feminine pulchritude trying to throttle me. Despite the mud and grime and darkness I found her extraordinarily attractive, the scent of her hair dizzying; at the time, I put it down to oxygen starvation.

'With pleasure,' I croaked, finally managing to unwind her from around my throat. 'If you could just...'

'They're coming!' she shrieked, wriggling in my grip like a downhive dancing girl. Under other circumstances I'd have enjoyed the experience, but there's a time and a place for everything, and this was neither.

'Who are you, miss?' At least Jurgen was paying attention; Grear and Mulenz were just staring at her, as though they'd never seen a pretty girl falling out of her dress before. Maybe they didn't get out much.

'Them!' She pointed back they way she'd come, where something else was thrashing its way through the undergrowth. The stench preceeding it was enough to confirm the presence of at least one of the Chaos troopers we'd encountered before. Shaking her off like an overeager puppy I raised my arm and fired.

The crack of the lasbolt broke the spell; Greer and Mulenz raised their lasguns and followed suit. Jurgen took slower, deliberate aim.

Something shrieked in the darkness, and burst through the surrounding undergrowth. A smoking crater had been gouged out of the left side of its body, a mortal wound to any normal man, but it just kept coming. Jurgen fired once, exploding its head, and it fell in a shower of putrescence.

'Sir! There's another!' Grear fired again, setting fire to a nearby shrub. In the sudden flare of light the enemy trooper stood out clearly, running towards us, a filthy combat blade in its hand. Jurgen and I fired simultaneously, blowing it to pieces before it could close.

'Is that the last of them?' I asked the girl. She nodded, shaking with reaction, and slumped against me. Once again I found the sensation curiously distracting; with a surge of willpower I detatched her again. 'Mulenz. Help her.'

He came forward grinning like an idiot, and I handed the girl across to him. As I did so a curious expression flickered across her face, almost like surprise, before she swooned decorously into his arms.

'Any movement out there?' I asked, crossing to Jurgen. He turned slowly, tracking the barrel of his lasgun, sweeping the perimiter of firelight. Welcome as it had been at the climax of the fight, now it was a hindrance, destroying our night vision and rendering everything outside it impenetrable.

'I think I can still hear movement,' he said. I strained my ears, picking up the faint scuff of feet moving through the forest detritus.

'Several of them,' I agreed. 'Back towards the road.' Almost the opposite direction to the one our guest and her pursuers had come from.

'Commissar, look.' Grear managed to tear his envious attention away from Mulenz long enough to point. Flickering lights were moving through the trees, heading towards us. He levelled his gun.

'Hold your fire,' I said. Whoever it was out there was moving far too openly to be trying to sneak up on us. I kept my pistol in my hand nevertheless. 'It might be...'

'Hello?' A warm, contralto voice floated out of the darkness, unmistakably feminine. A tension I hadn't even been aware of suddenly left me; even without seeing the speaker I felt as though here was someone to be trusted.

'Over here,' I found myself calling unnecessarily. The lights were now bobbing in our direction, attracted by the glow of the gradually diminishing fire, and quickly resolved themselves into hand-held luminators. Half a dozen girls, dressed like the one clamped firmly to Mulenz but without the mud and rents appeared; like her they all seemed to be in their late teens. All except one...

She stepped forward out of the group, almost a head taller, the hood falling back from her cape to reveal long, raven hair. Her eyes were a startling emerald colour, her lips full and rounded, pulling back to reveal perfect white teeth as she smiled. She extended a hand towards me. Even before she spoke I knew hers would be the voice I'd heard before.

'I'm Emeli Duboir. And you are?'

'Ciaphas Cain. Imperial Commissar, 12th Valhallan Field Artillery. At your service.' I bowed formally. She smiled again, and I felt warm and comfortable for the first time that night.

'Delighted to make your acquaintance, commissar.' Her voice tingled down my spine. Listening to it was like bathing in chocolate. 'It seems we owe you a great deal.' Her eyes moved on, taking in the corpses of the traitors, and the girl who still seemed welded to Mulenz. 'Is Krystabel all right?'

'Shocked a little, possibly,' I said. 'Maybe a few minor scrapes. Nothing a warm bath couldn't put right.' The words were accompanied by a sudden, extraordinarily vivid mental image of Krystabel luxuriating in a steaming bathtub; I fought it down, bringing my thoughts back to the necessities of the present. Emeli was looking at me with faint amusement, an eyebrow quirked, as though she could read my thoughts.

'We need to get her inside as soon as possible,' she said. 'I wonder if your man would mind helping to carry her.'

'Of course not,' I said. Judging by Mulenz's expression we'd need a crowbar to separate them.

So we accompanied the women home, which turned out to be a large, rambling manor house set securely in its own grounds. A plaque on the gates announced that this was the Saint Trynia Academy for the Daughters of Gentlefolk, which explained a lot. To my relief I saw that the forest track was paved from that point on, which would speed up our journey considerably when we set out again. But of course Emeli wouldn't hear of it.

'You must stay, at least until the morning,' she said. By this time we were in the main hall, which was warmed by a roaring fire; I'd expected the Valhallans to be severely uncomfortable, but they didn't seem to mind, crowding into the benches along the polished wooden dining table with the students.

We were certainly the centre of attention during dinner. Grear was surrounded by a small knot of giggling admirers, oohing and ahhing appreciatively as he enlarged on our day's adventures. Although he was making me out to be the main hero of the piece, he was painting himself a fairly creditable second. Mulenz had seemed remarkably subdued since Krystabel was detached from him and packed off to the infirmary, but he perked up as soon as she reappeared, chatty and animated now.

She perched on his knee as he ate, the two of them gazing into one another's eyes, and I found myself thinking I was going to have trouble getting him back aboard the Salamander in the morning. Even Jurgen was being flirted with outrageously, which struck me as truly bizarre. The only female I'd ever known to take a romantic interest in him before was an ogryn on R&R, and she'd been drunk at the time. He picked at his food nervously, responding as best he could, but it was clear he was out of his depth.

'Is the grox all right?' Emeli asked at my elbow. Protocol demanded I sat next to her at the top table.

'It's fine,' I responded. In truth it was excellent, the most tender I'd ever tasted, lightly poached in a samec sauce that was positively to die for. Which I nearly did, of course, but I'm getting a little ahead of myself. She smiled dazzlingly at my approval, and again I found my senses overwhelmed by her closeness. The sound of her voice was like the caress of silk, smooth and fine, like the fabric of her gown; it was the same shade of green as her bewitching eyes, clinging to the curves of her body in ways which inflamed my imagination. She knew it too, the minx. As she leaned over to pick up the condiments she brushed my arm lightly with her own, and a lightning strike of desire swept the breath from my lungs.

'I'm glad you like it,' she said, her voice bubbling with mischief. 'I think you'll find a lot here to enjoy.'

'I'm sure I will,' I said.

* * *

AFTER DINNER THE company separated. Emeli invited me up to her private apartments, and promised to arrange accomodation for the gunners, although by the look of things Greer and Mulenz had pretty much taken care of that for themselves. While Emeli went off to do whatever finishing school principals did in the evening I caught up with Jurgen in the hallway, and prised him away from his giggling escort.

'Jurgen,' I said. 'Get back to the Salamander. Vox the battery, and give them our co-ordinates. This is all very pleasant, but...'

'I know what you mean, sir.' He nodded, relief clearly visible in his eyes. 'The way the lads are acting...'

'They're acting pretty much like troopers always do when there are women around,' I said. He nodded.

'Only more so.' He hesitated. 'I was beginning to think they'd got to you too, sir.'

Well they had, nearly. But my innate paranoia hadn't let me down. If it's too good to be true then it probably is, as my old tutor used to say, and even though I wasn't sure exactly what was going on here I knew something wasn't right. I just hoped I could keep reminding myself of that when I was with Emeli.

Of course I should have been wondering why Jurgen wasn't affected like the rest of us, but that particular coin wouldn't drop for another decade or more; in those days although I'd read the manual, I'd never met a psyker, let alone a blank.

'Don't worry girls,' I reassured his hovering fan club. 'He'll be right back.' Jurgen shot me a grateful look, and disappeared.

'Ciaphas. There you are.' Emeli appeared at the top of the stairs. 'I was wondering what had happened to you.'

'Likewise.' I turned on the charm with practiced ease, and moved to join her; although I told myself I was climbing the stairs of my own volition, something drew me towards her, something which seemed to grow stronger and muffle my senses the closer I got. She

moulded herself to the inside of my arm, and we drifted
across a wide hallway towards her apartments.

I had no memory of entering, but found myself inside
an elegant boudoir, smelling faintly of some heady perfume. Everywhere I looked were soft pastel colours,
flimsy fabrics, and artworks of the most flagrant eroti-
cism. I'd seen quite a bit in my time, I have to confess, but
the atmosphere of sensual indulgence inside that room
was something I couldn't have begun to imagine.

Emeli sank into the wide, yielding bed, drawing me
down after her. Her breath was sweet as our lips touched,
tasting faintly of that strange, sensual perfume.

'I knew you were one of us the moment I felt your presence in the woods,' she whispered. I tried to make sense
of her words, but the sheer physical need for her was
pounding in my blood.

'Felt?' I mumbled, drawing her closer. She nodded,
kissing my throat.

'I could taste your soul,' she breathed. 'Like to like...'

The little voice in my head was screaming now, screaming that something was wrong. Screaming out questions
that something kept trying to suppress, something which
I now realised was outside myself, trying to worm its way
in.

'Why were you out there?' I asked, and the answer suddenly flared in my mind. Hunting. Krystabel had been...

'Bait,' Emeli's voice rang silently inside my brain. 'Enticing those Nurglite scum. But then you came instead.
Much better.'

'Better for what?' I mumbled. It felt like one of those
dreams where you know you're asleep and try desperately
to wake. Her voice danced through my mind like laughing windchimes.

'That which wakes. It comes tonight. But not for you.'
Somewhere in the physical world our bodies moved
together, caressing, enticing, casting a spell of physical
pleasure I knew with a sudden burst of panic was ensnar-
ing my very soul. Her disembodied voice laughed again.

'Give in, Ciaphas. Slaanesh has surely touched your soul before now. You live only for yourself. You're his, whether you know it or not.'

Holy Emperor! That was the first time I'd heard the names of any of the Chaos powers, long before my subsequent activities as the Inquisition's occasional and extremely reluctant errand boy made them all too familiar, but even then I could tell that what I faced was monstrous beyond measure. Selfish and self-indulgent I may well have been, and still am if I'm honest about it, but if I have any qualities that outmatch that one it's my will to survive. The realisation of what I faced, and the consequences if I failed, doused me like a shock of cold water. I snapped back to myself like a drowning man gasping for air, to find Emeli staring at me in consternation.

'You broke free!' she said, like a petulant child denied a sweet. Now I knew she was a psyker I could feel the tendrils starting to wrap themselves around my mind again. I scrabbled for the laspistol at my belt, desperation making my fingers shake.

'Sorry,' I said. 'I prefer blondes.' Then I shot her. She glared at me for a moment in outraged astonishment, before the light faded from her eyes and she went to join whatever she worshipped in hell.

As my mind began to clear I became aware of a new sound, a rhythmical chanting which echoed through the building. I wasn't sure what it meant, but my tingling palms told me things were about to get a whole lot worse.

SURE ENOUGH, AS I staggered down the stairway to the entrance hall, the sound grew in intensity. I hefted the pistol in my sweat-sticky hand and cautiously pushed the door to the great hall ajar. I wished I hadn't. Every girl in the school was there, along with what was left of Grear and Mulenz. They were still alive, for whatever that was worth, rictus grins of insane ecstacy on their faces, as the priestesses of depravity conducted their obscene rituals.

As I watched, Grear expired, and an ululating howl of joy rose from the assembled cultist's throats.

Then Krystabel stepped forward, her voice raised, chanting something new in counterpoint to the other acolytes. A faint wind blew through the room, thick with that damnable perfume, and the hairs on the back of my neck rose. Mulenz began to levitate, his body shifting and distorting in strange inhuman ways. Power began to crackle through the air.

'Merciful Emperor!' I made the warding sign of the eagle, more out of habit than because I expected it to do any good, and turned to leave. Whatever was beginning to possess my erstwhile trooper, I wanted to be long gone before it manifested itself properly. Not that that seemed likely without a miracle...

Lasbolts exploded over my head, raking the room, taking down some of the cultists. I turned, the sudden stench behind me warning me what I was about to see. Sure enough the entrance hall was full of the pusbag troopers, and for the first time I realised that Slawkenberg was under attack from two different Chaos powers. No wonder they were more interested in killing each other than us. Not that I was likely to reap the benefit, by the look of things.

The Slaaneshi cult was rallying by now, howling forward to meet their disease-ridden rivals in what looked like a suicidal charge; but it was only to buy Krystabel enough time to complete her ritual. The daemonhost which had formerly been Mulenz levitated forwards, spitting bolts of energy from its hands, and laughing insanely as it blasted pusbags and schoolgirls alike. I fled, ignored by the Nurglites, who grouped together to concentrate their lasgun fire on the hovering abomination. Much good it seemed to be doing them. I could hear screams and explosions behind me as I sprinted across the lawn, shoulderblades itching in expectation of feeling a lasbolt or something worse at any moment.

'Commissar! Over here!' Jurgen's familar voice rose above the roar of an engine, and the Salamander crashed through an ornamental shrubbery. I clambered aboard.

'Jurgen!' I shouted, dazed and delighted to see him. 'I thought they'd got you too!'

'No.' He looked puzzled for a moment. 'I ran into some of those enemy troopers in the woods. But they walked right past me. I can't understand it.' I caught a full-strength whiff of his body odour as he shrugged.

'The Emperor protects the righteous,' I suggested straight-faced. Jurgen nodded.

He crossed himself and gunned the engine.

'At least we know what they were doing in this sector now,' I said, as we raced down the paved track towards the road. 'They were trying to stop the summoning... Oh frak!' I grabbed the voxcaster. 'Did you vox in our co-ordinates?'

'Of course,' Jurgen nodded.

'Cain to command. Full barrage, danger close, immediate effect. Don't argue, just do it!' I hung up before Mostrue could start pestering me with questions, and waited for the first shells to arrive.

If being close to the first strike had been worrying, getting caught in a full barrage was serious change of undergarments time. For what seemed like eternity the world disappeared in fire and smoke, but I guess the Emperor was looking out for us after all or we'd never have made it to the road in one piece.

When we went back at first light the entire building had been obliterated, along with several hectares of woodland. I left out the bit about the daemonhost in my report; I'd been the only one to see it, after all, and I didn't want the Inquisition poking around in my affairs. Instead I made up some extravagant lies about the heroism of the dead troopers, which, as usual, were taken as a modest attempt to deflect attention from my own valour. And, so far as I knew at the time, that was the end of it.

Except that sometimes at night, even after more than a century, I find myself dreaming of green eyes and a voice like velvet, and I wonder if my soul is as safe as I'd like to think...

ABOUT THE AUTHORS

Dan Abnett and his army of clones live and work in Kent. He is well known for his comics work and his considerable output for the Black Library includes *Lone Wolves*, *Darkblade*, the best-selling Gaunt's Ghosts novels and the Inquisitor Eisenhorn trilogy.

Darius Hinks is the product of an ungodly union between man and beast, a shambling monstrosity who looms pungently in the darkest recesses of the Black Library, lording over his design team lackeys.

Andy Hoare works on Games Workshop's games development team, and has recently completed work on *Codex: Witch Hunters* alongside fellow games developer and Black Library stable Graham McNeill.

Sandy Mitchell is a pseudonym of Alex Stewart, who has been working as a freelance writer who produces science fiction and fantasy in both personae, as well as television scripts, magazine articles, comics and gaming material.

Mitchel Scanlon is hot new writing talent from the valleys of South Wales. His first break was with the Black Library's *Warhammer Monthly* comic and the character Hellbrandt Grimm.

Simon Spurrier has become a frequent contributor to 2000AD and the Black Library whilst attempting to reconcile the zany lifestyle of a neurotic writer with the sombre existence of a student.

James Swallow has written *The Butterfly Effect* and *Judge Dredd: Total Eclipse* for our Black Flame imprint, as well as short fiction for *Inferno!*

MORE ACTION FROM THE
WAR-TORN FAR FUTURE!

1-84416-005-X

1-84154-136-2

1-84154-154-0

1-84154-230-X

'A terrifying ground-level glimpse into
the carnage.' – SFX

Buy them now from:

www.blacklibrary.com

A MIND WITHOUT PURPOSE WILL
WALK IN DARK PLACES!

The all-action adventures of Inquisitor Gideon Ravenor
and his band of desperadoes begin in this storming
novel by Dan Abnett!

'Dan Abnett truly is a master of
his craft.' – Starlog

(Hardback) £16.99 / $19.99
ISBN: 1-84416-072-6

INFERNO!™

Inferno! is the Black Library's high-octane fiction magazine which throws you headlong into the worlds of Warhammer. From the dark, orc-infested forests of the Old World to the grim battlefields of the war-torn far future, Inferno! magazine is packed with storming tales of heroism and carnage.

Featuring work by awesome writers such as:

- **Dan Abnett**
- **William King**
- **Graham McNeill**
- **Ben Counter**
- **Gordon Rennie**

and lots more!

Published every two months, Inferno! magazine brings the grim worlds of Warhammer to life.

For subscription details call:

US: 1-800-394-GAME
UK: 0115 91-40000
Canada: 1-888-GW-TROLL
Australia: 02 9829-6111

For more information visit
WWW.BLACKLIBRARY.COM/INFERNO